To my wife Liz, my editor and partner.

To Tracey,
Merry Christmas
Taylor Pensoneau

Chapter One

The summer of 1950. The day was hot as hell. Nothing stirred under the late afternoon sun on the deserted campus of Hanover College. Peter Stine had the place to himself as he stood on the crest of a bluff, staring down at the silvery Ohio River in the valley below. Stopping at Hanover was a refreshing breather for Stine, an incurable idealist who was letting his mind wander, dreaming that he might someday escape from the daily grind to a haven like this.

A slender fellow in his upper thirties, Stine had just come from the nearby Indiana town of Madison, where he'd made stops at the Jefferson County Courthouse and the local newspaper. He was prowling for background on a matter that, for him, was an irresistible hot potato. While he hadn't pinned anything down in the musty documents he'd scoured a few hours earlier, he was sure he'd score when he resumed the search the next morning. For the moment, though, he needed to find a motel room for the night, which should be easy judging by the vacancy signs he saw back out on the highway.

Returning to his car, Stine drove slowly across the empty campus, wondering where he might have landed had he spent his college-age years in a private school refuge such as Hanover instead of sweltering back rooms of printing shops and small newspapers. The return drive to the highway was scenic, winding through a dense woods for a mile or more. Suddenly, Stine noticed another automobile, rounding a turn. As it drew closer, it abruptly swerved across the road and stopped, forcing Stine to do the same. Wondering what in the world was going on, Stine watched as a man in a dark summer suit jumped from the other car and walked briskly toward him. Even though the other guy's face was partly obscured by a wide-brimmed straw hat, Stine could see he was older.

"Is something wrong?" Stine asked, sticking his head out of the window. The only reply was a slight grin. As the eyes of the two locked for a second, Stine's visitor deftly moved a hand inside his suit coat, pulled out a pistol and fired once into the astonished face of Stine. As birds flapped loudly out of trees, Stine slumped sideways onto the passenger seat of his car, his steel-rimmed glasses askew while a hole in his forehead yielded a bright-red trickle. The assailant then leaned through the window and pumped another bullet into Stine's head.

Turning quickly, the triggerman raced back to his car, absolutely certain that no life remained in the crumpled body of Peter Stine.

Chapter Two

Jacob Samuel Brosky. His byline had been appearing on front-page crime stories in the *St. Louis World* for as long as most readers could remember. Brosky was as widely known as many of the gangsters and other assorted creeps he'd tracked in a career with the *World* going back to the start of the 1920s. More than the cub reporters on the staff speculated about the dangerous, secret sources that Brosky must have to disclose the doings of so many underworld figures. Everyone realized he swam in shark-infested waters, and his Smith and Wesson was common knowledge. Now, as to whether he had ever fired it, the old hands at the newspaper liked to insinuate that he had. Brosky was mum about it, figuring that by not denying it he only added to the air of mystery surrounding him. More than once, he had brought it out and conspicuously laid it on a table to discourage reckless behavior by some less-than-bright punk prone to being trigger happy. It was Brosky's security blanket all right—that little five-shot snubby.

Whenever possible, Brosky took the old Eads Bridge across the Mississippi. The reason was unusual for a man as tough as Brosky. Licorice. He loved licorice. The tollbooth at the St. Louis end of the bridge sat right next to a licorice factory, which smothered everything with an overwhelmingly sweet fragrance. Great side benefit for the toll takers, he thought. Lucky fellows.

Once off the bridge on the Illinois side, the odor was different. East St. Louis really did smell, he thought. It was just like all the St. Louis patricians insisted during a lifetime of looking down their noses on the East Side—the uncouth cousin on the far side of the river. Even the punky name East Side was part of the put-down. Slaughterhouses reeking like rendering works. Noxious fumes from chemical plants insulting nostrils and taste buds. People literally coughing when they passed the chem monstrosity on the south edge of East St. Louis.

Brosky himself was hacking as he sped through the town in his forest-green Oldsmobile 88 convertible, enroute to a southern Illinois funeral service. Couldn't blame the East Side this time, he had to admit, knowing full well his dry cough started with the Lucky Strike he lit after crossing the bridge. He had sworn off heavy booze a long time ago, but not the smokes. Two extra packs of Luckies were stashed in the glove compartment, right along with his Smith and Wesson revolver.

As Brosky's Olds, a powerful V-8 with hand straps attached to the back of each front seat, traded the congestion of the East Side for bucolic countryside, the car radio began to emit static.

"Damn it," he muttered as he drove beyond the range of his favorite St. Louis station. He was catching the news for the last time.

"With the approval of President Truman," said the broadcaster, "the Joint Chiefs of Staff have ordered Marine ground and air units from the West Coast to General MacArthur's Far Eastern command. The move comes as Communist North Korean invaders continue their advancement through South Korea...."

"Commie bastards," interjected Brosky.

"Stan Musial extended his blistering hitting streak yesterday by slamming a homer, double and single," the commentator continued, "to lead the Cardinals past the Brooklyn Dodgers, 8 to 4, at Sportsman's Park. If Stan the Man stays this hot at the plate, he'll be on a fast track to his fourth National League batting crown.

"In other news, funeral services are scheduled for later today in Grandville, Illinois, for newspaper publisher and editor, Peter Stine, who was found shot to death Monday in Indiana. Authorities say they have no leads in the killing of Stine, who had turned his small newspaper into a hard-hitting voice against...." The rest was drowned out by static.

Stine's funeral was the first stop Brosky intended to make

while nosing around in southern Illinois for a background piece on the murder. Foul play involving a journalist was always of more than passing interest. But even more so this time. Stine had generated considerable attention because of his crusade in his weekly *Cypress County Banner* against the wide-open but patently illegal gambling rampant in parts of downstate Illinois—including Stine's own backyard in the bottom part of the state.

"Jake," the city editor of the *World* told him, "it looks like southern Illinois is threatening to take center stage again." Brosky knew that was a mouthful.

Year in and year out, southern Illinois was a newsy gold mine, a fountain of the juicy stuff that sold newspapers. Prohibition era gang wars. Klan turbulence. Violence in the coal fields. The sum and substance that hooked readers. The *World* had been on top of most of it. The paper was not only the biggest in St. Louis, but one with a healthy circulation over in Illinois.

Brosky had a big hand in a lot of those Illinois stories. Snooping around over there was old hat for him. He'd made it his business to get to know the place quite well as a young reporter in the Roaring Twenties, years in which he came up with articles revealing uncanny insight into the bloody fighting during Prohibition between the rival bootlegging outfits terrorizing southern Illinois. Most of the veteran reporters in St. Louis back then shied away from Illinois as much as they could, regarding it as a second-rate assignment not helpful to career advancement. Brosky jumped at the chance, though, to come up with headlines out of Illinois that would go on to bolster his credentials for later becoming the *World's* ace reporter on the naughty characters in St. Louis too.

An unlikely thing happened along the way. Brosky, a two-fisted young man from the west end of St. Louis, Jewish to boot, grew fond of many of the people and the towns he encountered across the river—so much so that he resented the snideness toward Illinois of many at the *World*. Brosky's affection may have been gruff, but it also was sympathetic, an empathy born out of his firsthand awareness of how hard pressed life was for many in southern Illinois. Brosky hung in there with this view in spite of some things he'd witnessed or heard in Illinois, like the anti-Zionist diatribes of hooded Ku Kluxers circling burning crosses in the black dead of night.

Sucking on another Lucky as he drew closer to Cypress County and its seat, Grandville, Brosky mulled over the Stine murder in his mind. It was tough to figure.

For sure, Brosky assumed, Stine's articles and editorials made a lot of people nervous. He wasn't giving anybody a pass. Not the operators of the gambling clubs. Not local officials who, because they were on the take, refused to pursue any serious crackdown on the gambling even though it was clearly in violation of the law. Not Governor Sanderson, who took office the year before as a reformer, but was yet to tackle the widespread gaming drawing unfavorable attention to his state. Stine had even turned his pen in the weeks before his death to the strong rumor that longtime East Side rackets boss Harry Fontane was out to get his mitts on the wagering in southern Illinois. Brosky had to hand it to Stine. For a fellow with a piddling paper, he had chutzpah. Sitting down there in Grandville, pretty much alone, crossing swords with rough characters in an unlawful business that was helping plenty of influential people get better heeled while providing fun for a lot of other folks. But Brosky could not fathom who involved in the gambling would be dumb enough to bump off Stine.

Rubbing out newspaper types was just out of character for gangsters, especially an old pro like Fontane. Jake had Fontane's organization wired, and he'd already been tipped that Fontane was furious over the execution of Stine because of the revved-up heat it was sure to ignite. No, as much as Brosky personally despised Fontane and many in his mob, he could not see sticking the crime godfather with this baby. Maybe one of the independent gambling chiefs farther south, or one of the local officials named in Stine's stories, could be tied to it. If so, Brosky could only shake his head at such idiocy.

Jake would only be a spectator at the funeral. A *World* feature writer was assigned to cover it for the paper. That sort of story was not Jake's shtick. Anyhow, he was one of the worst writers on the staff. Brosky actually did not write his own stories. He was paid well above the newspaper guild scale because very few reporters had the temerity to play footsie with the underworld and ferret out a true picture of what was going on. Wordsmiths, on the other hand, were a dime a dozen. There was one particularly seasoned writer in the city room who, for years, took Brosky's findings and converted them into fine journalistic prose. Nobody outside the *World* knew this because the rewrite man never got his name in the paper. Bland, balding Herbert Overman didn't exist in the public's eye.

Following the service, Brosky planned to head without delay to Smithburg for a huddle with an individual who'd certainly done his share to contribute to the unseemly side of southern Illinois' past. Cecil Langston was an old news maker, which at this stage was all he wanted to be. He'd gone straight in the years since he and a brother ran a very conspicuous gang in the booze-smuggling trade. Ironically, Langston and Brosky took to liking each other when Langston was a rough-hewn, locally grown bootlegger and Jake a reporter in his salad days, eager to make a name. His taking a shine to Brosky led Langston to feed Jake with much of the inside dope that catapulted him to the front of the reporters covering the bootlegging wars. In turn, Jake had been wont to gloss over in his mind and his stories the misdeeds of the Langston gang, even though it employed guns and muscle against rival whiskey runners while, like the competitors, paying off authorities.

Jake could hardly believe that it was close to two decades ago when Cecil and his brother, Arthur, stood up to the ruthless incursions into Langston territory by Fontane and his hoods, whose aim was to extend their tentacles throughout southern Illinois. Wild and woolly it was, with Fontane and the Langstons going for jugulars and Fontane putting out the word that Brosky also was a marked man because of his buddying up with the Langstons.

What came of it? For Brosky, nothing but a reputation. For the Langstons, a different outcome. Arthur ended up with a bullet in the back, a murder never solved. Not long after Arthur bought it, Prohibition went out the window, and the bootleggers had to find other ways to make money. Fontane easily shifted gears. Prostitution and labor racketeering were two undertakings quite lucrative for him in the Great Depression years. He then became the natural beneficiary on the East Side of the gambling boom that hit full stride during World War II and continued to expand in the years afterward. Cecil Langston sought to go legit after the manufacture, transportation and sale of alcoholic beverages again became legal. He rediscovered religion, the bible-thumping kind. He moved his wife, Dorothy, and two sons, Marvin and Lucius, to an old family farm outside Smithburg. Corn and beans replaced shotguns and roadhouses in his life. He operated an auto repair garage behind the farmhouse and was willing to do about anything else that might turn a dollar, including wildcatting for oil.

When Brosky tried, after learning of Stine's death, to reach Cecil by phone—his first attempt to contact Langston in a great while—he got an apprehensive Dorothy on the line. A visit by Jake would be welcome, she said, because "Cecil is down these days."

"Jake," Dorothy went on, "things have been happening to us that's got us worried. Somebody took a shot at Lucius.

Marvin, he's spending all his time working at that gambling club in Grandville. We wish he'd get out. Cecil, he just thinks there's big trouble coming down here. We don't want it no more, Jake."

Chapter Three

They descended like locusts on the funeral parlor. Society matrons, civic honchos, judges, state legislators and local officeholders—some of whom were targets of Stine's typewriter—pressed shoulders with curiosity seekers and reporters at the standing-room-only service for the murdered publisher. Ceiling fans whirred, women whipped hand fans back and forth, and men wiped their brows in the thick air.

Photographers from newspapers and magazines jostled to take pictures, drawing angry glances. The undertaker said "no photos," but he was overruled by the lanky, white-headed figure standing by the closed coffin, the individual who had jumped at the invitation to command the occasion. The last thing the Reverend Sterling Kincaid desired was to exclude photographers from capturing the service and his role in it.

The farther south in Illinois, the more fertile ground for hellfire and brimstone preachers. And he could stand with the best on any given day.

Kincaid was not officiating simply because his church, the Tabernacle of the Living Lord, had soared to the pinnacle in southern Illinois evangelism. If Stine had any interest in religion, it was a secret. No, Kincaid got the invite from Lyle Hathorn because the reverend was the leader of Ministers Against Gambling, a downstate group dubbed MAG whose cause Kincaid pursued with the same grandiloquence he brought to his pulpit.

Arranging for Stine's funeral fell to Hathorn, the chief associate of Stine at the *Banner*, because the deceased never mentioned having a family. Stine just surfaced in Grandville out of the blue a few years back with enough money in his pocket to secure a loan to purchase the *Banner* from its decrepit owner. In the process, Stine inherited Hathorn, the paper's only full-time news-editorial writer. The two proved to be a workable team, and it was only to Hathorn that Stine dribbled out bits and pieces of his past. Not much, though. Stine spent his years as a youngster in an orphanage. Later on came his period of toiling at small papers in Missouri and Kansas. Hathorn recalled Stine once saying that he'd served as a printer's devil for William Allen White, a country editor who was an icon in his industry. But Stine never referred to any kinfolks.

If the good reverend knew what he was talking about, Peter Stine "was sent to us by God to fight the sin and dark forces of evil that grip so many in our part of the world.

"Let us not," Kincaid exhorted the funeral crowd, "forsake the just and righteous cause for which this brave man was so brutally slain. The Lord has called Peter Stine home, to a place in heaven where he will find his eternal reward for the good that he has done." Amens were heard around the parlor, even from those in the pockets of gamblers. "Now, it falls to us—to each and every one of us—to not betray this man any more than we would the Lord almighty himself by surrendering to the wicked men who did this horrible act, to those among us who do the bidding of Satan by corrupting the souls of God's kingdom." More amens.

Looking down at the casket, Kincaid lowered his voice as he said in an almost confiding way to the body of Stine, "Your slayers are the enemies of Jesus." Slowly, very slowly, the minister raised his head and scanned his audience. "And as with all enemies of Jesus," he concluded in a most forceful tone, "we must cast down upon them the fury of the Lord, a wrath so powerful they will fall to their knees and beseech forgiveness for the damnation they have caused." The amens reverberated again.

Kincaid was giving Stine a terrific send-off from this world, Brosky had to admit. Jake, of course, had no idea where Stine or his soul were headed since Brosky had never convinced himself there was an afterlife. Brosky had no faith in the spiritual. Few hard-boiled reporters did because, in their questioning of so much in everyday life, religion was easy prey. Jake could not remember the last time he set foot inside a synagogue, but he knew it was not to worship. Still, he believed in heaven and hell. He saw both of them right on earth, in St. Louis. Monarchs lived not one whit better, Jake was convinced, than the families in those castles on the private streets. By the same token, he felt hades couldn't be much worse for the Negroes and poor whites in the segregated neighborhoods of similarly teeming ramshackle tenement houses.

As he stood along a wall, taking in the service, Brosky had to concede that Kincaid was right about all the evil people in the world. In some respects, allowed Brosky, and he was not being sarcastic, he and Sterling Kincaid were in the same line of work, crusading. The minister's unrelenting attacks on gambling already had gotten his picture in the papers more than once. His featured role this day was frosting on the cake for him. Jake had been on the verge of contacting Kincaid a year ago about all the noise he was making over the gambling spots. But, he was sidetracked by an investigation of highway construction fraud in Missouri that only wound up recently.

Now, with the spotlight on southern Illinois gaming, Brosky had to think again of seeking a sit-down with the reverend. Maybe the next time Jake was down this way.

The presiding minister received rapt attention from most in the parlor. As for Brosky, his eyes began skipping around the crowd, looking for familiar faces. He spied a well-known Illinois legislative power broker, a canny old fox from this neck of the woods who was covertly scheming with a band of other politicos to establish a dog racetrack a few miles up the way. Jake might be having fun with that in the future, he suspected. Brosky also waged a bet with himself as to which of the pallbearers was Hathorn. He would know for sure tomorrow when, as agreed to in an earlier phone conversation, they'd meet at the *Banner*.

Moving on, Brosky focused on an impeccably dressed twosome in the front row across from the pallbearers. She was easy on the eyes, a beauty who'd stand out in any crowd. With no wife to worry about, Brosky was free to vent his taste for flashy women, gals as showy as those squired around by many of the gangsters Jake shadowed. His dates were invariably gentiles; he shied away from Jewish women. There was a shakiness there, an inferiority complex, which went straight back to coquettish Sarah Goldman, the daughter of old dry goodser Levi Goldman. Blame it on her. It had happened long ago, but always seemed like yesterday. She was the one who'd asked him to spend an evening with her, not the other way around. It was her idea to go to the soiree with her rich girlfriends and their pretentious boyfriends. He might as well have been a goy the way they put him down because he had dropped out of college and, oh yes, because of his threadbare look next to those dandies decked out in all the latest—knickers, oxford shoes and those frigging hip-hugging coats. Ashamed at having shown up with Brosky, Sarah acquiesced in the belittlement. Never, ever again, he swore. He'd stuck to it.

Yet, he'd catch himself wondering at times, even after all these years, about the reaction of Sarah Goldman, if by chance she'd paid attention, to his journalistic success. He'd even envision himself showing her and her fancy friends his prize, the 1934 Hupmobile that he kept under cover in a St. Louis garage. He'd see them oohing and aahing over its yellowish cream body, leather rumble seat, burgundy fenders, whitewalls. Of course, he'd not tell them how the little coupe came into his possession. Couldn't do that. Couldn't talk to anybody about it. The day would come, though, when he'd bring it back out into the world and drive it around with no second thoughts. He'd have a drop-dead gal cruising with him too, hopefully as attractive as the knockout in the funeral parlor that summer day in 1950.

As for that one, Jake's curiosity was aroused, had to be, as he gazed at her profile. Darn if she didn't remind him of Lilli Palmer, one of Brosky's favorite actresses. Only Lilli's hair was dark, and the gal's in the parlor wasn't. And Brosky doubted that Palmer's cheeks in magazine ads were as porcelain-like as this woman's.

Others in the parlor could have told Brosky that he was staring at Sloan Dillard, and that the considerably older gentleman parked next to her was her husband, Arkell. The line on the two was common knowledge.

Arkell Dillard was a man who reminded more than one astute observer of that English nobleman, the Duke of Windsor. Dillard's manner was so formal he was nearly regal. He was a fashion plate, too, as was the Duke. When Dillard sallied forth on business ventures, he'd be asked in Chicago and New York if his suits were tailored on Savile Row. Like the Duke, Dillard hated the old, high, English waistbands on trousers, and he had no use for suspenders. A golfer, Dillard stood out like a sore thumb when he hit the links in baggy plus fours or wildly checked pants. Yet, it was attire the world was accustomed to seeing on the Duke.

Dillard didn't come out of a womb, it was snickered. No, he grew out of a cutout of an English dude in one of those kiddie doll rags. Well, those who knew better, and there were a fair number of them, remembered a time when Dillard's grandpa, a storekeeper, was anything but flush. But the family kept its nose to the grindstone, and by the time Arkell was growing up the Dillard wallet was fat enough to send him to a haughty private school in Indiana and then Brown University. Time and money also were made available to young Arkell for travel to places the folks back home only dreamed about.

Given a head start in life, he was not about to squander it, to sit back and relax. Returning home after his Ivy League years, he went on to broaden his handed-to-him wealth by gaining control of several of southern Illinois' large quarries and, with the passing of years, a bank. He also added a trophy wife to his holdings.

Sloan just happened to be the daughter of Reverend Kincaid, and the price tag for her acquisition was, well, anybody's guess. This was one Illinois marriage that made the society pages in St. Louis—Sloan's favorite destination for cavorting on shopping sprees and other excursions. Frequently she was alone, as she was down home. Her husband often was not to be seen as Sloan flitted around, putting on the ritz, always capturing stares.

Theirs was a captivating marriage, a union of aristocracy and fundamental religion. Kind of. A bred Episcopalian like

Arkell was hardly comfortable with the zealous ardor at the Tabernacle of the Living Lord. Dillard probably was, as reputed, the biggest contributor to the church of his father-in-law, but he drew the line at revivalistic clapping with the hardscrabble farmers and miners and oil field workers who flocked to the tabernacle in a feverish search for redemption. Sloan also had pretty much stopped going to the services. The farmers, miners and oil roustabouts noticed that more than the absence of her husband.

A day or two or three could easily pass without Arkell straying from the Dillard residence, a columned mansion on a remote rise south of Grandville. It was the best overlook in the county for a panoramic view of the surrounding Shawnee Hills, and also to trace the snaking below Grandville of the sluggish little Cache River into the great low-lying swamp of cypress trees where most feared to venture and those who did treaded carefully.

When Brosky finally forced his eyes away from Sloan Dillard, he zeroed in on a strapping hunk of a man standing across the room at what might be described as parade rest. Jake recalled with a bit of amusement meeting the fellow, Jud Parkins, a few years back. It must have been at somebody's cocktail party, right after Parkins was elected sheriff of Cypress County. Parkins' capture of the office was noteworthy because he was a local hero running as a Republican in a Democratic county on a pledge to protect the integrity of the county, which may have meant different things to different folks. Jake had asked Parkins in the course of the small talk what he planned to do differently from the previous sheriff, who ignored illegal wagering. Parkins had a wry reply, recollected Jake, that had nothing to do with gaming and everything to do with Parkins being a onetime star center for the old purple and white, the Grandville High School basketball team, a topic of greater interest for most Grandvillians than even life or death.

Parkins was decked out for the funeral in his fanciest sheriff's garb. Nobody could miss the two pearl-handled revolvers that he wore like his own personal hero, General Patton. Brosky reckoned the time had arrived for a hardball confrontation, not cocktail bullshit, with Parkins. But later, because Parkins was to lead the funeral caravan to the grave site in Grandville's cemetery.

Craving a Lucky, Brosky elbowed his way out to the front porch as the service was ending. He was not the only one lighting up, once outside. Everyone's clothes were rumpled from the heat, except for the Dillards'. Jake pronounced them wrinkle free as they came out, passing him without so much as a side-glance.

Max Slattery of the *World* and other photogs continued to snap away as the coffin was carried out of the parlor, trailed by the lean figure of Kincaid, his head bowed and his long, thin fingers clasping a bible. Retreating for a wider-range picture, Slattery backed into, of all people, Brosky.

"Got enough pics, Max?"

Turning around, Slattery saw the square-jawed face of the reporter that younger cameramen at the *World* found intimidating. The wiry little Slattery did not, having been around the horn himself. With a wink, he retorted, "Got this one figured out yet, Jake?"

He got no reply from Brosky. Just a grunt.

Time to make tracks for Smithburg, Brosky realized, and he set off for the parking lot. However, he was intercepted by a drawly voice he recognized all too well. "Yoo-hoo, Jacob. If you've got a moment, I'd like you to meet some people." In the home office, Brosky usually could avoid the insufferable Martha Tanner, the veteran *World* feature writer assigned to cover the funeral. But not this time. Besides, she was standing with the Duke of Windsor and his wife.

"Jacob, I know you are on the run, but I do want you to meet Mr. and Mrs. Arkell Dillard. I'm sure you've seen their names in the paper associated with many worthy causes in Illinois."

Facing the Dillards, Martha said, "Jacob Brosky is the best reporter at the *World* who can go into grisly things and find out who did them, and why. He's famous for it."

"Mr. Brosky," said Dillard, extending his hand, "I am glad to meet you. I was just telling Miss Tanner here how sorry we are that something like this has happened to a man who was trying to make such a difference in our part of the world.

"I informed Miss Tanner, and I hope she includes it in the story she is writing, that some of my business associates and myself are going to establish a journalism scholarship fund at our university in the name of Mr. Stine. In fact, I have a friend who knows your publisher and is going to put me in contact with him. Your great newspaper may be interested in contributing."

Jake had been paying more attention to Dillard's bar-stripe silk rep tie than to his words. Until mention of the publisher. That usually got the reporter's attention. "Speaking of my publisher," Jake chimed in, "he's paying me to get to the bottom of situations like this killing. Is there any chance, Mr. Dillard, that you might have some ideas on places to look or people to talk to?"

Dillard appeared surprised. "Oh no, Mr. Brosky, I wouldn't think so. I hardly believe that's my cup of tea."

Brosky did not expect the stuffed shirt to be of any help, but he'd had to say something to steer Dillard away from the subject of the publisher, which Jake found awkward to talk about.

Brosky glimpsed at Sloan. She could not have been more striking, or more disinterested. Brother, how'd he like to usher this cool honey blonde around St. Louis for a night. But, watch it, he warned himself. Better get his mind off Sloan Dillard and back on the murder of Peter Stine.

Chapter Four

The Autumn Moon at Grandville was the best of the southern Illinois gambling clubs. There was a string of them, stretching down to the tip of the state at Cairo, with names like Colony, El Patio, Flamingo and Thunderbird. Unlawful gambling was having a heyday across the country, but few areas were singled out in the ballyhoo over it like downstate Illinois. A committee of the United States Senate was embarking on a series of hearings on wagering in the nation, and everybody and his sister knew southern Illinois would take a big hit. So what else was new? *Life* and *Look* and other magazines sold a lot of copies on the back of southern Illinois through the years. The shooting of Stine just further fed an already hot fire.

Harry Fontane's place on the East Side may have packed 'em in from St. Louis, but the Autumn Moon, a two-hour drive south, had a great clientele from everywhere else. They came from Paducah, Evansville and Cape Girardeau, and even from Memphis and Nashville. Men wore ties, which wasn't the case at other clubs in the region. Many brought their wives, girlfriends or mistresses, all dolled up. No sneaking in the backdoor. For all the world to see, patrons paraded up to the rambling, two-story building, passing under a large royal-blue canopy at the front entrance. "Autumn Moon" was lettered on the awning in bright yellow.

A few hours after the body of Stine was lowered into the ground, the Autumn Moon was abuzz with its normal activity. Nobody, nothing at the club broke stride.

Yvonne Fitzgerald threw her new white Cadillac into reverse and backed into her regular spot under the huge oak tree in the Autumn Moon's parking lot. Hastily she grabbed her handbag and paraded under the canopy, ready to make her usual grand entrance into the club. Like most nights, she was greeted by Dayton Mansfield. As part owner of the establishment, Mansfield, habitually dressed to the nines, personally welcomed his customers early in the evening. As the night progressed, he'd wear many hats—club manager, casino operator, pit boss and, if necessary, runner. Once in a while, in the absence of burly Marvin Langston, the front door gorilla, he'd fill in as bouncer. But he wasn't in shape for that.

The widow Fitzgerald used to ignore Langston when she entered, but no longer. Now it was, "Hi, sweetie." The other night she even interrupted her dinner at the club to ask Langston if he could spare time for tasks begging to be done at her place. Plus, she asked if he preferred scotch. When word of this got around, that was all it took for Marvin to be projected the likely winner of the most popular game being played beneath the surface at the Autumn Moon. Yvonne Fitzgerald may or may not have known it, but she was the prize in the surreptitious contest known as "Who can get into Yvonne's knickers?" And a fortunate fellow it would be because she had exactly what most guys wanted—big boobs, tiny ankles and a fat pocketbook.

A looker she still was. She wore her hair long and curly like Rita Hayworth's, with soft ringlets dangling above big brown eyes. Yvonne's late husband Bill had loved the look. After he died, leaving her well-off from his trucking company, she stuck with the hairdo even though she knew it should have been taboo for someone past fifty. It just seemed like the respectful thing to do.

Bill wouldn't have liked it, but the Autumn Moon became an important part of Yvonne's life. She frequently dined at its restaurant, which was top drawer, and enjoyed the daily entertainment, except for the Sunday night strippers whom she boycotted. Their firm, hard bodies depressed her.

Gambling six days a week was not a problem for her. She could easily afford it, and she did it with regularity. Sometimes she took home more than she lost, which made it even greater fun. At first, she just played the slot machines. Then she graduated to blackjack and, on evenings when she felt lucky, roulette.

She was hardly a high roller, but Yvonne Fitzgerald was probably the Autumn Moon's best-known patron after a widely read tabloid somehow got ahold of her for a story on the gaming craze sweeping the land. Pictured as a lonely widow, she said her life "would be damn dull without the Autumn Moon."

"Hey," she was quoted as saying, "it's my money and my choice, isn't it? I'm not an addict or anything like that. So, I just don't understand why some nosy people think gambling is wicked. There's sure lots of things I know people do that are far worse than gambling. If you win, you just can't beat the feeling."

The article was accompanied by a photo of Mrs. Fitzgerald standing by Mansfield's most prized possession, a rare Liberty Bell slot machine, a member of the first family of slots invented in San Francisco in 1895. It was the only slot in the Autumn Moon not part of the action. The others were everywhere, including the men's and ladies' rooms.

Yvonne grew fond of blackjack because it was competitive, yet seemed easy. She was not a reckless player, refusing to draw another card when she held 16 points or more. Still, the advantage laid in the fact that the dealer got the last card, and in a professional gambling operation like the Autumn Moon the house was always the dealer. Whether it was blackjack, the dice games or the roulette wheel, the odds were resolutely against the players. They were not likely to walk away with much more at clubs with an up and up reputation like the Autumn Moon than at the mob-bossed "steer joints" up north. Any club not coming out ahead was not going to stay in business.

The Autumn Moon housed its blackjack tables, craps games and roulette in the private club room, a misnomer in that nobody was kept out. Of course, Mansfield and his crew had to closely watch the crowd to guard against the house getting taken by skilled gambling cheats known as "mechanics," who endeavored to look harmless enough as they made their way to the tables with the inexperienced wagerers—fondly described as "chumps, marks and chippies"—as well as the "deadwoods." The last moniker was slapped on the hangers-on or players without money.

Yvonne had that providential feeling tonight, really did. It started with the way Marvin blushed when she walked in. The bettors were more numerous than usual at the big roulette wheel in the bowl, where the wagering limit was $20 on a single number or $200 on the red or black—bets made under the keen eye of a suspender-wearing croupier spinning the wheel and dealing the game. Roulette actually gave the most favorable odds of any game in the room, but one wouldn't know it by the anxious faces watching to see if they bet correctly. More popular most nights were the fast-paced dice games, where the sticks of the "cane men" never rested. Gawkers hovered around the shooters, watching them curse for luck as they threw the dice. Mansfield insisted that the dice used in craps had to be "perfects," true cubes, not the rigged kinds like "shapes" or "six-acre flats." The same went for the slots. Mansfield would not tolerate dishonest machines such as "ten stoppers," slots fixed so that of the 20 symbols on each reel only 10 could appear on the pay line.

Mansfield looked every bit as taut as the men and women praying for something for nothing at the roulette wheel. The service for Stine earlier in the day, Mansfield did not doubt, was a precursor of the fired-up indignation to be emotionally vented without letup by Reverend Kincaid and the other antigambling zealots. Added to that, Nat Coyne was out in the club's restaurant, waiting like a poised leopard to ambush him. Coyne, the top lieutenant to Harry Fontane, was at the Autumn Moon for one more, and maybe the last, chat on a proposition by Fontane. It would spell the end of the Autumn Moon's independence. Mansfield could not duck Coyne all night.

Yvonne Fitzgerald's shrill cry of delight snapped Mansfield's attention away from his headaches. She had placed winning bets while the wheel and ball were in motion, and the dealer was quickly paying her off with the large amount of chips due her. "Dayton," she proclaimed exuberantly after spying him, "I think I just might break the house tonight." That, Mansfield told himself, was the least of his worries.

"Yvonne, I'm getting you a drink on the club to see if I can slow you down and get your luck to turn." Both laughed because drinks for persons gambling were always on the house.

"Mirla," ordered Mansfield, "a scotch and soda over here for Mrs. Fitzgerald."

Mirla Hornick, the cocktail waitress, returned in her own time with the drink on a tray. Handing it to Yvonne with a glare, Mirla walked away in a huff.

Chapter Five

"**S**crew you, I know what's going on," Mirla snapped at Marvin, her face flushed with anger. She was so upset she accidentally rammed the corner of her cigarette box into the Liberty Bell slot as she stomped off, leaving packs of Camels, Luckies, Pall Malls and Chesterfields scattered on the floor.

Taking after her, hoping his quick movement would not distract customers, Marvin caught her by the shoulder. "Wait just a minute, Mirla, I haven't done a damn thing."

"Yeah, sure. Of course. You're just innocent little Marvin. Well not tonight, buster. You can go to her house. I'm sure she's expecting you."

Dammit, Langston did not need this, not yet at least. The attention from the widow Fitzgerald was quite flattering. Cashing in on it was already on his mind. But, it might be only a

one-night stand. Who could know? He was certain it was too
early to brush Mirla off. She was the best he'd had. Almost
every night, in the remaining early morning hours after the
Autumn Moon closed, he was ending up in Mirla's bed in the
small cottage in which she stayed a short hike down the road.

Plenty of other guys would have jumped at a chance to
take his place. Mirla got hit on regularly as she peddled drinks
or cigarettes or checked coats and hats. She was fetching all
right in that scanty outfit, accentuated by the dark hosiery and
spike heels, and oh that hair, black as Manchester coal. Marvin
thought he caught Nat Coyne giving her the eye from his table
in the restaurant. Marvin could not let anything develop there.
He had too much pride.

Marvin grew up with the bad blood between his family and
the Fontane gang. He could not hide his irritation over Coyne's
increasing visits to the Autumn Moon. The patrons may not
have known Coyne from Adam, but the employees did. They
kept a wide berth from him, well aware that he was trouble. It
ticked off Marvin to no end.

Jake could not help it. After getting away from Grandville and
the funeral, his mind stubbornly insisted on slipping back to
Sloan Dillard. Sizing up her hubby as a rich wimp would have
been easy enough, but Brosky suspected that such a hasty
reading might prove to be wrong. The Dillards didn't pass out
of his consciousness until he turned into a filling station for
gas. The station resided where the rolling hills ended and the
land became much flatter, more monotonous, along the route

heading north to Smithburg. From this point on, the farms were primarily corn and soybean, as opposed to the orchards and pastureland on the hill places back to the south.

Brosky had been at this service station before, more than once. Years ago, it was in front of a roadhouse kept well stocked by the Langston brothers. Not many more rip-roaring outposts were found in Langston territory. As an attendant in an oversized blue overall filled the tank of the Olds—from an age-forgotten red gasoline pump topped by a glass cylinder through which the fuel surged—Brosky sauntered behind the station for old times sake. The speakeasy building was still there, but it was a sad sight with its windows boarded up, a no trespassing sign on the door, the tar paper on the roof flapping forlornly and tall weeds closing in.

The establishment never closed, at least not when Prohibition was in full bloom. On weekend nights, it was a challenge to elbow a way into the jammed interior. The dance floor vibrated with a gaggle of sweaty men and women, including high school girls kicking up their heels in their first Charleston or feverishly strutting to ragtime. More than a few of the gals hung with guys old enough to be their fathers. At the cramped tables, chicks from hoity-toity families squeezed up against more experienced women of the night, all downing tepid beer while surveying the field of males constantly surging to and fro.

Jake well remembered one less crowded weeknight at the place when a drunken professor from God knows where treated Jake and the Langstons to gin and then asked to sit at their table. Discovering that Brosky was a dropout from Washington

University at St. Louis, the prof scolded him. The erudite gentleman also shed light on something Brosky had wondered about, why southern Illinois was called Egypt. The explanation sounded so good to Jake that he repeated it through the years to those who thought he knew nothing more than gangster chasing. According to the prof, the nickname went way, way back and was based on the area's great fertility, which resulted partly from river overflow in the region suggestive of the Nile. Consequently, southern Illinois was a provider of grain shipped down the Mississippi to New Orleans and also a source of grain for Illinois farmers up north when severe weather killed their crops. Likewise, ancient Egypt was a supplier of corn to the world. Jake liked the admiring looks he got when he related this, true or not.

The heart of the matter was that Jake savored being looked upon as a guy in the know about a whole bunch of things people were curious about. Being the rabid St. Louis Cardinals' fan that he was, he'd get asked in Illinois to settle arguments over the background of the name Gashouse Gang for the Cards. This weighty subject arose frequently, and Jake had a pat answer on it, one he believed was accurate. Well, accurate enough anyway.

"It was back in the summer of '35 that they began calling the Cards the Gashouse Gang," Jake would relate. "A Chicago baseball writer was the first to pin the name on the team."

Jake's version never varied.

"Their uniforms had a lot to do with it. You couldn't play ball as hard as they did and keep your uniforms clean. Certainly not with the afternoon sun beating down on them every day, sweating their uniforms through and through. The most colorful of them, Pepper Martin, Ducky Medwick and Dizzy Dean, what characters they were, had the most responsibility for the Gashouse Gang tag. But it was mainly Martin, the wild horse of the Osage. He was famous, you know, for his great flying leaps on those hands-first slides. He'd just get so damn grimy. He looked like he worked in a gashouse."

Nobody in Illinois ever challenged Brosky on any of this. They accepted it word for word.

Back on the road to Smithburg, Brosky fished aimlessly on the radio for something of interest. He caught a popular music station playing "Autumn Leaves," a song he loved. He hoped a Sinatra was next. But no—it was a song he could not stand, "A Bushel and a Peck." He suffered through it on the chance that, if not a Sinatra, the next selection would be a Bing Crosby or, better yet, a number by the soothing baritone voice of Pierino Ronald Como, known to the world as Perry Como. Brosky had settled pretty much on Como as his favorite crooner; Jake's initial punch on jukeboxes the last few years was for Como's million-seller smash, "Till the End of Time." However, when no Como, Sinatra or Crosby was forthcoming, Jake turned the dial. As he did so, he recalled a recent story in the *World* that upset him, an article about the large number of radio superstars, like Bob Hope, leaving for the burgeoning world of television. Jake finally stopped twisting the knob when he stumbled on a voice he recognized. It was Eleanor Roosevelt, whom he regarded highly not because he was a Democrat but because of her grit. She was conducting her weekly forum on the topic, "What to do with the hydrogen bomb?"

He did not flick off the radio until he saw the horizon ahead punctuated by a grain elevator, water tower and spindly steeples. It was the skyline for Smithburg, but could have been for Every Town, USA.

So many of these downstate Illinois burgs were cut from the same mold, Brosky noticed. He never detected anything different on the square in the middle of Smithburg. Everything centered around the redbrick, turreted courthouse with the olive green cannon on the lawn, its barrel aimed away from the nearby granite monument engraved with the names of men from the town killed in World War I. Jake could never see the timeless storefronts of the prosperous merchants passing away. Certainly not the awning-shaded edifice housing the J.C. Penny store, where gingham and muslin for dressmaking and every other kind of merchandise imaginable were available, right down to the heavy boxes of chocolate-covered cherries Brosky couldn't resist.

Just as seemingly eternal had to be the little movie theater that started as a nickelodeon, its metal and glass marquee now heralding the opening of *All the King's Men* with Broderick Crawford. The firehouse with the elegant stonemasonry remained conspicuous, but no more so than the absence of taverns. Smithburg had stayed dry. One small building that otherwise might have been a saloon provided space for the local historical society. Its genealogical collection traced many of the families from Tennessee and Kentucky that moved northward to become the dominant group in this section of southern Illinois. The Langston family was one. Next door to the historical society stood the Masonic hall, and two doors down was the cramped office of the local newspaper, *The Clarion*, right where it was two decades ago when a crowd swarmed to grab copies of an extra edition announcing that Arthur Langston was shot to death.

Reaching the Langston farm on a narrow road a few miles out of town, Brosky saw right off the bat the sinewy figure of Cecil Langston. He was walking to the farmhouse from the auto repair garage, which was partly ringed by junked cars. The warm welcome Cecil gave Jake could not hide the anxiety written on Cecil's face, once quite handsome but now weather-beaten, its skin a duller copper than Jake recalled.

Jake offered Langston a cigarette, but he declined to take it, reminding his visitor that he rolled his own. Jake had forgotten that, although he did recall the way Cecil employed only one hand to strike a match, light up and discard the match, wind or no wind. Brosky used to try the one-handed bit himself, but he always fumbled the match.

As Langston motioned to Jake to follow him to the house, Brosky spotted Dorothy smiling at him from the porch, standing by a cream separator outside the front door.

"My oh my, it really is Jacob Brosky. In person. The best reporter on the *St. Louis World*. The best reporter on any newspaper anywhere." Dorothy added, with a laugh, "In fact, Jake, you are the only good reporter there is anywhere at all. I wouldn't give one pig's tail for any of the rest of 'em.'"

She was wiping her hands on an apron over her cotton dress, which she made herself. Her long hair, streaked with gray, was pulled straight back and braided into a bun at the nape of her neck. Her face with the deep set eyes had taken on those stark features that Arthur Rothstein and other Farm Security Administration photographers frequently seemed to capture on pitiable but defiant southern Illinois women in the hard years of the 1930s.

"Dorothy's cookin' us a real true meal, Jake. Nothin' like you get in those fancy St. Louis restaurants." Cecil spoke in a low rumble with hardly any of the southern accent of so many in his part of the world.

Brosky was no stranger to Mrs. Langston's down-home dinners. He did not understand how her husband stayed thin. Jake wasn't carrying any extra weight back when he first met the Langstons, but he had beefed up since. Not that he had turned flabby or anything like that.

A mantel above the living room fireplace advertised the past. There was a picture of the brothers, Cecil and Arthur, both in their twenties, smiling in their Sunday-go-to-meeting finest. They were raking in money at the time, just like other successful bootleggers. Beside that photo was another of Cecil's family taken near the end of Prohibition. Dorothy's dress had puffed sleeves and her hat, trimmed with ribbons, flowers and quills, was enormous—a dead ringer for the showy head coverings of women in the clubhouse at the Kentucky Derby. The boys weren't quite teenagers, but Marvin, his sandy hair slicked back, was already ruggedly attractive. Dorothy had a soft spot for Marvin, the eldest, who had given her such a difficult time at birth.

Really, though, the first thing in the room that caught Jake's attention was the smoothbore shotgun ominously standing upright by the front door. When Brosky eyed it again after sitting down, Cecil felt compelled to explain.

"Yep, it's loaded, and I'm keepin' it there, right handy, cause I don't have much choice," Cecil said. "There's somebody up to no good. I don't know who, Jake, but there's plenty I guess who maybe think they got some good reason."

Dorothy had mentioned to Jake on the phone that somebody had fired at Lucius. What was going on?

Langston hashed over a series of mysterious doings. They started a month back with the shooting of several Langston cattle. Next, an old barn at the far edge of the farm was nearly destroyed by a fire set by an arsonist who didn't even bother to carry away the gas can. Then fencing was torn down. But this was minor league stuff compared to the Lucius incident a few nights ago. As he was driving from Smithburg on the road to the farm, a bullet crashed through the windshield of his car. He escaped injury, luckily, but his mother was horrified. Who would bear a grudge so strong after all these years, Dorothy questioned, so as to try to commit murder? Her husband had no answer.

"We haven't had any of this rubbish for a long time, Jake. We've spent all these years getting it right with the Lord." Before taking another breath, Cecil quickly corrected himself.

"I don't mean Dorothy had to ask to be forgiven. She's the best woman God put on this earth."

"Cecil," Brosky interjected, "you know people have long memories, especially on bad things. You'd better believe that some can sit around quietly for years waiting to strike at you when they think you've forgotten. You might be surprised, Cecil. It might be somebody, or more than one, you'd never think of. I've seen that happen."

Pausing, Brosky appeared to be deep in thought. Then, seeking to steer the conversation to what he came for, he said he'd find it hard to accept that "Fontane has anything to do with all this stuff." At the same time, Jake pointed out, "Fontane would never forget or forgive, as you and I know, how you refused to give up your territory to him. That made him look bad to the Chicago bosses, especially when you roughed up a few of his boys."

Langston replied by shaking his head in bewilderment.

"Now, on the other hand," Jake said slowly with unusual deliberation, "there are people who think Fontane is behind the killing of the newspaper publisher over in Grandville."

"Let me tell you, and you've got to think this yourself, his crowd is mean enough to do that," Langston shot back immediately. But, he went on, "lots of others would have liked to see it done too. That paper fellow was writing all of them up. Maybe a stupid thing to do, but it took some guts, I'd have to say.

"Marvin's over at the Autumn Moon, I know Dorothy told you. You should hear him talk about the money that place takes in. Course they got to pay a lot of people off. Just like the old days, huh? That tinhorn sheriff over there, and he's only that because he could shoot the basketball, he's in on it. You met him, Jake?" After Brosky nodded, Langston added with an eyebrow twitch, "Ain't he a squirrel?"

Ignoring the last comment, Brosky jumped on the concern of Cecil and Dorothy over Marvin's employment at the Autumn Moon.

"Well," Cecil replied, "she's most worried, but, yeah, I am too. There's trouble, real bad trouble coming down. It's not just what Marvin tells me. I've got friends at some of the other clubs too. They're scared."

Langston got to the point quickly, a touch Jake admired, even though he would only hear what he already knew or guessed. As the former bootlegger put it, the clubs were facing a squeeze between that old rock and a hard place. If Fontane didn't get them, it was an increasingly safe bet the state would. Rumors about Fontane's mob "sucking up the southern Illinois clubs," Langston said, "are more than bunkum. Marvin sees Fontane's big thug at the Moon all the time. When it falls, the others down there will go pretty fast." If that doesn't happen, Langston predicted, the state "will be coming down on the gambling." The clubs, he said, "have got to be a real burr under the butt of this governor up there."

Dorothy summoned the men to the next room, where the linen-topped table was piled with fried chicken, mashed potatoes, milk gravy, homemade butter and green beans and tomatoes from her garden. There was also squash stew, which

Brosky had never had at anybody's table but Dorothy's. A freshly baked cherry pie laid back in the kitchen.

Bowing his head, Cecil intoned in his deep rumble the blessings in his life traceable to the Lord. The list was long, requiring some time. Brosky was deaf to it. Instead, he thought to himself what Dorothy explained years ago about southern Illinoisans like the Langstons, the ones who came up from the hills of states to the south. They were still mountain people, she said, undaunted, short on schooling and definitely not willing to be controlled by others. They bowed to no one. Why would they? So many adhered to Jacksonian democracy, the championing of greater rights for the common person. They brought with them to southern Illinois their prejudices, family pride and god-awful mulishness. And another trait. They were so easily aroused. Violence came almost naturally into the lives of many. Jake couldn't believe how prone they were to it.

Brosky's mind passed to the chicken. He had not eaten since grabbing two doughnuts earlier in the day at St. Louis. He was relieved Cecil's prayer was winding down. He'd heard enough from Reverend Kincaid at the funeral parlor to last him for years.

"And lastly, God," Cecil concluded, "I ask thee to watch over and protect my Dorothy and our sons, Marvin and Lucius. In thy name we pray. Amen."

Chapter Six

As Brosky left the Langstons for a drive back toward Grandville, the night at the Autumn Moon was not getting any better for Dayton Mansfield. "Fix me a manhattan," he ordered the bartender, breaking his personal rule against drinking during the club's peak hours.

The band was lousy, which served him right for not following the advice of his idol, Sherman Billingsley, the owner of New York's Stork Club. When Mansfield visited the world- famous night spot, Billingsley told him to always book peppy little dance bands because they were good for business. But Dayton had hired a jazz outfit for this night after he was told the clarinetist sounded like Benny Goodman. But the cat didn't. His group talked the jive okay, but its bebop stunk. Mansfield should not have strayed from Sherman's admonition. But hell, it was the way the night was going.

Nat Coyne still loomed in the restaurant, cooling his heels, and Mansfield knew he could not ignore him much longer. Later on, when the club closed, Mansfield anticipated another awkward visitor, the Cypress County "iceman."

Coyne was the main event, though. Mansfield's financial partners in the club, pretty much invisible, wanted him to stall Coyne as long as possible. However, Dayton knew that further stonewalling of Coyne and his boss, Fontane, was dangerous. Tonight, especially, Mansfield could not shed the fear that Coyne was going to warn him that Fontane had run out of patience waiting for an answer to his request for a piece of the Moon action. Mansfield ordered another manhattan, heavier on the whiskey this time.

It was Fontane's most fervent desire to install a wire room in the club. Operated by Fontane bookmakers, it would be an action-feigning setup where horse players listened to loudspeakers blaring the fluctuation of odds at the tracks and jockey changes before providing a phony running description of the races. Afterward, the names of the in-the-money ponies and the official track payoff figures were announced. If it sounded suspiciously like something Damon Runyon might script, it was. Funny it would not be, though, since with that cute little horse room Fontane would have his hooks in the Moon. That would be that. Once the Moon capitulated, nobody doubted the other southern Illinois clubs would tumble into Fontane's web like falling dominoes.

The thought of taking orders from Nat Coyne chilled Mansfield. He could not believe how much Coyne, Fontane's point man for corralling all the gambling in southern Illinois, resembled a movie gangster. The romanticized variety. Tough as concrete and every bit as cocky, and debonair in his specially woven threads. On the tall side of six feet, his face was too boyish for his forty years. The jet-black hair was perfectly coiffed, making it hard to picture a strand ever out of place. It wasn't difficult to imagine that Coyne had his first killing under his belt before he turned twenty, done with his bare hands when he was just one more young punk clawing to survive on the mean streets of "Kerry Patch," the notorious St. Louis Irish ghetto.

Women did not disregard Coyne, who if he was married kept it a secret. Mirla Hornick had to play it nonchalantly when Coyne gave her the once-over, keeping in mind Marvin's seething hatred for the mobster. This night, though, ticked off over Yvonne Fitzgerald, Mirla was thinking Marvin needed a lesson. It also happened that the vigilant Coyne sniffed the tiff between the little cigarette gal and her bouncer boyfriend. When she passed his table, Coyne took a shot.

"Is he still treating you okay, baby?"

This was a first, Coyne getting personal with Mirla. She realized she was blushing under her rouge. She was tempted to walk away, but she gave in to another voice inside her that said don't. Marvin deserved a comeuppance. Turning her face into a pout, she shook her head from side to side. No, the gesture read, she was not being treated right.

Out of the corner of his eye, Coyne saw Marvin watching. Coyne couldn't pass this up. "You need somebody to talk to? I'm a good listener." He added, with a straight face, "What's ever the problem, I don't like to see people crapped on."

Mirla could not help it. Tears welled in her eyes.

Coyne jerked out a handkerchief. "Here, take this. You keep it." As he handed it to her, he gave Langston a take-that-buddy look. Coyne was not through. Reaching in a side pocket of his coat, he pulled out a wad of money. Peeling off a hundred-dollar bill, he motioned to her with a finger to bend down close to him. She complied.

"You've got a friend here, little baby, when you want one," Coyne said, close to her ear. Then, with his thumb and forefinger, he stuffed the bill down into the top of her skimpy attire, snug between her sassily uptilted breasts.

Langston was over there in a flash.

"You keep your crummy hands off her," he blurted out, jabbing a finger at Coyne. Staying calm, Coyne answered, "I was just telling this pretty little lady that she's got a friend in me." Repeating his warning to Coyne to "keep your hands off her," Marvin bumped against the table, causing Coyne's drink to spill. Coyne was on his feet quickly.

Mirla moved to step between the two, but Coyne forced her back with the palm of his hand. Eyeballing Langston, the gangster's voice had dropped the nicey-nice. "Listen you son of a bitch, you're even dumber than your old man. Do you know who you're talking to? You may need me, buddy boy, to keep your job."

"Well let me tell you, mister," Langston rejoined hotly, "I can show you outta here. This ain't no East St. Louis where we kiss big shots' asses."

Mansfield, seeing the altercation and alarmed at the attention it was drawing from others in the restaurant, ran over. On the way, he signaled wildly to the band, coming off a break, to play something pronto.

When he reached Coyne and Langston, Mansfield found the shirt of each in the grip of the other. "Gentlemen, please, please," he pleaded, "not here." He managed to push the two apart.

"You'd better learn your boy some manners," Coyne snapped at Mansfield, "or others are going to do it for you."

"Who? You?" Marvin yelled at Coyne. "Well, up your fancy butt, mister!"

Mansfield shoved his bouncer hard toward the front door, declaring firmly, "I'll handle this."

"Look," Mansfield said after turning back to Coyne, "I don't allow—

Coyne cut him off in a sardonic tone. "I've been waiting out here, Mr. Mansfield, for you to find time to talk to me. I was starting to think, Mr. Mansfield, that maybe you don't want to talk to me, that I'm just somebody you can ignore."

Mansfield exhaled a sigh of resignation. His stall was over.

"I apologize, Mr. Coyne."

The man who did it all at the Autumn Moon asked Coyne to follow him.

The office at the rear of the club wasn't much bigger than a broom closet. It was so cramped Mansfield smelled Coyne's cologne. The thick fragrance further aggravated a throbbing ache in Mansfield's head, a consequence of no food, the manhattans and the unwelcome presence of one very dangerous gangster. While Coyne looked down, slowly straightening his tie, Mansfield snuck a glance at his own hands to see if their twitching was conspicuous. It was.

Still fingering his tie, Coyne got to the point. "Harry doesn't understand, Mr. Mansfield, why the delay—

"Please, Mr. Coyne," Mansfield interrupted, "call me Dayton."

"If you so wish, Dayton," said Coyne. He had not ditched the sarcasm. "As I was saying, well, Harry, he just can't understand waiting around any longer to give your place the best horse parlor this side of Louisville." He mistakenly pronounced the Louis in the city's name like the Louis in St. Louis. Dayton pretended not to notice. "He cannot understand, and I sure can't give him an answer, why we're holding off one more day on something that would be so good for everybody. You, Mr. Fontane, those people out there."

Mansfield was certain his Adam's apple was bobbing. Damn his financial partners. It was so easy for them to tell him to handle this guy, to keep him at bay with double-talk.

"As I've told you, Mr. Coyne," replied Mansfield in a voice he knew not to be convincing, "my partners just want a little more time—

"Mr. Mansfield, or Dayton, if you could only see how excited Harry has been about this, and how difficult it's been for me to tell him I can't get you to do your part."

Mansfield prayed for a knock on the office door, hoping somebody would say he was needed out in the club. But the only voice he heard was Coyne's.

"This is business we're talking about, Dayton. And every day we dick around is money gone bye-bye, for you and for us. Harry has shown so much patience with you, the kind of waiting around I've never saw with anybody else. Now he's angry, which is sad to see since he's been so excited about coming in down here to make this a very big money-maker."

Coyne's face assumed an expression of pain. In a softer voice, he said: "Dayton, I was not told to come down here for mealy mouth talk. Harry, he thinks you don't respect him. He thinks you should be shown he deserves respect."

Pausing, waiting for a reply from Mansfield that did not come, Coyne went on. "It's not what I want," he said, aiming the index finger of each hand at his own chest. "It's what the boss wants. Do you see?"

Mansfield sat still, his complexion completely pallid. He harbored a morbid fear of being hurt. All he could think about was how Coyne would do it. Or have it done. Would one of Mansfield's arms be broken? Or just a finger or two? The mob might have something else in mind, maybe far worse. His head was pulsating painfully, and he was trying to remember if there was a bottle of aspirins in the little office.

Coyne had Mansfield intimidated, the gangster could see that. Dayton looked as terrified as guys in the past who Coyne really intended to maim. This time, Coyne had no doubt, progress was visible with the genteel Mr. Mansfield.

"Now what I think, Dayton, is this," Coyne resumed, suddenly acting as if Mansfield was an intimate. "We got this guy who set up part of the Desert Inn. He will show us how to do the wire room here. He'll make it look very good. The customers will love it. Harry's got a very nice suite out there, you know. He's got an in. He's got it lined up for this guy to come back here and do this for us. You don't have no worries. You just have to figure what to do with the big take your place gets out of this. That's all you got to worry about, Dayton."

Mansfield nodded his head in what Coyne took to be a sign of approval. Inside, Mansfield was relieved he would not be hearing the sickening snap of his arm bone. His partners could go to hell.

Coyne, the embodiment of the new partner, was continuing to lay it out as if he and Mansfield were conspiring to outfox everybody else with a stake in the matter. Mansfield did not dare laugh.

"What I tell Harry, Dayton, is that you're wanting the Vegas guy here in a couple of weeks to get our room going. I tell him he was right in being patient with you, that you just needed time to line all the things up. That's what I'll do, and you can forget there was ever a problem. I'll square you with Harry. I don't want you to worry."

It occurred to Mansfield that this was how a political leader must feel signing away his country's independence. His headache was no longer as bad, though.

"Say," asked Coyne, "when were you in Las Vegas last?"

"I've never been there, Mr. Coyne."

"No kidding," Coyne said, as if in disbelief.

"Well let me tell you what," he added, putting a hand on Mansfield's shoulder. "Harry and me are going to take care of that. We're going to fly you out there, put you up at Harry's suite at the Inn. It's all first class, Dayton. We'll have the boys talk to you, show you things, like how your house can get a bigger vigorish, increase the gravy for you and your partners. We're going to do that for you, Dayton."

And what else, Mansfield was tempted to ask, will Coyne and Harry Fontane be doing for him? Not that he'd have posed the question anyway, but their attention was diverted by loud squealing from a woman who'd hit a jackpot on a dime slot machine outside the office door. Coins were clanking into the tray in a gush.

Coyne rose to leave. Mansfield stood up too, still intent on searching for aspirins after Coyne's exit.

"Oh, one more thing," Coyne added. "You'll be needing a new gorilla." Marvin Langston will be going, he assured Mansfield. Real soon.

Chapter Seven

Sure enough, there he was. Just as Mansfield expected. His car was sitting over on the far side of the Autumn Moon parking lot. Mansfield spotted it the moment he came out of the closed club with Marvin Langston and the overnight watchman. Seeing the coast was clear, the watchman went back into the club. Without a word, Mansfield handed a heavy sack of currency to Langston, who had a pistol protruding from the waistband of his trousers. Carrying the night's receipts over to his old army jeep, an antsy Marvin had his fingers crossed the boss would not take long because he had Mirla on his mind. He needed to get down to her cottage to try to smooth it over with her.

As Mansfield walked over to the car at the edge of the lot, he realized he was feeling better than before during the long night. The throbbing in his head was just about gone, and his final visitor, though no more invited than Nat Coyne, was a piece of cake next to the gangster. The iceman was, so the saying went, the lesser of two evils. By a long shot.

Reaching the auto, Mansfield saw one occupant, a big fellow. Like always, the iceman came alone. Mansfield slid in on the passenger side.

"Hello Sheriff," Mansfield said.

Most places, the "ice"—the protection money paid by gamblers to police and politicians—was collected by front men. But in Cypress County, the iceman was the chief law enforcement officer himself.

Mansfield could have written the script. "Got to talk, Dayton," Jud Parkins said. "The cost has got to go up. Right away. All of us need more."

Parkins was in casual attire. Gone were the pearl-handled revolvers and the rest of the ceremonial uniform he sported eleven hours earlier when he'd escorted Stine's body from the funeral home to the cemetery. Before that, in the morning, the sheriff had gotten word from Oscar Gratiot that Springfield demanded more dough from the southern Illinois clubs to call off the dogs. Old Oscar, the longer-than-anyone-could-remember commander of the state police district covering much of the lower region of Illinois. Parkins never was sure just who in Springfield was getting the protection cash that the sheriff funneled with regularity to Gratiot. When the previous governor was still in office, all aboard understood that a large amount of the dough went right into his personal political kitty. However, the guy currently in the governor's chair was not playing along, according to everything Parkins heard. The sheriff would not have been surprised to learn that plenty of the pay-off money he collected never got beyond Gratiot and his boys.

Irregardless, as long as Gratiot was hiking the ante, Parkins figured he might as well claim more for the slice of the protection pie he controlled. Mansfield and the other club operators were making killings, Parkins assumed. Yet, they would not have a pot to pee in without the blessing of the sheriff and several other locals. Parkins knew that the head commissioner of Cypress—who'd just invested in property down in Florida—thought he deserved more. As for Jud himself, well, he could not run for re-election as sheriff under the state constitution. And, thanks to the Stine murder, nobody could say what was going to happen anyway. So, the way Parkins looked at it, he had to strike while the iron was hot.

"It's this Stine thing, Dayton. It's really rough on all of us."

Mansfield had hardly uttered a word. The whiny buzz of a mosquito was competing with Parkins for Mansfield's attention. When the humming stopped, Mansfield wondered whether it would be him or the sheriff getting bitten. The answer came when Parkins slapped an open hand against his own bare arm and cursed, "The little bastard bit me good."

As the drone of another skeeter, maybe the same one, cut through the humid air in the car, Mansfield was asking himself if he'd really ever find out where all the payoff money went. He was not positive he cared to know.

The sheriff tried to convince him that most of it was

shipped to the state capital. Dayton had to believe, though, that a good chunk did not advance beyond a coffee can buried in Parkins' yard. Mansfield was aware, from sources, that the top county commissioner received a cut, maybe a very healthy one. Dayton was not sure about the state's attorney.

The ice was one thing. The other stuff Parkins brought up did not cheer Mansfield either. The sheriff said his counterpart over in Jefferson County in Indiana was convinced Stine was bumped off because of his activities in southern Illinois. "The guy over there," said Parkins, "is pushing this in my lap, and making no bones about it. So I just can't shove it under the rug." To make it worse, Parkins added, "the sheriff in Indiana thinks we should get the FBI involved."

Parkins also mentioned the press, the unlikelihood of it allowing the Stine case to be shelved. In his heart, Mansfield thought to himself, he really didn't want the Stine killing to go unsolved either. "I've got *Life* magazine," Mansfield heard Parkins complaining, "wanting to come down to interview me on why it's tough for a little sheriff like me to stamp out you big-time gamblers.

"Hell," continued Parkins, "they asked me if I knew Illinois was a gambling 'meckuh' or some screwy word like that. Whatever they say we are, Dayton, it don't sound good."

The ache in Mansfield's skull may have subsided, but it struck him that his whole being was drained. When was this miserable night going to end?

"Oh yeah, another thing," the sheriff noted. Brosky. Jake Brosky, that hound dog St. Louis reporter. "I spotted him at the funeral. I know who he is. I met him once. He's snooping around. You can bet he's trouble. The bastards won't let us alone, Dayton."

"Sheriff, it's late," Mansfield said, fighting to suppress a yawn.

"Sure, I understand, partner," said Parkins. He handed Mansfield a slip of paper with a figure scribbled on it. Unable to read in the dark of the unmarked car, Mansfield slipped the note into his shirt pocket. He could wait to see how much. He knew the price of doing business was going up, way up.

Chapter Eight

For crying out loud, what was taking Mansfield so long? Marvin was squirming in his pants he was so itchy to get to Mirla's place. He did not intend to ignore the big invite from Yvonne Fitzgerald. No way, though, was he going to kiss off his little Mirla. He'd have them both. But the bird in the hand first. He had to patch it up with Mirla quickly, but he couldn't tend to that until he dumped Mansfield.

After Mansfield finally escaped from the iceman and walked to Marvin's jeep, he was barely inside the small vehicle before Langston's foot hit the accelerator. They sped through the darkened town to the bank, where the currency satchel was shoved into the night depository, and then shot over to Mansfield's home, where the wrung out boss of the Autumn Moon could not wait to get inside.

Racing back through the hushed streets of Grandville, not even slowing for stop signs, Langston tore past the club and, seconds later, slid to a halt at the small driveway for Mirla's cottage. The place itself was a short hike off the road behind a clump of trees.

Turning into the driveway, Marvin was surprised to spy, in the nearby weedy grass, a well-seasoned, two-door sedan; a car he knew was not Mirla's. He was jarred. Who would be visiting Mirla at this early morning hour? If it was another guy, Mirla had found a replacement for him in record time. For God's sake, could the fellow already be in bed with her? Marvin knew there was only one way to find out, and he steeled himself for the confrontation.

Climbing out of his jeep, he saw through the trees a light burning in the cottage. The glow riveted his attention as he stood by his vehicle, attempting to contain a surge of jealous anger long enough to calculate a plan of action. Marvin should have been looking the other way.

Silently, like a slithering snake, a man had stolen up behind him. With a move deft from years of practice, the darkish figure smashed a billy club across the back of Marvin's head, a vicious blow that sent Marvin tumbling to the dirt of the driveway. While Marvin, half unconscious, moaned in pain, the attacker cracked the rear of his skull again with the heavy truncheon. The groans stopped.

The club man was no weakling. Although shorter than the coldcocked Langston, he managed quite capably to lift him into the front passenger seat of the sedan. In so doing, he discovered Marvin's handgun. Stuffing it under his own belt, he jumped quickly into the driver's seat, backed the sedan out onto the road, shifted gears and took off.

With the lurching of the car, the eyes of the paralyzed Marvin slowly opened. The face of the driver was visible in the light of the moon. The oldest son of Cecil and Dorothy Langston was filled with unspeakable terror.

Back in her cottage, Mirla thought she had heard car door and engine noises out near the highway. Maybe Marvin had come, she said to herself, but then had decided at the last minute she did not want to see him. Mirla laid in her bed, alone, sobbing.

Chapter Nine

Midsummer brought sultry dog days to Springfield, but on the day following the burial of Peter Stine the Statehouse was far from dead as a doornail. A thousand kids at a state youth convention, bused down from the state fairgrounds and turned loose in the big old place, tramped from floor to floor, glancing fleetingly at the marble mosaics, expansive historical murals and ancient oil paintings. Not many paid any attention to a string quartet playing in the rotunda alongside the bronze statue of a woman with outstretched arms that had welcomed visitors since the last century.

Hundreds of the young persons in white T-shirts found their way up to the galleries of the empty legislative chambers, where lawmakers only sat six months every other year. Visible disappointment showed on the faces of youths who thought they'd be seeing senators and representatives passing important statutes. On the other hand, something was happening in the reception room serving the governor's office. A large group of individuals was milling around, prompting a bunch of the kid conventioneers to press against the glass walls of the reception area, wondering who they were watching.

Some of those in the reception room were doing their own wondering. Sterling Kincaid and others in MAG, waiting to see Governor Elijah Sanderson, were anxious to learn if the biggest of the state's big shots was going to get off his duff on the gambling issue.

Kincaid had a notion that he and his troops were not going to be brushed off. The reverend encountered no resistance when he asked two days ago for a meeting with the governor on the heels of Stine's funeral. The pot was boiling, and Kincaid was not about to turn down the heat. The crusade against gambling was a game to Kincaid. He knew the killing of Stine was a tremendous break for his team. MAG was energized to high heaven. The opponents' goal line was in sight. Only a push from the governor was needed for a touchdown.

"Reverend Kincaid," said a prim woman coming out of the sanctum of Sanderson's office, "the governor will see you and your group now."

Without another word, she led Kincaid and the others past a desk occupied by a blue uniformed trooper, through another anteroom and into the high, fresco ceilinged office of the governor. It was commodious to say the least, but not, Kincaid observed, overdone with elaborate furnishings.

Two other things struck Kincaid immediately. The office was much cooler than the rest of the building and, more importantly for him, men and women with pencils and notepads were scattered around the fringes of the room. Reporters. Great! Kincaid was counting on press coverage to make the day count. Naturally, the presence of the scribes meant he'd have to embellish his pitch with more colorful quotes than would have been necessary in a private session with the governor.

Another door in a far corner of the office opened and in came Sanderson, a thin man whose hair was in serious retreat from his forehead. Trailing him was a severely groomed young man the governor would introduce as Whitney Charles, his executive assistant. The governor's press secretary was already in the room.

After apologizing for a shortage of seating "making it necessary for some of you to stand," Sanderson slowly settled into his own chair, an antique with timeworn distinction.

"I appreciate all of you being here," the governor began, "because I know this is a matter of concern, not only to you, Reverend Kincaid, and others in your organization, but certainly to myself and many other people in Illinois."

Sanderson went through the motion of surveying all in the room before focusing on Kincaid, who had taken the seat closest to him. The governor recognized, of course, that this was really a meeting between himself and Kincaid on an irritating issue and that everybody else was window dressing. Some may have been wont to dismiss Kincaid as just another hillbilly preacher, but Sanderson knew better. The silver-haired minister had a large following, and he came to the table today in his suit of funereal darkness with plenty of leverage. He had to be handled delicately. Yet, the governor was not about to surrender the playing field to Kincaid. He had decided what he was going to do on the gambling, and he intended to put his plan into action in a few days. The big political picture no longer gave him any other choice. But he was not about to reveal his intention at this moment because that would let Kincaid grab all the credit. Which would not do.

From his perch a few feet away from the governor, Kincaid was taking his own reading. Elijah Sanderson, Kincaid suspected in his gut, had to try hard to tolerate southern Illinoisans. We surely come off as yokels, the minister assumed, to a fellow from Chicago with his obviously fine breeding and cultivation. The way the governor pronounced words with such precision reminded Sterling of his son-in-law, Arkell Dillard. He hardly doubted the governor would be as uncomfortable in the Tabernacle of the Living Lord as Arkell, which was too bad since Sanderson was about to get a taste of the tabernacle.

The Book of Genesis, the always reliable first round of scriptures in the Old Testament, was perfect for the occasion. It came down hard on wickedness and recounted God's unsparing punishment of it. The reporters scribbled furiously when Kincaid jumped to the heart of the matter.

"We are letting our great state become another story of Sodom and Gomorrah, with our evil places choking with vice and corruption. God in his ultimate wisdom knew what he had to do, and he destroyed Sodom, and Gomorrah too, with a horrible rain of fire and brimstone."

Kincaid thought he detected a slight wince in the governor's countenance, just enough to prompt the reverend to rush to the logical follow-up.

"Governor, we know you are a man of great wisdom, and we know you see that what is happening in our cities is wrong and tragic. Yes, I believe, tragic. And when we think of tragic, nothing certainly is sadder than the brutal slaying of the fine newspaperman who gave his life in the fight against the forces of gambling."

"Governor Sanderson," concluded Kincaid, "the time is now to act, to stand up for a high morality that will let the whole country know that Sodom and Gomorrah are not going to be tolerated any longer in Illinois."

This was a governor who knew when to listen; he was a rarity in politics because he was a good listener. Being politically skillful also meant recognizing moments not to remain silent. Or, in the case of Reverend Kincaid, a time to forcefully speak up. Such a juncture had arrived, Sanderson's aides realized, when the governor pressed his fingertips together in front of him—a tip-off to his being annoyed—during Kincaid's play on sinfulness in Illinois cities. Like Kincaid, Sanderson was well aware of the note-taking reporters.

"Reverend Kincaid, I want to assure you, and everybody else in this office, that Illinois is not a state of Sodoms and Gomorrahs. Furthermore, sir, it will not be so!" The governor's voice was pungent. His fingertips stayed pressed together. He was not through.

"I also must remind everybody that proper authorities are pressing hard to find whoever is responsible for the death of Peter Stine. It was a shameful crime." Nevertheless, the governor tacked on, his voice still piquant, "it is unfair to point a finger at gamblers or anybody else until somebody is arrested for the crime."

Upbraided, Kincaid sought to rebound. "Now Governor Sanderson, sir, I only intended in a biblical way to make the point that gambling is an evil that people of good faith cannot ignore." But he suspected the governor had quickly gained the upper hand in the exchange.

Sanderson sensed this too. His fingertips no longer were pressed against each other as he went on. "I took office as governor last year with a promise to return government to a place of honor and respect in the minds of Illinoisans. To do this, I have already addressed many problems, numerous areas of concern. You all surely must be aware of this.

"Now, I agree that gambling, illegal gambling I mean, is a problem. I have waited, I have hoped, and patiently I might add, for local law enforcement authorities to do their job when confronted by open and illegal gambling. It has been my belief that frontline responsibility for this matter has resided with local officials."

"But Governor," interrupted a member of MAG standing at the back of the room, "it seems clear, your honor, that in the towns we come from the local officials are just sitting on their hands."

The timing of that remark could not have been planned any better by Sanderson. Once again looking around his office, not just at Kincaid, the governor carried the subject to the exact point he desired—at least for the moment.

"I want every one of you to know that I share your lack of indulgence for people who flout the law, be they gamblers or public officials. It is not just your patience or my patience that's running out. The patience of other Illinoisans is also at an end with those who boldly thumb their nose at the law."

Chapter Ten

Lyle Hathorn had a bad case of the heebie-jeebies. Brosky could see he'd cut himself shaving. Calling Hathorn disheveled was not stretching it.

Jake guessed at the reason; he figured right. The heir to Peter Stine's mantle at the *Cypress County Banner* admitted he had already received calls suggesting that, for the sake of his health, the newspaper ought to back off from its war against the gambling industry. Live and let live would be a smart policy, he was told.

"Are they getting to you?" Brosky asked. "I'm not sure," Hathorn replied. Brosky bet they were.

Sitting in the front office of the *Banner*, Brosky sheltered mixed feelings of relief and respect. He was thankful that his life in journalism had not taken him to a paper like this one, which seemed so small-time next to the *St. Louis World*. But he also took his hat off to people at papers like the *Banner* because everybody there had to handle many different jobs and, as a result, learned more about putting out a newspaper than a narrow reportorial specialist in the business like Jake ever did. A lot in the crowd back at the *World* would have gotten uppity at having to rub shoulders with their smaller town brethren. Not Brosky.

"Is it okay if I smoke?"

Jake looked at both Hathorn and Mrs. Tolliver when he posed the question. Mrs. Tolliver, an overweight woman who was the *Banner's* business manager, was seated at a desk a few feet away from Brosky and Hathorn and was the only other person in the office. Brosky normally did not ask for permission to light up, certainly not in the joints he frequently haunted. He did it this time because he was trying to show respect.

"No, go ahead," Hathorn replied. "People smoke in here all the time."

Brosky hoped the gesture did not come across as phony. He also made a stab at sincerity by asking, in a voice as sympathetic as he could muster, what changes Hathorn contemplated in putting out the *Banner* since the publisher, editor and star reporter was murdered and gone. Hathorn was wrestling with that, he nervously replied, but did add, with a jerk of his thumb in the direction of the composing room, that the *Banner* was fortunate to have a veteran master printer.

From where he sat, Brosky could see back into the composing room, which would have taken up just part of the spacious first floor lobby in the *World* building. To Jake, composing rooms remained only convoluted, rackety places with an unforgettable smell where stories from reporters' typewriters were miraculously turned into galleys of type. Hundreds labored back at the *World* to accomplish what a handful of persons did in that back room of the *Banner*. It was true, as Hathorn said, that the *Banner* was lucky to still have one of the diminishing number of master printers—an individual who needed little help with typesetting, page makeup and presswork. He could cast his own type and, if need be, mix his own ink.

Hathorn seemed uncomfortable discussing any further with Brosky the future operation of the *Banner*. This was fine with Jake because it was none of his business anyway. Jake only stopped at the *Banner* to query Hathorn about the death of Stine.

Brosky could not help but notice the section of the front office dominated by a desk far more ornate than the other furniture. Stine's desk. Rococo in style, it was loaded with drawers, including a serpentine one over a kneehole flanked by two short drawers, all inlaid with leafy scrolls. Hunkered down on the desk was the workhorse of a newspaperman, a typewriter. A shopworn Remington, black as a politician's limo and heavier than hell. With its faded keys, it had to be a cousin of the old clacker that Herbert Overman hunched over to bang out Brosky's stories at the *World*.

On the wall behind the desk was a baroque Ansonia clock

in a walnut case, which like the desk had belonged to the *Banner's* previous owner. There, on the wall, also hung a large framed picture of a gentleman Brosky did not recognize. William Allen White was the subject, and it was Stine who'd put up the image of the man he once served. Down a bit from White on the wall was the obligatory Cardinals' calendar featuring two smiling faces that Brosky did recognize, hustling 1946 World Series hero Enos (Country) Slaughter and that most graceful of shortstops, Marty (Slats) Marion.

Shifting the conversation to the investigation of Stine's death, the detective in Brosky was curious about the contents of those fancy drawers in Stine's desk. Hathorn insisted that a thorough search of them, and every nook and cranny at the *Banner,* revealed no clews to the solving of the murder.

Hathorn averred that he, himself, had shed no light on the mystery when questioned at separate times by an assistant state's attorney of Cypress County, an investigator from the Jefferson County sheriff's office in Indiana and, of course, Sheriff Parkins. At the mention of Parkins' name, Jake cut in.

"Tell me if you can, Lyle. Was Stine about to write a story linking Parkins to the payoffs from gamblers?"

Hathorn fidgeted before answering. "I don't personally know if Sheriff Parkins is part of any of that, Mr. Brosky."

"But still, Lyle, I'm sure you would know if Stine was about to hit Parkins in your paper."

"Mr. Brosky, I wouldn't know that or hardly anything else Peter planned in the gambling series because he never discussed any of those pieces with me beforehand. I never thought it was because Peter did not trust me. It was more...well it was just that he was secretive about so many things. His personal life, his own background, for example. I don't even know where the orphanage was that he lived in when he was a kid."

Mrs. Tolliver waddled over with glasses of iced tea for the two men. She also turned the only electric fan in the place more in the direction of Hathorn and Jake. "I know it's hot in St. Louis, Mr. Brosky," she said. "But, I'm sure it's not like this frightful heat we have in southern Illinois." Beads of glistening perspiration on her neck and thick arms attested to the suffocating humidity in the room.

As Brosky yielded to the desire for a long sip of the tea, the paper's front street door flew open and a tall, gangly woman burst into the office like a Marine storming a Pacific island. Paying Brosky no heed, she pulled up in front of Hathorn and thrust into his hand a bundle of pages scribbled in cursive. "Here is my column," she declared in a no-nonsense voice. "There's not a word in this that you can change." There was, of course, never a word to be altered any week in her column, a faithful but mumbo-jumbo recitation of the comings and goings of Grandville's finer families.

Although momentarily caught off guard by the abrupt interruption, Hathorn rose for the purpose of an introduction.

"Mr. Brosky, this is Frieda Shepwinkel, who writes a popular column in our paper, 'Inside Grandville'."

"And," he followed up, "this gentleman, Frieda, is Mr. Jake Brosky from the *St. Louis World*."

Well, well, calculated Brosky as he stood up, so this was the Walter Winchell of Grandville, disguised to look like the nasty witch in *The Wizard of Oz*. Jake forced what he hoped was a smile, and she did too, if only for a second. Just long enough to reveal one of the most outstanding rows of horse teeth he'd seen.

With not so much as a sound to Brosky, she pirouetted and barked to Mrs. Tolliver, "You make sure he doesn't change anything in my column.

"You might want to even place it on the front page since I started off with Henry and Violet Hortense visiting her first cousin in Walla Walla. That's the Walla Walla in the state of Washington. On the drive out, they stopped off in Omaha, Nebraska, to look up a second, or maybe it was a third, cousin on Violet's side...."

"We'll see," Mrs. Tolliver broke in, "if we can run it closer to the front. And don't worry, Lyle won't change anything. Just don't bother yourself about it, Frieda."

Jake was ready to resume with Hathorn on the subject of Stine, trusting that Mrs. Tolliver could keep Shepwinkel's attention. No such luck. She spun back to Hathorn. Something else on her mind couldn't wait.

"Lyle, some of my readers think we should run a picture that is more flattering of me with my column."

Hathorn's face went blank.

"Well, I...I haven't thought about it. I guess we could, though. But what is wrong with the picture we are using, Frieda?"

"Oh, you know, there's been some talk. I've heard things."

"Heard what?"

"It's just that the picture, some seem to feel, makes my neck look...well, look too long. They think I deserve a better likeness of me in the paper."

Jake had turned away, was gazing in fact at the Cardinals' calendar on the wall. This was not his fight. If it had been, he'd have told her that she was afflicted with what was commonly known as a goose neck, except that the stem connecting her head to her body would have made many geese jealous. But this was Hathorn's baby to handle.

"I was wondering," she said.

"About what?" Hathorn rejoined.

"If the paper would pay for a new picture of me...since it's only fair...."

"Well, I guess we could consider—

"Fine. Then I'm going over to Carbondale, to a professional photographer over there who Violet Hortense and Elsie Botkins went to because he makes people look as good as they really look. They say he's one who can bring out my best features...and it's only fair...."

"Yes, I'm sure we can do what we have to do to get a picture of you for the paper that makes you look as good as you truly do. But right now I have to get back to my discussion with Mr. Brosky, whose time—

"Say," she interrupted, turning from Hathorn to Brosky, "can that be ice tea you're drinking?"

Surprised by the sudden question, Jake was slow to reply.

"Oh, why, why, yes it sure is."

"That's sure a fooler. I always thought you big city newspaper people drank something a lot stronger than tea."

While Jake rummaged for a retort, she flashed a "gotcha" grin with a drawing back of her lips that gave him another eyeful of those teeth. And that was it. She was gone, as quickly as she came in.

Brosky cracked a smile, and Hathorn did too, but his smacked of embarrassment. Returning to Stine almost seemed to be a relief for Hathorn. Yet, as the conversation got back on track, Hathorn was soon again emphasizing that Stine was a very private person who refused to share his personal life with anyone of whom Lyle was aware.

To underscore this, Hathorn related that, just a month ago, Stine had left one morning without any advance notice for what he said would be a drive through Missouri. While Brosky wanted to get Hathorn back on the subject of gambling, he did ask, almost unthinkingly, about what in Missouri attracted Stine.

"Oh, probably nothing in particular, Jake." Sometimes Hathorn called him Mr. Brosky and other times by his first name, Jake noticed. Hathorn apparently could not decide which one was appropriate.

"Peter just said he needed a break and wanted to roam some of the out-of-the-way roads in Missouri he got to know when he was over there cutting his teeth in newspapering. He was back in Grandville the next day, and he never said a word about it."

"Stine's trip to Indiana," interjected Brosky, "is the one people are interested in."

Hathorn succumbed to the jitters again at the mention of Stine in Indiana. No, he told Brosky, he had nothing to add to what the authorities surmised about it. One and all, Hathorn included, assumed Stine drove to Indiana in pursuit of a significant new angle for the *Banner's* antigambling crusade. Nobody had discovered what it was, though. Predictably, Stine had left Hathorn in the dark before departing for Indiana. Stine only mentioned to him, Hathorn maintained, that he was off to the Hoosier State for a day or so to follow up on some recently obtained information.

The investigation into Stine's death, Hathorn recounted, turned up that he surfaced in the county courthouse in Madison, where a clerk seemed to recall him searching through birth records. However, no notes were found on his body. Stine also dropped by the office of the Madison daily newspaper, *The Pilot*, and paged through bound editions of the paper from earlier decades. A woman there remembered Stine saying he'd be back the next day to continue his perusal.

"You have no idea at all, Lyle, what he was looking for?"

"Mr. Brosky, I'd tell the investigators, and you too, anything that Peter might have said to me. But he just didn't let on what it was about."

"Are you certain, Lyle, that you cannot remember anything?"

Hathorn blushed. He looked away from Brosky, chagrined that he was absolutely no help to those trying to find out who killed his employer and friend, Peter Stine. Shame flooded Hathorn at the thought of what Brosky must think of him.

Jake caught Hathorn's cheeks turning to a rosy tint. He could not see pushing Lyle much further. Maybe just another question or two.

"Lyle, do you have any reason to believe Peter went over to Indiana on a chase involving something different from gambling?"

"I just can't say, Mr. Brosky. I have no idea what it would be."

"Think for a moment, Lyle. We know the gambling crowd had reason to take out after Peter. But who else was mad at him? He was certainly not bashful about using the paper to stand up for what he believed in. Whom else did he cross?"

Well, responded Hathorn after some thought, Stine editorialized in support of a fledgling effort by blacks to integrate the public swimming pool down in Cairo. In moving to blunt such a development, white segregationists angrily threatened to firebomb the *Banner* office. Scorn also was piled on Stine by several of the major loggers in the nearby Shawnee Hills as a result of the *Banner's* call for preservation of certain stands of trees.

Brosky knew about the white supremacists in this part of the world; he'd put nothing past them. Logging was foreign to him, but he didn't picture lumberjacks as killers. The situation down at Cairo, though, might merit a look. Jake just could not convince himself that the gaming crowd bumped off Stine.

At the conclusion of the meeting with Hathorn, Jake made one more pitch for assistance from the man who, in Brosky's eye, had to know something that could shed light on the slaying of his boss. "Please," Brosky implored Hathorn, "call me in St. Louis if anything comes to you in future days."

Thanking Mrs. Tolliver once more for the iced tea, Jake departed. As he stepped out onto the sidewalk, he heard a familiar jingle from down the street before his eyes had readjusted to the glare of the midday sun. When his vision cleared, he saw, sure enough, that the clinking and tinkling came from a Good Humor ice cream truck stopped on the other side of the wide thoroughfare in front of a small flower garden snuggled between the gray Grandville Post Office and the yellowish frame home of Western Union. Prompted by his sweet tooth, Brosky strode toward the squat white truck with an ice cream bar painted on its side, one of a fleet contributing to the good life on the streets of America. He found himself fifth or sixth in the quickly formed line awaiting service from a smiling gentleman in a starched, white uniform that made him look cooler than a polar bear. If he'd been in St. Louis, Jake would have glanced around before joining this particular line since it often was dominated by gleeful kids. A man with his reputation wasn't known for patronizing Good Humor trucks. But Jake was a stranger in this town. He could let his guard down.

While Brosky still was in Grandville, hitting the Good Humor driver for a vanilla bar, Mrs. Tolliver asked Hathorn to take a telephone call to the *Banner* that she thought it best for him to handle.

"There's a woman on the line who says she is a Miss Sadie," explained Mrs. Tolliver. "I think she's calling long-distance. She asked for Peter. I don't know but that you ought to talk to her, Lyle." As Hathorn moved to the phone, Mrs. Tolliver added softly, "I'm sure she is an older woman."

Out of curiosity, Mrs. Tolliver listened to Hathorn's end of the conversation. She heard Hathorn tell the caller that Peter Stine had said nothing in the office about a story that he was writing about the caller. No, Hathorn went further, he had never heard Peter mention anything about Miss Sadie. After that, Mrs. Tolliver judged that Hathorn was getting an earful since he listened for a time without saying a word. He took some notes on a scratch pad, though.

Finally, Mrs. Tolliver heard Hathorn deliver the bad news. "Miss Sadie, I am sorry to have to tell you that Peter died a few days ago in an unfortunate incident. Otherwise, I am sure he'd have gotten back to you if he said he was going to." A pause followed. Then Hathorn said, "We are all in shock also. Yes, I know it's terrible." Those were his last words before he placed the receiver back on its cradle.

The call added to Hathorn's uneasiness. He decided to tell Mrs. Tolliver only that it was "a strange call, but nothing for us to worry about." However, he couldn't be certain of that. Maybe Brosky should know about Stine and Miss Sadie. Sheriff Parkins and the other investigators too. Hathorn would think about it. He just wished he wasn't so edgy.

Not long after Brosky left Grandville for the drive home to St. Louis, his Olds 88 cruised by the Big Dog Mine of Burning Diamond Coal Company. Several hundred yards beyond the mine's tipple, the workers in a crew constructing a new portal for the colliery were taking a break on the surface. Their respite was a noisy one, thanks to three or four mangy coy-dogs yapping like crazy behind a mound of dirt left behind as a result of bulldozing for a new fresh water pond for the mine.

Suspecting that the carcass of some animal was laying back there, two of the workers walked to the heap for a look. As the dogs scattered, the chaps found more than they bargained for.

One of them shouted excitedly back to the others, "Holy Jesus, get over here!"

Within seconds, the entire crew was staring at the corpse of a man, an obviously tall fellow, clothed in a ripped shirt and trousers. The layer of dust coating the body was doing little to discourage the ants and flies swarming over his every inch.

Chapter Eleven

While state police and sheriff's deputies were racing toward the Big Dog Mine, the sirens of two St. Louis city police cars wailed loudly as the vehicles sped along fashionable Kingshighway. When they approached the majestic President Hotel, everyone stopped to watch them pass. Even some hotel guests rushed to their room windows to see what was going on.

Not among the curious, though, were two people in an elegant suite fourteen floors above the din of the street. They were in a world far removed from sirens, and all else for that matter. Lovemaking—the feverish brand—was like that.

The guy could have had his pick of almost any of the lovelies tanning along the pool in the hotel courtyard below. But for Nat Coyne, his only interest was the woman whose curvaceous body was writhing under him on satin sheets. Coyne lived for the hours he could have her, and more and more he was finding it impossible to think of anything but her.

They were in a marathon today. Over and over again, she whispered her love for him; for Nat Coyne, her guardian, the man who'd protect her from all comers.

She wore only a sheer brassiere, which she knew drove him wild. Even after halting to catch their breaths, Coyne couldn't stop sliding his fingertips over the bra. She twirled the crucifix dangling on a chain around his neck.

It took a hell of an effort for him to take his hands off her and turn to a bedside table holding a bottle of Seagram's 7 Crown, ice in a bucket and glasses. He mixed two highballs. His woman, wiping golden strands of moist hair from her forehead, reached to a stand on the other side of the bed for a yellow pack of Old Gold cigarettes. The silence between them was electric. She lit up, took her drink from Coyne and leaned against the headboard, gazing silently at this strong, untamed man who so secretly brought an erotic side to her life. Before him, Sloan Dillard never knew a world of passion in her upbringing and marriage.

When her very being was threatened, it was this man, Nat Coyne, to whom she turned. Not to her father, not to her husband. Coyne was the one, the only one, Sloan wanted to turn to.

Chapter Twelve

The lights were burning later than usual in a ground floor office of the Governor's Mansion. Troopers remained stationed at the entrance, but the inside staffers, meaning the cook and the butler, had been directed, just hours before, to take the night off. Elijah Sanderson, one of the country's few unmarried governors, wanted to huddle with as little interruption as possible with Whitney Charles and the person who was the governor's closest confidant, Adrian Lee Burke.

Even before his morning meeting with Reverend Kincaid and the other clergy, Sanderson knew he did not have much time left before he had to act forcefully on the gambling issue. Now, to top it all off, there had been a murder.

The body of Marvin Langston, a son of a former bootlegger, Cecil Langston, had turned up at a southern Illinois coal mine. Langston had been strangled, and the back of his skull was bashed in. Since he worked at the popular Autumn Moon gambling club, the wire services were wasting no time speculating that his murder might signify an outbreak of old-time gang warfare for control of lucrative downstate gambling enterprises. The reporters also saw a possibility of some connection between the Langston and Stine killings. Sanderson had on his hands, as Chicago political writers often put it, a tempest in a teapot.

Fear not, though, Sanderson was telling himself. By the end of the day tomorrow, he was sure his feet would no longer be in the fire.

When the governor had been informed of the Langston slaying, he realized he could not wait out the few more days he had intended before playing his hand. Prior to leaving his Statehouse office to head for the mansion, he telephoned Chicago. It was time to put the plan into action. The man would be joining the governor, Burke and Charles at the mansion before the night was over.

When Sanderson ordered Charles late in the day to report to the mansion in several hours, he told his boyishly looking executive aide to grab a bite on the way. Otherwise, he'd have to raid the mansion kitchen because the cook would not be around. Sanderson also had asked his personal secretary to call Adrian Burke at the hotel he used in Springfield on his visits from Chicago, the St. Nicholas. Tell Adrian, the governor instructed, to consider eating before coming because the leisure evening together the two had planned would now be "serious business."

Sanderson remembered well the words of Burke when they had chatted by phone the previous day. How prophetic they were. "I've got to tell you, Elijah, I think the time is now, right now, to put your fist down hard on this gambling stuff," Burke said. "I see a hot potato here, and you're going to have to stop being wishy-washy about it. I know what you plan to do, Elijah, and it needs to be done now. You have to look bold and decisive."

Well, Sanderson would have the satisfaction of telling Burke at the mansion that the button triggering the game plan was pushed. Twenty-four hours from now, Elijah Sanderson would look very bold and decisive.

Few persons called Sanderson by his first name to his face. And who, besides Burke and perhaps the mayor of Chicago, could accuse the governor in so many words of wishy-washiness? But nobody else had a relationship with the governor like Burke, which was interesting since Burke was nigh invisible to most in state government, as well as to other Illinoisans.

Burke was not a public official; his name didn't surface anywhere on the state payroll. It made no difference. There was always a person like Adrian Lee Burke who had the ear of a governor, who went back a long way with the top dog. Burke, a son of an Irish Catholic plumber who became rich, and Sanderson, from an old-moneyed WASP family, did not know each other as they grew up at the same time in Chicago, but in different environs. They met and grew chummy at the University of Pennsylvania, where each majored in economics, chased the same high-hat eastern girls and snuck into speakeasies together when Prohibition set in.

The 1920s saw Sanderson emerge as a reputable economic theorist while still a junior member of the faculty at the University of Chicago. When Franklin Delano Roosevelt captured the White House during the Great Depression, he reached out and plucked Sanderson to serve with a select group of young academic eggheads entrusted with the execution of his New Deal. Sanderson got high marks for his administration of the National Recovery Board's programs across the land. His deputy, at his insistence, was his Chicago buddy, Adrian Burke.

Sanderson wore an army uniform during World War II, but remained stateside. When the fighting was over, the feds sent him to Europe to help oversee the rebuilding. Afterward, it was back to the University of Chicago, but not for long. Burke saw to that.

As the 1948 election approached, Burke was a rock-solid member of Chicago's Irish elite. An investment brokerage he founded before the start of the war was going great guns, and he was potent politically. He was looked upon as a financial conduit for the city's ruling Democratic machine, a kind of one-person exchequer handling the receipt and care of major donations from bigwigs in the Jewish, Polish, Italian and other ethnic communities supporting the machine. Being a shirttail cousin of the mayor—one his honor listened to—did not hurt Burke's standing.

The Democrats knew they had a chance to wrest the governorship in 1948, but only with a blue-ribbon candidate, a fresh face pledging reform. Burke had the perfect choice, and he went about selling him to the mayor and other party bosses. The gamble on Sanderson paid off in the voting booths. But Burke and Sanderson could not see stopping with their state's governorship. They'd gotten a good taste of Washington back in their National Recovery Board days, and the intoxicant power of Washington settled in their blood. Getting back there, at the top of the totem pole, was now more than a pipe dream.

Every major move that Sanderson made as governor had to be orchestrated to gain favorable national attention. His showing was a good one, so far. If there was a fly in the ointment, it was the ruckus over the gambling.

Sanderson's vacillation in confronting the gambling issue couldn't have been more understood by Burke. Neither man saw gaming as inherently evil. Certainly not charity raffles or church bingos. And if people who could afford it wanted to throw away money in the clubs, then that was their business. Not government's. But an issue could be propelled out of control by circumstances—events and things never planned or anticipated. A person in a position like Sanderson's could get trapped. When that happened, self-interest came first. Political survival always took precedence.

So, Burke truly was relieved when he learned, moments after arriving at the mansion, that his friend, the governor, had set the wheels in motion on the course of action they had been privately discussing for weeks. Too, when Burke found out about the murder of the bootlegger's kid, he definitely felt Sanderson was acting none too soon.

Charles was quick to point out that *Life* magazine was pressing for an interview with Sanderson within a week or so on the subject of gambling. The governor's press secretary, said Charles, "tells me they're doing a special issue on gambling because of the Senate investigation and that they're going to give Illinois a good ride."

The inquiry on the spread of gambling nationally by a special committee of the United States Senate never was far from the minds of Sanderson and Burke. The chairman of the panel, a pious senator from a southern state who expressed moralistic outrage over gaming as stridently as Reverend Kincaid, was determined to include Chicago among the committee's hearing sites. The senator also coveted the White House. Great political moxie was not necessary to see that something had to be done in Illinois before the traveling committee show hit Chicago.

For a man who glided smoothly through the corridors of power in Chicago, Burke remained surprisingly uneasy dealing with downstaters. The further south they came from, the more antsy he got. They used a different playbook; the culture, the life-style down there was so alien to Chicago it was hard to accept that everybody lived in the same state. Many of Burke's big-city friends routinely dismissed southern Illinoisans as yahoos. Not Burke. He certainly didn't buy the poor country boy line spewed by innumerable politicos from the lower end of the state. Dumb like foxes, that's what they were. Give them a chance and they could sell bridges to a lot of Burke's acquaintances should they ever venture south of Joliet, which they would not if they could help it.

Sanderson tried to convince Burke that he'd handled Kincaid well enough, but the two had no doubt that the reverend would remain a pain in the ass until he saw some results. The worst thing that could happen would be for Kincaid and others to go before those United States senators in Chicago and lambast Sanderson for doing nothing.

The plan of action to preclude such a nightmare was more Burke's idea than the governor's. The individual selected to make it happen was suggested by Burke. With the approval of Sanderson, Burke had contacted the person several days ago to see if he'd do it. Yes, he said, he was their man.

Finally, he was in Springfield. There was a knock on the door of the office in the Mansion.

"Yes, what is it?"

"Governor, sir," said the trooper, "the plane from Chicago has arrived."

"Thank you."

Turning to Charles, Sanderson asked him to drive to the Springfield airport to bring the man back to the mansion as quickly as possible because the hour was getting late. Much still had to be gone over before the press conference in the morning.

Chapter Thirteen

The notice went up on the bulletin board in the smoky Statehouse pressroom early in the day. The governor wanted the reporters in his office in an hour for a very important announcement. Sanderson's press secretary, himself a onetime Statehouse scribe, personally notified the correspondents for the Chicago papers and the wire services to make sure they knew. The *St. Louis World* fellow received a call too.

Walking en masse down to see Sanderson, in the elephant herd style they often used in traipsing through the Capitol, the reporters for once were not exactly sure what the governor was up to. Not a word had been leaked. Their guess was that the topic just might have something to do with the previous day's events—the visit to the Statehouse by Kincaid and the discovery of the murdered gambling club bouncer. They seldom guessed wrong.

After they were escorted into the governor's office and the door closed, each of the newspeople was handed a press release. It read as follows.

FOR IMMEDIATE RELEASE

Springfield, Illinois—Governor Elijah Sanderson announced today the appointment of Lawrence Dantello as superintendent of the Illinois State Police, effective immediately.

Dantello replaces Lawton (Burly) Carruthers, who ended a 25-year career as a state policeman with his resignation as superintendent today.

Dantello, 34, has been the chief of a special vice squad of the Chicago Police Department the last three years. Under an agreement with the City of Chicago, he is being granted a leave of absence from the city police department to serve with the State Police.

"I am very pleased for my administration and the citizens of Illinois to be able to obtain the services of Lawrence Dantello at this time," said Governor Sanderson. "I also want to emphasize that we have been fortunate in Illinois to have benefited from the fine public service for many years of Burly Carruthers. We all wish him well."

Governor Sanderson said he was confident that "the role of the State Police in enforcing the laws of Illinois will continue to be pursued with utmost vigor by new Superintendent Dantello."

Dantello is a native of Chicago. After graduation from Saint Peter's High School, he joined the Chicago Police Department and started as a patrolman. Attending night school at DePaul University, he was graduated from a widely recognized criminal investigation program. He left Chicago after the start of World War II to join the Marine Corps. Serving in the Pacific, he received numerous decorations for his participation in the successful invasions and capture of Guadalcanal, Tarawa and several other islands. Dantello returned to the Chicago Police Department after his discharge from the Marines. Last year, the special vice squad operating under his command received the highest commendation awarded by the Chicago Crime Commission.

While the release was being scanned by the reporters, the governor entered his office, flanked as usual by Whitney Charles and behind him the star attraction of the news conference. Sanderson sat down at his desk, Charles moved in robotic fashion to the side of the room and Dantello, a short, broad shouldered man, stood behind the governor, stiff and unsmiling. The *Chicago Herald* reporter, for one, confided in a low voice to a colleague, "I've heard the police beat guys in the city say this fellow is a tough little bastard."

The customary procedure was for the governor to read his announcement, which he did, and then take questions. They came in a rush, all asking in different words the same thing. Did the naming of Dantello mean that Sanderson was ordering a crackdown on wide open gambling?

The governor was a bit cautious in replying, but thought the reporters should get the message. "This administration is committed, as I have said over and over, to full enforcement of all the laws of Illinois to the maximum extent possible," he told one reporter. To another, Sanderson said, "If people are violating the law any place in the state, then they are not going to escape the attention of either this office or Superintendent Dantello."

One member of the press corps who didn't like Sanderson—he disparagingly called him "the professor" behind his back—moved to get the governor on the defensive.

"In view of recent events, Governor, do you think your administration has been lax in confronting illegal gambling?"

Sanderson always steeled himself to be ready for that kind of question, particularly from this reporter, but the governor could not completely hide his irritation when he replied, "As I indicated yesterday to Reverend Kincaid's group, and as I'm sure most of you know, I've felt that local offiicials have the primary responsibility for dealing with that matter."

"Then, Governor, are you saying that county and other local officials have been derelict in upholding the law where gambling is concerned?"

"I am not saying anybody is derelict. I certainly have not used that word. I am simply saying that while I am governor the law is going to be enforced." Wanting to get off the subject, Sanderson quickly added, "Are there other questions?"

Most of the reporters were beginning to fidget, knowing they'd better be running back upstairs to the pressroom to phone their home offices on a story unquestionably destined for page one. However, nobody could leave the governor's office until the press conference ended. As long as one unsatisfied news hound kept posing questions, it was not over.

Looking at Dantello, one of the scribes, hoping to catch him off guard, bluntly asked, "Mr. Dantello, when do you plan to begin the crackdown on the gambling joints?"

A brief smile crossed Dantello's wide face. He was prepared for the question. "I am sure that you gentlemen of the press, knowing as much about law enforcement as you do, realize that a question like that can never be answered."

Another reporter took a swing at him. "You are not saying are you, Mr. Dantello, that you have no plans to go after the gambling establishments?"

"Sir," Dantello calmly countered, "the governor has given me a rare opportunity to head an organization responsible for upholding the laws of this state, and I intend to do everything I can to justify the faith and confidence that Governor Sanderson has shown in me."

The reporters with deadlines looming were getting jumpier. However, one in the pack was not through. Maybe he thought he still could get a pound of flesh out of the occasion.

"Mr. Dantello, are you aware of persistent rumors that some state policemen may have received payoffs or bribes to ignore open gambling, especially in southern Illinois and certain other places like Peoria?"

Dantello did not flinch. "I would say this to that question," he responded. "If you or anybody else has specific information about a member of the state police accepting bribes, then I invite you to come to my office and give me the details. If any of you are familiar with my record at the Chicago Police Department, you know that I have no tolerance of any kind for corruption among law enforcement officers."

"Gentlemen," Sanderson spoke up, "I am aware that you have to be phoning in your stories. If there are no more questions...."

"Thank you, Governor," the senior member of the press crew, an old "don't rock the boat" fellow, piped up. Before he finished saying the words, his colleagues were hastily on their way out of the office. One did not escape, though, before being pulled to the side by Whitney Charles. He wanted a quick word with the correspondent from the *St. Louis World*.

While the reporters were racing back into the pressroom, a grieving Dorothy Langston walked slowly to her mailbox, which was a bit of a hike down on the narrow road leading to her farmhouse. Reaching the box, she looked inside. It contained only a package, or something resembling one, messily wrapped in dark paper.

Withdrawing the small bundle, she found it heavier than it appeared. Peeling away the paper, she gasped upon finding a pistol inside the wrapping. Along with it was a note on a torn piece of soiled white paper.

Laying the weapon down beside the sunflowers alongside the road, she held the note between two fingers of a shaking hand. She did not want to read it, but knew she had to.

Scrawled in pencil were words that left her reeling as if

she'd been hit in the chest by a cannonball.

"Youse shud have this gun. It was on Marvin, but poor Marvin just dont need it no more."

Chapter Fourteen

R-r-r-ring.
R-r-r-ring.

The goddamn telephone. It was an indispensable tool of his trade, but he still hated being jolted awake by it. Only when he was ringing somebody else out of their sleep was it okay.

R-r-r-ing. Seldom did he not get to it after the third ring. He couldn't stand a fourth shrill, but it took a considerable effort with one very lifeless arm to pick up the phone.

"Yeah," he mumbled groggily into the receiver.

"Jake," said the familiar voice at the other end of the line, "I know you just got to bed, and I'm sorry to hit you with this, but you have to be getting back over to Illinois. A big one is going to be breaking."

The city editor of the *World* was one person Brosky could not put off. "What is it?" he growled hoarsely. "What's going on?" Rubbing his eyes to wipe out the sleep, he glanced over at the clock. It was mid-morning.

The *World's* reporter in the Illinois Statehouse was dictating a story, the city editor rapidly explained, on Governor Sanderson's naming of a new state police chief. Beforehand, the *World* man relayed a tip to the city editor that he'd just received from a young assistant to Sanderson named Whitney Charles. The new head of the state cops was gung ho. So zealous that he planned to cap his first day on the job with a surprise raid on the Autumn Moon gambling club. No more details were available, but the *World* editors knew the next day's top story was being handed to them.

A reporter was never in the business too long not to get excited over his byline on a front pager. When it was no longer a thrill, it was time to get the hell out. Jake was positive his story on Marvin Langston's murder was the lead or "turn" article in today's paper, the first edition at least. He'd been up all night working on it. Now he was looking at two days in a row in the limelight. He'd been there often, but it never became old hat.

Brosky's throat was raw and clogged. When he coughed to clear it, he felt a stab of pain down into his lungs. "Are there any phone messages?" he finally asked.

Two were of interest. One from "Mr. Brown," an alias for a Brosky stool pigeon in the Fontane gang, and the other from Lyle Hathorn.

The city editor said he'd hang up to give Brosky a chance to get going. Jake realized, of course, that the city editor was the one who could not talk any longer. His desk was the busiest in the *World* news operation, the funnel between the newspaper's large cast of reporters under him and the managing editor and his assistants—individuals to whom the city editor answered in the chain of command. A good city editor needed three heads and six hands.

Brosky designed to call the stoolie right away. First, he struck a match to fire a Lucky and walked over to the bedroom window of his high-rise apartment overlooking Lindell Boulevard. The building happened to be around the corner from the President Hotel and the suite so steamy the day before from Nat Coyne and Sloan Dillard. Opening the curtains and venetian blind, Jake was caught off guard by the blast of sunlight. He coughed again, hard, grimacing at the sting.

Back at his desk, he fumbled in his little black book for the stoolie's number on the East Side. He reached him on the second ring. Meet me at the usual place in an hour and a half, Jake told the guy. He said he'd be there. This was one underworld character who always jumped at a chance to talk to Brosky. It made him feel important.

Heading for the bathroom, Brosky looked longingly at his empty sack. He felt like he'd just left the city room of the *World,* where he spent the early morning hours putting together background that only he could supply for the Langston piece.

Jake did not stray far from the wire services' line that the killing smacked of the days of the bloody gang wars in downstate Illinois over the liquor-running trade. That was easy to infer, and the readers ate it up. Brosky being Brosky, he fed poop to his rewrite man that nobody else had. He and he alone secured from Dorothy Langston the account given her by Mirla Hornick of the run-in at the Autumn Moon between Marvin and Coyne. The editors ran it high up in Jake's story for extra zing.

Brosky really found it hard to swallow that Coyne was dumb enough to bump off a guy right after an open confrontation with him. Brosky saw Coyne here and there, but he and the tough dandy always ignored each other. True, Coyne was known as a hothead. But would he knock off Langston just like that? Nah. Brosky didn't buy it.

The roughest part of the night for Jake was talking to Dorothy, listening to her beautiful dialect gone weepy. Cecil wouldn't come to the phone. Dorothy said he refused to come out of the auto repair garage, where he was holed up with his bible and shotgun. "He won't even hardly say anything to me, Jake," she uttered. "He just sits there, staring. I can't even get him to eat."

Brosky developed a thick skin long ago to the murders on his beat. He never blinked at the body of this or that gangland victim because he knew most of the stiffs got what they deserved. Marvin's death was different, though. Jake hardly knew Marvin and, furthermore, the kid was flirting with trouble working at a place like the Autumn Moon. But Brosky had a kinship with Cecil and Dorothy that he'd never admit, at least not to anyone at the *World*, because it flouted the tenets of objective reporting. Callous Jake Brosky was saddened by this turn of events. He did something quite extraordinary when he talked to Dorothy. He tried to console her. However, he did it in a voice low enough to preclude anybody else at the *World* from hearing him. Sympathy did not square with his persona.

Jake's story had to delve into a lot of things that the Langstons and others in southern Illinois didn't want to be reminded of. The no-holds-barred combat between the Langston boys and Fontane for territory. The midnight calls on those unfortunate enough to be caught in the middle. Burned out roadhouses. The still unsolved shooting of Arthur Langston and other killings. Brosky himself hadn't thought about a lot of it for some time, but the murder of Marvin forced a rehash in print.

When he'd left the city room, Brosky was in the doldrums. After the telephone forced him out of bed, he was still in a slump. Only following the shower, shave and cup of Borden's instant coffee did he begin to snap out of it. The clean white dress shirt and drops of Vaseline tonic in his hair helped. Also, he reminded himself, the call from the city editor was his ticket to the top of the front page in tomorrow's paper.

If he needed any more incentive to get rolling, he got it when he went to the window of his living room for a look down at Lindell. Over on the corner he could see the small yellow and black stand where the same geezer hawked the *World* day after day. Business was brisk. The old, gray-bearded newsie who reminded Jake of the ancient mariner was working his changer to death as he dispatched copies to walk-up customers and passing motorists. The first thing in the paper they saw had to be Brosky's story. It was hard not to gloat.

Jake checked his watch to make sure he was leaving himself enough time to make the rendezvous with the stoolie across the river. He had to go. But, wait a second, there was the other call he wanted to return, the one from Hathorn. He'd almost forgotten it. Brosky had asked him to get in touch if anything came up about Peter Stine.

Mrs. Tolliver answered when the operator put Brosky through to the *Banner*. Was Lyle there? No, she replied. The woman sounded exasperated.

"He's gone, Mr. Brosky, and we don't know exactly when he's going to be back. At least not for a few days it looks like. He told us he had a personal family matter down in Tennessee that he had to take care of right away."

"When did he leave?"

"Couldn't have been any more than an hour ago."

"Well, my office said he placed a call for me earlier this morning."

"He made several calls when he was here, Mr. Brosky, and he took some. That's all I can tell you."

Jake needed to hit the road. Still, he asked the woman if she knew where Hathorn came from in Tennessee."

"We are not really sure. Somewhere in the eastern part maybe."

"Well, if he checks in, I'd appreciate it if you'd tell him I'm sorry I missed his call."

"I will. I surely do hope he'll be coming back to us real

soon because we've got a paper to get out here, and he's left us real short handed." In a less serious tone, she added, "We could use some help from you, Mr. Brosky, if you could find the time."

Jake forced a croaky laugh, a small one. Putting him to work at the *Banner*, he shot back, would reveal "how damn little I know about getting out a newspaper."

Chapter Fifteen

The place was a dingy hole-in-the-wall, a bona fide greasy spoon nestled among the maze of tracks in the switchyard hogging the riverfront on the East Side. Few besides brakemen and gandy dancers were aware of the little eatery, which specialized in sliders with the suspicious smell of horse meat. Brosky and the stoolie could not find a more perfect spot to meet.

Jake never ordered anything in the place except for the full-bodied coffee, brewed from visible tins of Old Judge and always poured by the squat woman in the umber stained apron behind the counter. Brosky didn't know her name because he never told her his name. No names, no questions. He did go so far as to nod to her when he came in and saw she was alone in the joint with Mr. Brown.

Brown was really Norton Raven. He despised the name Norton, though, and wanted to be called Sam Raven, which his acquaintances did because mention of the name Norton brought out the mean streak in him. Raven was an errand guy for the Fontane mob. Being such, he was close enough to the palace guard to pick up things. He was not exactly a stool pigeon in the literal sense since Fontane knew Raven got his jollies exercising his jaws to Brosky, which was copacetic with Fontane as long as Raven passed on stuff the gang leader didn't mind Brosky hearing. Brosky, not having been born yesterday, naturally assumed this was the case. But, he never let on to Sam's face that he viewed him as anything but a true canary.

Brosky joined Raven at the oilcloth-covered table farthest from the counter, but neither said a word until the short-legged gal brought over the cups of hot java and moped away. Like always, Raven, the last of the zoot suiters, was resplendent in a black ensemble with vertical white stripes. Wide ones. The coat overly padded in the shoulders was outrageous on the lapels; the sharply pleated pants tapered down to narrow cuffs. Other sports had quit taking this garb out of their closets in the early '40s. The only thing Raven had abandoned was the knee-length key chain.

"Saw your story this morning, Jake, right up at the top of the front page." When they'd first sat down together, Jake was Mr. Brosky to Raven. But the surname went by the wayside as Raven assumed, in his mind at least, an increasing state of familiarity with the crime reporter.

"But you know, Jake, it ain't what you think. Yeah, I can see how it looks like the way you wrote it. But, I'm telling you, it ain't that way."

Brosky certainly did not need convincing that his story might not be on target, especially the tying of Marvin's death to a new flare-up of the old gang war days in southern Illinois. However, Brosky felt he had to play a devil's advocate with Raven, even though it was a needless charade since Raven was going to convey the Fontane message of the day in any event.

"You tell me, Sam," Brosky said in mock wonderment, "how else I'm supposed to see it."

The situation appeared clear enough, Brosky professed. Fontane trying to muscle in on the gambling action down south. The Langston kid, son of an old Fontane enemy, somehow getting in the way. Ticking off Coyne was probably sufficient cause alone to get Marvin killed. And then there was the murder of the newspaper editor, a person fighting the whole gambling industry. "So, as I am saying, Sam," snorted Brosky, "I don't see how else to play all this."

"Jake," Raven responded, "do you know what Fontane did when he heard about the death of that Langston punk? I swear to God, he—

The rest of his words were drowned out by the rumble of a switch engine lumbering by the cafe. It was so close the place shook.

When the engine moved on, Raven repeated what he said. "I was telling you, I swear to God, that Fontane threw a chair against the wall when he heard about that punk's death. He was so goddamn mad. He's trying to work out a business arrangement with the clubs down there, something which would be very good for everybody. The last thing we want is a killing to bring on the goddamn heat."

So as to convince Brosky that he was not spreading baloney, Raven crossed himself. Cool. But Jake, the skeptic, would have wagered that Raven hadn't been to Mass since he was a brat stealing bicycles.

Sticking to the devil's advocate game, Brosky asked, "But what about all that bad stuff in the past between the kid's dad and Fontane?"

"Harry could give a cat's ass about that Langston fellow. He ain't been heard from in years."

Jake brought up the altercation at the Autumn Moon between Marvin and Coyne. So what, Raven countered. "I read about that in your story, Jake, but Nat's got an alibi for the time the punk was bumped off. Anyway, you've gotta know Nat would never knock anybody off without Harry's okay. That's the last thing that'd happen, Jake, believe me."

Brosky did. This led to another question, but it had to wait as the engine went by again, moving to switch more cars from one track to another in the making of a new train.

When the two men could hear again, Brosky started off. "If Fontane's as innocent as you say, Sam, then who's doing all the killing?"

"We don't know," Raven replied. "There's some asshole out there who's doing it, but it's no Fontane guy. Maybe it's one of those local yokels down there. Whoever he is, he's trying to screw it all up."

More than just trying. Brosky had to believe the killer, or killers, were on the verge of success if causing trouble for the

Illinois gambling world was in fact the motive behind the murders. However, Brosky knew he could not tell Raven that he was heading to cover a raid that most likely was the beginning of a big state crackdown on unlawful gaming.

Time to leave, Jake indicated. The way they worked it, Raven would not depart from the eatery until he figured Brosky was away from the switchyard. As Jake rose, Raven got in final words.

"If Fontane finds out who's doing the killing, the coppers won't have to worry about making any arrest."

Later that day, as the sun slipped in the sky to the west, two cars were parked side by side in a clearing off a dusty road in a remote section of Cypress County. The vehicles were unmarked, even though each was occupied by a single individual wearing a uniform. One was Sheriff Parkins and the other Oscar Gratiot, the state police commander in the area. They conversed without getting out of their cars. When they finished, Parkins peeled off, leaving billows of dust as he headed for Grandville and the Autumn Moon.

Chapter Sixteen

Like predators, they glided at twilight onto the half-filled parking lot of the Autumn Moon. Two black and white cars of the state police. They conveyed a platoon of eight men, two in uniform, who emerged from the vehicles and gathered without a word behind the shortest guy in the group, a wide-shouldered fellow wearing a tan suit. One behind him brandished a long-handle ax and another a sledgehammer with a mean head. Still another had a camera.

As the crew moved briskly toward the club's entrance, six other individuals not accustomed to hanging around the Autumn Moon emerged from the shadows of dusk. Three of them were armed with cameras—photogs from the *Associated Press* and *Life* magazine and Max Slattery of the *World*. Each was accompanying a reporter. One was the AP bureau chief for southern Illinois, another the *Life* correspondent in Chicago and the third was Brosky. Besides the *World*, the governor's man, Whitney Charles, had covertly tipped off the wire service and the magazine as to the raid. He wanted to assure national coverage of the governor's first dramatic strike against the spread of gambling in the state. The governor's office decided, probably with good reason, not to alert any local press in an effort to bolster the chance of the raid coming off as a true surprise.

When the raiding party reached the entrance, the reporters and cameramen were waiting under the blue canopy. So was Sheriff Parkins, and he was standing smack-dab in front of the door.

The press guys licked their chops. They'd hoped for something like this in scurrying down to Grandville. The photographers were taking pictures as fast as they could change their camera bulbs; Brosky and the other reporters were hastily making notes. An opportunity to cover a standoff firsthand did not come along every day. Or a live raid for that matter. Raids by the feds were old hat back in Prohibition, but few reporters on the scene then were still around.

The standoff commenced with the sheriff in full regalia putting up his hand, palm outward, in the face of the fellow in the tan suit, not unlike a cop stopping traffic. "You are at a place of business in my jurisdiction," Parkins declared sternly. "If there is a problem, it is my job to take care of it."

The guy in the tan suit did not blink. "Sheriff," he said calmly, "I am Superintendent Dantello of the state police. I have a warrant to enter this premise on the sworn word of several citizens of this state that illegal gambling is going on here. If you try to stop me—

"Sir," interrupted Parkins, "I am the law in this county. If there is something going on in the county that you want to talk to me about, I am willing—

He was cut off quickly by Dantello. "Sheriff, I am sworn to uphold the laws of the state of Illinois. Should you try to stop me, I will arrest you for obstructing a law enforcement officer in the performance of duty." He added in a voice still unwavering, "Now step aside!"

"You, sir," Parkins insisted, "are going to be a sorry man." Yet, as he muttered the words, he was retreating from the entrance.

With the sheriff out of his path, Dantello did not even give him a second glance as he pushed open the door and burst into the Autumn Moon, trailed by his men and the press gang. Commotion quickly set in. The AP scribe would write that it was "pandemonium," but that may have been a little strong.

Numerous startled patrons exited as fast as they could, some abandoning dinners half eaten. This was no problem with Dantello since he wanted everybody to disappear anyway— except for Mansfield and the employees. The cop and his men shooed out those who didn't go voluntarily, including a few who had choice words for the raiders and their ultimate boss, Governor Sanderson, before departing.

"You oughta be out there chasing real crooks," one person shouted. A shapely woman confronted Dantello and let him know what she thought. "Sweetie, that old governor up there in Springfield is going to hear from me." Behind her, another gal chimed in, "You tell him, Yvonne." Turning away from the widow Fitzgerald, Dantello bumped squarely into a graying individual a good foot taller than the state police chief. Extending a hand, the man introduced himself as State Representative Ernest Bigelow from the next county over.

"I am right pleased to meet you, mister," remarked Bigelow in an almost nonchalant manner. "I can see you are very busy at the moment, but when you have time back up in old Springfield I want you to give my very best to my good friend, Governor Sanderson." Bigelow started to walk off, but then hesitated. His face took on an expression like he just had a second thought. "Oh, you probably don't know this," the legislator said to Dantello, "but I am my party's ranking member on the House Appropriations Committee. I'll be sure to keep an eye out for you when you come before me on the request for money for the state police."

Encountering Bigelow was the first thing to give Dantello pause in the Autumn Moon, but not for long. He knew he couldn't let anything interfere with the raid, or his control of it. A great deal was riding on the execution of this incursion, for himself and the governor.

The reporters were tempted to follow Bigelow out of the club to seek further comment, but they realized they had to hang close to the maestro of the action, Dantello. When the raid started, Dantello informed Mansfield he was under arrest. The employees were ordered by Dantello just to stay put. After all the customers finally were ushered out, Dantello told the employees that each would be fingerprinted in short order, a step necessary to permit a check to see if any had criminal records. He directed Mansfield to accompany one of the raiders, a state revenue agent, to the club office, where Mansfield was to hand over account books.

Then the real fun began.

With a flip of his head, Dantello barked, "Go to it men!"

The officer with the sledgehammer, a bull with thick upper arms and no visible neck, teed off on the Liberty Bell, slamming it with a force that sent the venerable slot crashing to the floor. It was more than Mirla Hornick—already upset over the murder of her lover—could stomach. She bolted toward the guy wielding the sledge, yelling tearfully that "there's no reason to destroy the place." Dantello intercepted her by grasping her arm and swinging her around. "Stop right there, lady," he snapped curtly, "or you'll be in very big trouble." Every camera in the place flashed. For the photographers, the raid was a pictorial bonanza, a feast.

They couldn't change bulbs fast enough to capture it all. One raider impounding the currency in the cashier's cage in the private club room. Following the Liberty Bell, the smashing of the sledge into other one-armed bandits. The resounding thuds of the ax being smacked with ferocity into the craps and blackjack tables, splitting their tops. The sickening, splintering sound of the destruction of the handsome roulette wheel, another victim of the ax. What a waste, Max Slattery thought in concluding to himself that the raiding party was laying it on too heavy. He was sure Dayton Mansfield's face was ashen.

Brosky buttonholed Mansfield, trying to pry a verbal reaction to the brutal disintegration—within a matter of minutes—of his gambling enterprise. He sucked out a lament by Mansfield that "this is such a shame." The proprietor was obviously distraught; Brosky detected liquor on his breath.

"Why haven't the state police raided you before this?" questioned Brosky. "What's happened that you're getting hit now? What's changed things?"

Mansfield deflected the queries with a woeful shake of his head. He'd been downing manhattans ever since Parkins tipped him off late in the afternoon that the club would be raided in the evening. Neither Parkins nor Oscar Gratiot were even supposed to know, the sheriff admitted, that the newly appointed superintendent of the state police was heading south with a handpicked crew to personally invade the Moon. Well, Gratiot did get wind of it, but there was not a darn thing he could do to stop it, Parkins noted. As for the sheriff himself, he promised to do what he could. Mansfield saw how far Parkins got.

As big dollar signs reverberated in his head with every destructive swing of the sledge or ax, Mansfield had to bite his tongue to refrain from talking to the reporters. He wanted to tell them that they were witnessing his reward for paying off the bastards constantly putting the bite on him, the shysters assuring protection in exchange for the bribes. All the damn payments, and the Moon gets it rammed up its fanny. You bet Mansfield would have loved to level with that guy Brosky, to sit down with him right then and there on the up-and-up. But that would have left Mansfield a dead duck for sure in southern Illinois, maybe even dead literally, like his bouncer.

Mansfield also had to measure every word to this pugnacious fellow leading the raid, aware that any reference to the payoffs could land him and others before a grand jury, or worse. He had no choice but to tell his blackjack dealer, a chap with an invalid wife, a passel of kids and suddenly no job, to button his lip after he blurted out that the raiders were "acting like goddamn Nazis." Mansfield prayed that Mirla, nearly hysterical, didn't slug one of the invaders. If she did, he feared, she'd get a strong back of the hand in return before they slapped the cuffs on her dainty wrists. Mansfield felt compelled to put his arms around her, to console her. She trembled with every whack of the ax.

Brosky had no more luck drawing quotes from Dantello than from Mansfield. The World War II marine hero stuck to the obvious. The governor refused to tolerate unlawful activity in the state, and Dantello intended to clean house indiscriminately wherever the law was flouted. Beyond that, Dantello clammed up. Jake asked whether the raid was specifically prompted by the deaths of Peter Stine and Marvin Langston. No reply from Dantello. Jake knew he'd get no answer to another question, but threw it out anyhow. Where and when would the next gambling house raid come? Dantello countered with a look of incredulity, as if to say to Brosky, "Come on, man, get serious." The guy was certainly self-assured, Brosky had to conclude. A real cold-blooded dude.

The moon was afloat and stars had captured the rest of the sky by the time the raid ended. With everybody out of the club, Dantello padlocked the front entrance. He did it slowly so the cameramen wouldn't miss it. The AP reporter took off on a run to file the first story, taking his photographer with him. Max Slattery headed back to St. Louis. Ironically, nobody from the *Cypress County Banner*, whose late editor would have relished this night, ever showed up. The *Life* correspondent and photographer hung around because they had no deadline to worry about. Brosky knew his rewrite man was waiting for a phone call in St. Louis, but Jake needed and wanted to observe the arraignment of Mansfield before beginning to dictate the juicy information for the line story in tomorrow morning's *World*. Jake's deadline was not until after daybreak, so he had plenty of time. But he was dog tired, and hungry too, as he faced his second straight all-night outing. When it rained in his business, it usually poured.

Within an hour after Dantello secured the padlock on the Autumn Moon, the state police superintendent and one of his men escorted a handcuffed Dayton Mansfield into the only courtroom in the quaint Cypress County Courthouse in the center of Grandville. Sheriff Parkins surfaced in the back of the chamber. One couldn't tell if he was sullen or seething. Silence reigned as everybody cooled their heels until Circuit Judge Owen Harrold could be persuaded to leave the Cardinals' game on the radio in his home and come to the courthouse. When he arrived, he was not one bit amused.

He'd been summoned during an exciting comeback rally by the Redbirds against the New York Giants. While the judge was going out his door, bombastic Harry Caray, the Cards' raspy voiced announcer whom Harrold loved, was bellowing "Holy Cow!" This was Caray's trademark exultation whenever a Cardinal slammed one over the wall. Such a moment was always magic for the judge. He was definitely not happy that this damn impromptu business at the courthouse had spoiled it for him.

Voicing indignation at the cuffs on Mansfield, Harrold ordered them off immediately. Brusquely, he asked Dantello to come forward and tell him what was going on. As the state cop complied, the judge glowered at him. Then Mansfield stepped up at the judge's direction to be informed that he was charged with operation of an unlawful gambling establishment.

"How do you plead to the charge, Mr. Mansfield?" Harrold asked.

"Not guilty, sir."

"Very well. Your plea will be entered in the record, and the court will set a date for the commencement of further proceedings in this matter." Looking sympathetically at Mansfield, the jurist told him that he was "free to go until the court convenes again on the charge."

Dantello objected, arguing that the defendant should be required to post bail before being released from custody. The judge made no attempt to hide his anger in answering Dantello.

"This man is being released on his own recognizance. He is known to yours truly and to others in this community as a person of good standing. I am quite certain, very certain, he will not be leaving the state, Meester Duntullow."

With that, nobody in the chamber said another word. Didn't dare to. No one even moved—except for the photographer from *Life*, who maneuvered to obtain a picture of the whole courtroom scene. The judge took notice of him.

Admonishing the cameraman that taking pictures was verboten in the courtroom, Harrold asked the photographer where he was from. "*Life* magazine, your honor," the photog replied.

"*Life* magazine, huh? Now, how would *Life* magazine just happen to be down in our little part of the world tonight?" Sparing no sarcasm, Judge Harrold did not let it drop. "I wonder if there's anybody here who would know how *Life* magazine got down here tonight?"

He was looking at "Meester Duntullow" as he spoke.

Chapter Seventeen

If you didn't count the mayor of Chicago, Adrian Burke was the only person in the state put through to Elijah Sanderson right away whenever he called. The governor might not return calls from other elected Illinois officials, even the lieutenant governor, for hours. His own department heads usually had to wait much longer if there wasn't an emergency. Not Burke, though.

As a matter of fact, if Burke hadn't gotten on the horn to Sanderson the morning after the Autumn Moon raid, the governor would have tracked him down. Sanderson was about to pick up the phone when his personal secretary informed him that Burke was on the line from Chicago. The governor was ebullient, not a common characteristic for him, and Burke told him nothing to dampen the exuberance.

The appointment of Dantello and the follow-up strike

against a leading downstate gambling hot spot were all over the front pages of the Chicago dailies, Burke noted, confirming what the governor already knew.

"You're smelling like a rose today, Elijah," said Burke. "You're looking tough. The strategy worked." Neither man said so, but to both it had to seem apparent that Sanderson had taken a giant stride toward getting the most pestiferous monkey of his governorship off his back.

Burke also triumphantly conveyed to the governor the congratulations of a close friend of Burke at the Democratic National Committee in Washington. Adrian had just called the fellow, a party war-horse who had the ear of folks at the White House, even the President himself. Since the rumor factory had it that the President was fond of Sanderson, the DNC guy said he was sure the President would be pleased to learn that Sanderson had taken a step almost certain to bolster his already budding attractiveness in the national political picture. If nothing else, the individual added, Illinois was on its way to being up to snuff when the Senate committee on gambling opened its hearing in Chicago.

As if Burke and the governor did not know it. "We're covered on that one now, Elijah, and everybody's going to see it," Burke emphasized to Sanderson. One of the first, Burke bet, would be the highfalutin senator heading the panel. He had to be in a snit at having his thunder in Illinois stolen.

Which reminded Burke of another thing. "Elijah," he said, "there isn't any reason to delay that interview *Life* wants. You're ready for it now."

The smile on Sanderson's face grew wider. Before replying, he winked at Whitney Charles, who was standing quietly a few feet from the governor's desk.

"I have to tell you, Adrian, I'm ahead of you. The magazine already has been contacted. A writer and photographer will be coming to my office to see me the day after tomorrow."

The raid on the Autumn Moon the night before was also on the minds of many of the mourners gathered around the Langston family plot in the old cemetery on the prairie outside Smithburg. Marvin Langston's tie to the Autumn Moon left them even more sorrowful. Would the Langstons ever be free of the violence never failing to erupt from generation to generation in southern Illinois? The killings, first of the newspaper fellow and then Marvin, were matches lighting the fuses always set to detonate the explosiveness so ingrained in the region.

The bloodletting was all the outsiders seemed to remember, a sad reality in the eyes of those who knew southern Illinois as the home of God-fearing people trying to eke out a living in a land, as wildly beautiful as it was in places, that offered precious few ways to coast economically. Just putting food on the table was a robust chore, but this was a destiny of life countless southern Illinoisans felt to be willed in their souls. Honestly speaking, all but a few truly loved where they were. But, they hated the black-eye image from the violence; balked at talking about it with inquisitive strangers; and wished to all get-out the magazines and newspapers would give it up.

The burial of Marvin Langston did not help.

Many at the cemetery, including the Langston relatives from Kentucky and Tennessee, frowned at the photographers and note takers hovering around. Muffled cries of "let her be" and "leave the woman alone" were aimed at several of the camera guys who rushed forward to capture close-ups of Dorothy Langston falling to her knees beside the unadorned casket of her firstborn, extending her arms over it and bending down to press her lips against the sealed lid. They were acting like paparazzi, but this was Smithburg, not New York or Paris or Rome.

A reporter was rudely shoved aside when he attempted to question the grieving mother of Cecil Langston about the violent deaths stalking her family.

Nobody dared to ask Cecil any questions. His face was a stone mask, revealing not in the slightest the awful hurt eating away inside of him. He was uncommunicative when law officers paid him the obligatory visit. He knew their effort to find his son's murderer would yield nothing. He understood all too well that he and he alone would have to atone for the brutal slaying of Marvin. Arthur Langston's death had gone unrequited. Marvin's could not.

Finding her son's pistol in the mailbox unnerved Dorothy beyond anything Cecil could remember. The crude note with the gun was a gruesome touch, but Cecil knew it was not the style of professional killers. His son was murdered for a personal reason, Cecil was sure, by a person, or individuals, harboring an intense hatred for Cecil and maybe the other Langstons. No doubt, the firing at Lucius' car and the damaging incidents at the farm were done by the same hands. But by whom, or what persons? Cecil prayed that the Lord would show him the way, give him some sign or direction, to let him wreak revenge, to salvage his pride, his family's.

Cecil's impassivity remained unbroken as condolences were voiced quietly by those filing past his son's body at the mortuary. He deviated only once, when the cute young woman with whom Marvin had been dallying passed the casket. Cecil gently guided Mirla Hornick out of the line to ask her a few questions. No one heard what was said, but Mirla broke down in tears, prompting Cecil to embrace her in a fatherly manner.

Mirla was sobbing again as she stood near the grave site, not up with the immediate family but toward the back, next to some who were curiosity seekers out for a firsthand glimpse of the latest inopportune drama to afflict this dwindling, but still well known, family.

As the good reverend embarked on the final words for Marvin, before the lowering of the body into the earth, the blazing sun of midday took a hiatus behind a billow of clouds that brought a welcome breeze across the flatland. Too quickly, the light wind turned into a strong gust that whipped up a shower of dust from the parched fields of growth-stunted corn flanking the cemetery. A real wind, the kind that blows dirt into eyes and hair and between the teeth. Those lucky enough to have broad brims on their hats pulled them down, while others raised their hands to shield squinting eyes. Only those close to Asa Pollard, the pastor of the First Baptist Church of Smithburg, could hear him as he sought to instill a degree of dignity to the abrupt ending of Marvin Langston's life.

Reverend Pollard took a shot at bringing Shakespeare to the prairie, paraphrasing as best he could remember the wording in *Hamlet* about death being that undiscovered country from whose boundary no traveler ever returned. But for people who believed, who had faith, implored the minister, Marvin was passing on to a rewarding nirvana that promised everlasting life.

To those within earshot, Pollard had this to say: "We mourn the loss of Marvin, and we must search for the good things to remember him by to achieve solace. If we truly can see the nature of what is happening, then it will go far to give us comfort both now and in the future."

Because most standing on the prairie were covering their eyes, they failed to notice a hasty invasion of dark gray clouds from the west. Rain hadn't fallen for weeks, and the first drops caught everybody by surprise. Out of respect, nobody moved. But one or the other—the rain or the proceeding at the grave—had to quit. The rain didn't, so Reverend Pollard, with a makeshift homily, brought the service to a rapid conclusion. Then he wasted no time taking off his coat and wrapping it around Cecil's mother. He was her pastor anyway, not Cecil's, since the real Baptists in town had disassociated themselves from Cecil long ago over his booze running.

As the shower turned the dirt around the open grave into mud, all but Cecil, Dorothy and Lucius fled to their cars. Lucius strained to pull his mother away from the casket of his brother, which took some doing. Neither of them attempted to get

Cecil to leave. He just stood there, staring, continuing to silently plead with God to allow him to avenge this wrongdoing. He hardly noticed the rain as it turned into a downpour, the lightning suddenly cracking apart the sky.

Many miles away from Illinois, in Las Vegas, a land severely toasted by dry heat, Harry Fontane was damn riled. Bad things were happening back home, one after another, and Fontane could see his world spinning out of control. Just a few hours after arriving in Vegas, still steamed over the killing of the Langston kid—a stupid blunder by some horse's ass, every bit as idiotic as the murder of the newspaper editor—Fontane was paged away from the giant pool at the Desert Inn to take a call from one of his very jittery boys in East St. Louis. "We gotta tell you, boss," Fontane was informed, "the state guys shut down the Autumn Moon last night."

Harry's mouth dropped open. "Jesus," he replied into the receiver, his voice tinged with disbelief, "I can't believe that wimp of a governor would have the balls." Did that Mansfield fellow, that prissy straight arrow running the Autumn Moon, screw up by not making the necessary payments? Did he fail to touch all the bases?

Fontane assumed as far as his own Club Destiny was concerned that Coyne had everybody covered who had to be greased. Still, maybe he'd better go over it with Coyne. But sorry, the mob boss was told, his top lieutenant was not around.

"Where the hell is he?"

"We don't know, Harry."

"Well find him and have him on the goddamn phone up in my room in an hour!"

Slamming down the receiver, Fontane dressed hurriedly into casual clothes. He wanted to cool down, and he had a favorite little jaunt in Vegas that might help. Afterward, back in the hotel, a nice gratuity would await him in his suite.

The walk began across the landscaped grounds of the Desert Inn and continued past the far less luxurious Flamingo, an establishment that nevertheless brought out the closest thing to a warm spot in Fontane's heart. The Flamingo was the resort of the late gangster Benjamin (Bugsy) Siegel, whom Fontane had known and liked, better yet idolized. Siegel's construction of the Flamingo on an arid, forlorn Nevada highway paved the way for the incredibly rapid growth of the famous Vegas gambling strip. Heaven. To Fontane, that was Vegas. And Nevada. The state legalized gambling in 1931, and underworld money spawned the strip. Mob chieftains may have had Bugsy executed for his excesses, but Fontane's appreciation of him was rekindled every time he saw the Flamingo. Standing and staring at it, Fontane himself felt respectable.

Unlike home, Harry didn't have a bodyguard trailing him in Vegas. This was his brand of world run by his kind of people; a place offering fun and adventure for willing takers from all over. He was enraged that small-minded puritans denied the same in Illinois and other states.

The short hike calmed Fontane's angst. But not for long. Returning to the Desert Inn, he felt the hair rising on his neck again when the desk clerk told him no phone message was awaiting him. Coyne had not called.

Up in his suite, on the other hand, something was waiting for Fontane. Laramie, his woman in Vegas and the reason above all others for his frequent escapes to the desert oasis. Fontane had a wife, but he'd spent little time with her, much less shared a bed, in decades. His marriage was a charade, but his church forbid divorce. He had begun to doubt he could make love anymore until he was fixed up with Laramie, the only name she went by. She may have been the oldest gal in the Desert Inn's floor show, which would have made it on Broadway, but no cheerleader, or any other showgirl for that matter, had better legs. When the stage lights hit those strutting limbs, the faded Betty Grable pinups on barracks walls came to life.

Curse his luck, though, it was one of those days for Fontane. Nothing was going right. He couldn't cut it with Laramie. Their normal warm-up failed to spark a reaction from the gangster. Her attempt in soothing words to tell him to forget it until later did not clothe her disappointment. Fontane was humiliated. Then Laramie demanded more expense money from him, insisting she needed it and reminding him she had no other place to go because she limited herself to him. Remember, if there were more than Fontane, she always told him, she'd be a floozy. But Laramie with the Grable legs was no prostitute. Fontane forked over, but not without a reminder of his own. Any other guys found enjoying her favors could expect to end up buried in the desert.

Still, he knew she wasn't out of line. At any rate, he couldn't take out the day's frustration on Laramie. So he rolled out of bed, grabbed the phone off the French provincial desk in the front of the suite and ordered the hotel operator to connect him with East St. Louis. He'd take it out on Coyne.

But the boys hadn't found him. Nat was nowhere around.

Fontane was more than angry. He was befuddled. Where the hell was Coyne? He couldn't pick a worse time for a disappearing act. Shit, he couldn't even enjoy a moment's peace of mind in Vegas. He well might have to cut short his visit, but one thing was for sure. When he got back to Illinois, he'd be cracking the whip.

The long overdue rain that had begun earlier in the day was letting up as Arkell Dillard stood under the porte cochere on the south side of his palatial home. An early evening visitor, Johnny Bob Slocum, was taking his leave.

No individual could have been more different from the Duke of Windsor than Johnny Bob. Unpolished, almost doggedly so, Johnny Bob did not scrape the dirt from under his fingernails, not even for Arkell Dillard. But he'd do anything else for Dillard. Would and did. And there was not much that Johnny Bob could not handle. Nothing spooked him, not after growing up around rowdy Shawneetown where he'd gotten tough and meaner than hell brawling in taverns with the roustabouts.

Another fearsome thing about him, maybe the utmost, concerned catfish. He'd catch 'em with his bare hands in the murky backwaters of the Ohio, or in the mire of other sloughs down there. He loved having an audience as he waded into a muddy marsh to stick his hands into a log or hole and yank up a cantankerous thirty pounder. "Hogging" for the cats (also known as logging or "noodling") was his specialty, and he wore with pride the scars on his hands and arms where the doomed cats sometimes scored in a final chomping.

In one of those anomalies of life, the hogger supreme ended up close to Dillard. Stories varied as to how this came about, but the upshot was that Johnny Bob fit nicely into the slot in Dillard's world for someone who could tend to situations pertaining to the underside of the Duke's endeavors. Say certain individuals were trying to unionize a Dillard quarry, a frank discussion with Johnny Bob at the bottom of a sand and gravel pit might change their minds. Or a party stiffing the Dillard bank might be convinced to come across. Matters like that. Slocum was on the payroll of Dillard's Deep Valley Quarry, at a tidy sum, but he seldom was around. Johnny Bob answered to Mr. Dillard, and you could bet that when he did surface somewhere it had to do with a subject of special interest or concern to the big man.

Of course, the caste system prevented Dillard and Slocum from hardly ever being seen together. But the coarse fellow from the river bottom came up to the mansion pretty much at will, which Sloan Dillard, for one, found irksome. Naturally, Johnny Bob was aware the missus did not want him around, did not look kindly on any lowlifes. But that didn't deter him from matter-of-factly ending his visits to the mister with courteous references to Sloan, just as if she tolerated him as much as her husband did.

As Johnny Bob stepped back from Dillard, his shirt getting splattered with raindrops off the trees, he reminded his employer to "please give my regards to Miss Sloan, and tell her that I'm always ready to help her with anything that's got to be done."

Dillard nodded silently in assent. He had a feeling he'd be the one seeking assistance, not Sloan. Yet it would involve Sloan. Dillard was chewing in his mind the possibility of asking Slocum to shadow Sloan, find out where she went during her long absences. He'd never endeavor to tie her down; they'd gotten that straight at the start. She was spending more and more time away, though, and Arkell was not sure if she really went to St. Louis, like she said, or was being drawn elsewhere. He didn't know because he never asked.

His wife, the daughter of Reverend Kincaid, would not be seeing another man. She wouldn't do that, Dillard firmly believed, because there was too much at stake, and Sloan had a sizable interest in it all. Still, the growing hours unaccounted for were beginning to gnaw at him. If the unease persisted, he might be forced to sic Johnny Bob on her.

Take this evening. Tomorrow would be an important day for Dillard and southern Illinois. She ought to have been home by now, helping him plan for the occasion that would spotlight his prominence in the southern part of the state. His trophy wife should be at his side. It was the kind of thing he told her to expect when he persuaded her to marry him.

Chapter Eighteen

Not before or since the funeral service for Peter Stine had so many of the who's who of southern Illinois been under one roof. Arkell Dillard did not recognize everybody in the auditorium of the university at Carbondale, but the movers and shakers were there, he was confident, beckoned by an event that, for him, was certainly a crowning moment.

The only person on the stage eclipsing Dillard was Governor Sanderson, but even he seemed willing to defer to Dillard. Sitting, waiting for his turn to be introduced, Arkell basked in the realization that so many eyes were on him. Or, on his wife, who was seated between him and the governor.

Sloan had barely made it home before midnight, tramping in looking a bit dishevelled and without a word of explanation. Arkell was plenty hot under the collar, but confronting her last night could have ignited an argument that might have draped a pall over the next day and this gathering, where he definitely wanted to show her off. Putting Johnny Bob Slocum on her trail, though, was something he'd about decided to do.

Just now, southern Illinois had Dillard's full attention. His part of the world was looking in the mirror, recognizing that it could do a lot more with itself. Call it rebirth. Revitalization. Whatever. A fresh beginning was at hand, and the Duke of Windsor was assured a pivotal role.

Busby Caulfield, the stout old head of the State Chamber of Commerce, gave the governor a ringing introduction.

Nevertheless, for the leading honcho in the state, Sanderson didn't generate much in the way of applause when he rose to contribute his two-cents worth. Many in the auditorium had mixed feelings about the brutally abrupt closing of the Autumn Moon and the attendant publicity. However, when Sanderson recited the list of ways the state could help southern Illinois with extra manpower and funds, the coolness leveled off.

"This is an important day for southern Illinois, and for the rest of our great state, too," proclaimed the governor. "This is the day that we launch a drive that will bring a new era of unparalleled prosperity to this entire area.

"And nobody," Sanderson continued, "is going to be more important in making this happen than the distinguished gentleman seated on my left. You all know him. His name has carried a lot of respect for a long time. He's Arkell Dillard, whom I am proud to introduce as the first president of the new Progress League of Southern Illinois."

Stepping up to the microphone to the sound of lightly clapping hands, Dillard's first action in the spotlight was to slide his hand inside his buttoned suit coat in the style of Napoleon before introducing the woman resplendent in the pink summer suit. His wife would be, he said, "walking with me step by step as we try to make southern Illinois the kind of dynamic place that we all know it should and can be." More restrained clapping, led by the governor, followed. Men in the audience with their wives understandably had to be on guard to applaud with only mild enthusiasm, but they could see the mission of the Progress League taking on added luster if Sloan Dillard really was going to be around.

Arkell Dillard piloted the proceeding like the omniscient bank board chairman that he was. Since the objective was grandiose, nobody on hand hardly doubted that Dillard was a good choice to lead the charge. The Progress League was best explained as an umbrella organization for a caboodle of civic-minded groups and programs aimed at attracting new industries and other business to the lower region of Illinois. A big infusion of private money, solicited by Dillard and others capable of reeling it in, would be bolstered by taxpayer dollars funneled by Sanderson and state government. The mention again of bucks from the state triggered another round of scattered applause, which in turn prompted Dillard and the governor to exchange knowing smiles.

One subject on the agenda receiving a big play was a detailed report on all the potential for making southern Illinois the tourism and recreation center of the Midwest. The area was pictured as being stocked in a decade or two with man-made lakes and resorts and as making so much more of the Shawnee Hills and the great rivers bordering the area, the Mississippi, the Ohio and even the Wabash.

"We can do it, ladies and gentlemen, working together," Arkell Dillard concluded in his remarks winding up the meeting. "We'll roll up our sleeves, all of us, and when we get the ball rolling there will be no limit on how far we can go."

The thought of Dillard literally rolling up his sleeves to do anything did not strike many of his listeners as very likely. Nevertheless, if any one person brought enough to the table to make a difference in southern Illinois, the Duke of Windsor fit the bill.

Chapter Nineteen

After the kickoff for the Progress League of Southern Illinois, Sanderson, who tried to avoid flying when he could, was driven back to Springfield. As his dark limo sped northward, the governor was extremely tempted at one point around Nashville to direct the trooper at the wheel to cut over to the East St. Louis area so he could get a firsthand look for once at the next strike in his most exciting, and to some provocative, endeavor since taking office. He guessed the timing might be about right. The thought was quickly discarded, though. Governors never got their own hands dirty in such doings.

Had Sanderson given in to temptation, he would have witnessed a rerun of the Autumn Moon hit.

The target this time was the Club Destiny, snug in Dutch Hollow, a hilly no-man's-land nestled between East St. Louis and the well-groomed German city of Belleville to the east. The Club Destiny was the premier gambling spot on the East Side, or in the entire St. Louis area for that matter. Thanks to Harry Fontane's two big M's, money and muscle. In the bustling hours of night, the place offered high stakes gaming, entertainment and discreet sex for those who could afford it. Taking a cue from Bugsy Siegel's Flamingo, Fontane insisted everybody on the club payroll, from the top on down, wear tuxedos. But that was in the evening, not during the daytime, when Dantello and his men pulled up.

If the invaders found anything stirring, it was the gaggle of reporters and photographers milling on the narrow road leading to the establishment. The *World* and the other newspapers of any importance had been tipped only a short time before, by a trusted go-between for the cover-all-bases Dantello, that Fontane's jewel was next on the list for an uninvited visit by the state police super and his band. The city editors salivated at the prospect of a face-to-face confrontation between Illinois' new tough guy and the infamous Fontane. They had no way of knowing that the mobster was in Las Vegas.

Actually, just a handful of patrons, along with a few employees, were in the club when the two black and whites came around a bend in the road, braked by the front entrance and disgorged Dantello and the rest of the poker faces who had been at the Autumn Moon raid.

Dantello's choreography at the Club Destiny also mirrored his show at the Moon, starting with the quick heave-ho of the customers, mainly weary hangers-on jerking down the arms of slots. The workers were ordered to stand over to the side for fingerprinting, including the wisecracking manager on duty, who made an abortive move to place a quick telephone call to Fontane's office in downtown East St. Louis. The smart-aleck stuff wasn't dropped until the guy heard the first whacks with the ax and sledgehammer. Disbelief flooded his face, an expression Max Slattery captured so perfectly it graced the front page of the *World* the next day. The picture would win Max a coveted award.

When a fire-breathing dragon named Fontane arrived home the day after the raid and saw the photo, he threw the paper in the face of the luckless manager, a relatively mild rebuke in consideration of what he threatened to do to certain other individuals. Nat Coyne had surfaced by then, his face clear, almost bloodless, and he and Fontane went behind a closed door. Lord only knows what transpired. Those who could duck out did so.

After smashing to smithereens all the exquisite paraphernalia at the Club Destiny and padlocking the place, Dantello played it coy, again, with the reporters ganging around him to ask, "Where next?" They would not learn the answer to the question until twilight of the next day, when Dantello and his raiders appeared out of the gloaming to slam dunk a club along the Illinois River near Peoria, reputed for its classy strippers as well as the bulge of the bettors' wallets.

Afterward, in short order, three other gambling houses in downstate Illinois closed their doors, voluntarily. A rout of the unlawful gaming industry in the state clearly was afoot. The domino effect was in play. If any one event had touched it all off, it had to be the murder of Peter Stine.

The epilogue to the crackdown, or just call it the fallout, was pretty predictable.

Given their historic bent against wagering, even legalized betting, editorial writers largely extolled the governor for the antigambling blitz. As for Lawrence Dantello, well, he was caricatured as a modern swashbuckler, which was fitting since he liked to think of himself in that vein. He took as a particular compliment an editorial cartoon in the *Chicago Examiner* portraying him as one of Alexandre Dumas' three musketeers, swaggering around the state, sword in hand. Bravo! Bravo! You could hear the acclaim.

Sterling Kincaid and the rest in MAG praised the crackdown to high heaven. Hallelujah, a blight on morality in Illinois was removed. They were not bashful about pointing out that the long-sought raids began the day after their fervent appeal for action to Sanderson in his Capitol office.

On the other side of the coin, more than a few local officials complained that the shutdowns were a blow to local commerce, and even *Life*, in the text accompanying its pictorial spread on Sanderson and his attack against illegal gambling, pointed out that some county budgets would suffer from the loss of fines paid by club owners after friendly raids. Jud Parkins was not the only local law enforcement officer to bitch that Dantello and his men used the tactics of storm troopers, which were indeed a concern of greater magnitude in the eyes of certain civil libertarians than the targets of the raids.

More widespread, and of some worry to Sanderson, was the griping here and yonder by highly respectable frequenters of the clubs that the governor had spoiled their fun for purely political gain. Sanderson noticed that a sassy woman named Yvonne Fitzgerald, very photogenic and quite quotable, was warning of a backlash against high-and-mighty politicians who deprived honest citizens of even the simplest of pleasures. The governor hated to admit it, but he was a tad uneasy at all the ink she garnered.

Neither Dayton Mansfield nor any other operator of an illegal gambling establishment saw the inside of a jail. Punishment was limited to moderate fines or other light slaps on their wrists. Anyone so desiring was allowed to reopen the restaurant part of a club. Mansfield and a few of the others did so, for a while, but of course it was not the same. Most just sat and stewed over the end of a good thing. None more so than Harry Fontane.

Chapter Twenty

The summer of 1950 was on a downhill slide. As Labor Day approached, the excitement sparked by the murders and gambling club raids ebbed.

There was much else to think about. The Korean War was taking grave turns, Senator McCarthy of Wisconsin charged Communist infiltration of the State Department, and the amazing Whiz Kids playing for Philadephia's Phillies were heading toward a stretch run against the Dodgers for the National League pennant. The best die-hard St. Louis fans could yell for was that Stan the Man, coiled batting stance and all, would stay on track to the league hitting title.

Brosky, his pace toned down, blanked out a whole afternoon to catch the Cards out at Sportsman's. He also carved out time in the evenings to enjoy the company of Gloria DeForest, a divorcee he'd met by chance years earlier when she was still the spouse of a hard-driving St. Louis brewery executive.

Gloria satisfied Jake's standards for women. No husband. No imps hanging on her skirt. Never under dressed. In his estimation, she was a fashion plate, always neatly packaged. To a lot of other women, she showboated. Brosky loved her black and white combinations, worn year-round and always with glittery rhinestone jewelry. Her face, oval with a gracefully flaring nose, gave little hint about her age. Her makeup didn't completely obscure the lines of crow's-feet fanning out from the edges of her eyes, but he still couldn't pinpoint her age. He just knew she had "the look," like other women he'd squired around. But Gloria was also genuine and naturally confident of her power to please.

Best of all about Gloria, which separated her from others, Jake had fun with her, a darn good time. She dubbed him her "Jewish Dick Tracy," insisting, as she ran a delicate finger down Jake's forehead, nose and chin, that from the side he had the same stolid facial lines as the comic strip detective. Until Gloria brought it up, he'd never considered himself having any resemblance to Tracy, whose exploits he'd never stolen time to follow.

"Yes, Jake, you're my very own Dick Tracy, my Jewish Dick Tracy," Gloria said, "except that the bad people you chase aren't just a bunch of weird comic characters. You go after bad characters who have flesh and blood."

Obvious to Jake, the woman held an illusion that his work possessed special allure. He also suspected that Gloria—without saying so—envisioned a glamorous strain in the sordid types tracked by Brosky and brought to the pages of his newspaper. He didn't try to tell her differently, to straighten her out. He let her romanticize. He liked her just the way she was.

She had the ability to make him forget the *World* for hours at a time. He was the carefree person he'd never been as he escorted bejeweled Gloria into the old downtown movie palace, where he'd dreamed as a kid of actually being an usher, to catch Bette Davis and her huge eyes in *All About Eve*, one of the year's first-run hits. They perched up in the balcony with the lovebirds. They held hands. They spilled popcorn all over themselves while groping to share the same bag. They ducked down to the ostentatious lobby for a smoke, and then reclaimed their seats.

Not once, but twice, Gloria coaxed Jake to the Casa-Loma, the south side dance hall at Cherokee and Iowa where the big bands still stopped. Jake drew the line at venturing onto the floor for anything but a clumsy two-step to Ralph Marterie's orchestra, but he enjoyed the band's medley of old standards. After he suffered through his second sojourn to the ballroom on a night when America's self-professed polka king was booked, he let Gloria know she owed him one. He collected by dragging her to the civic auditorium to catch the legitimate world champion of straight wrestling, hometown St. Louisan Lou Thesz, in action. Gloria winced at the grappling in the ring and announced that she'd never accompany Jake to a boxing match, but she did heartily agree to his offer to someday introduce her to the rock-solid Mr. Thesz. Jake knew him well enough to know that he was pulling in more than $200,000 a year, a real bundle for a professional athlete.

During the days of dallying with the unfailingly upbeat Gloria DeForest, Jake dropped off the front page. The ongoing coverage of the antigambling campaign in Illinois was being handled by the straight news guys at the *World* and the wire services, but Brosky felt the stories were getting stale and deserved to be back pagers. Jake's task was to shadow the investigations of the Stine and Langston murders. However, a piece he dictated to his rewrite man revealed nothing new.

The sheriff in Jefferson County in Indiana was stymied by dead ends. Jake's impression was that the sheriff would leak to him if anything turned up on the Stine case, but it hadn't. Nothing panned out on the Langston inquiry either, beginning with the authorities' questioning of Nat Coyne about his altercation with Marvin during the last night of his life. Coyne produced verified accounts of how his time was spent in the hours after he left the Autumn Moon.

Peevish Sheriff Parkins down in Cypress simply stonewalled Brosky, period. Coming to the phone reluctantly, Parkins averred in a voice bitter as vinegar that he had absolutely nothing to say to Brosky on the killing of Marvin Langston or any other subject. When something was learned, Parkins made it clear, he'd be talking to his county's state's attorney and not to "any big shit reporters, Springfield nazis or any of the other goddamn outsiders who keep sticking it to our little county.

"And, Mr. Brosky, sir," Parkins added with even more

emphasis, "you can quote me on that in your damn newspaper."

If Brosky was to provide the *World's* readership with any revelations about these goings-on, he had to discover new sources. Or get a break. The trails were getting cold. Brosky feared he was trapped in a dry spell, a haunting realization for any reporter worth his salt.

It could not have been much longer than a couple of weeks after the Club Destiny's lights went out that Manny Manola was stunned by a tidbit reaching his ears. Fat Manny always was hearing things. The joke was that Manny was as savvy as any gossip columnist in the way he trafficked in information, even with the feds who slammed him for a huge wad of back taxes on the very lucrative race wire he ran out of St. Louis.

Manola had ties everywhere, the New Orleans mob included. One of his close associates down in Mardi Gras town happened to be the person who alerted Manola to the morsel that Manny felt his friend of long standing, Harry Fontane, ought to know. Manola's affection for Fontane was not contrived. The pair went back far enough that Manny was one of the precious few who could banter with Fontane about Harry being a son of an East St. Louis milkman, a point of extreme sensitivity with Fontane.

Ringing Fontane from St. Louis, Manola said he was in the mood for a drive and asked if Harry could see him. The reply was brief. "Come over."

Both recognized that conversation over the phone was dangerous if not impossible since there was no way of knowing who was listening in on the latest tap at Fontane's East St. Louis headquarters. Maybe Manola's place was bugged too. Shortly, Manny drove over to the East Side, taking the Free Bridge instead of the Eads Bridge because, unlike Jake Brosky, Manola got queasy from the sweet licorice smell at the St. Louis end of the Eads.

Fontane needed to hear, Manola knew instinctively, what he'd been told—hard as it might be to swallow. The world of Fontane had to be in an upheaval, Manola assumed, thanks to the collapse of the lucrative Illinois gambling ordered by a highbrow governor audacious enough to disregard the protection Fontane and the others had purchased from officials at the county level and on up. Manny had got wind that Fontane, trying to bounce back, was angling for the concession contract or another piece of the action at the horse racing track reportedly to be built outside East St. Louis by a secret trust dominated by powerful politicians. Fontane wanting to be the concessionaire added up because huge profits were virtually guaranteed.

Manola ascended with a glacial slowness to Fontane's office, which was on the upper floor of a two-story building the gangster owned among the commercial establishments on Collinsville Avenue. The premise also served as the command post for the notorious laborers' union local, for which Fontane supplied the strong arms to back up the local's extortions of construction firms.

Two rooms preceded Fontane's office. In the first, a small cadre of men with well-used faces hunched around a table, one of whom was Norton Raven, the hood with the wild threads who liked to bend Brosky's ear. In the second room, next to Fontane's office, Theresa Carmody, the wisp of an Irish lady functioning as Fontane's girl Friday, was parked at a large desk that had a considerable semblance of order. Right outside the door leading to Fontane hovered an expressionless bruiser noticeably packing heat. Spying Manola, he flashed a smile and flipped a hand with an air of indifference, a signal to Manny to advance.

Fontane's office was a small fortress. Brown stained paneling covered the walls. A window at the side was bricked up, a surefire way to stop bullets. Fontane sat with his back flat against a wall. Whether in his office, a restaurant or a car, the gangster positioned himself so as to preclude anybody from sliding behind him. One could never be too cautious.

Rising with effort, Fontane leaned across his desk to lightly embrace his corpulent friend from across the river. Manola was not pleased with what he saw. Since he'd last been with Fontane, cobwebs of bright red lines had flared across Harry's cheeks and nose, and Manola could not remember Fontane's lips ever being so purple. His eyes, set deep below the high brow, glowed like angry embers. Fontane wore one of his collection of black shirts, Manny noticed, along with the last of the white cravats an old Capone bruiser in Chicago had shipped down to him. Unfortunately, the tie dangling from Fontane's neck was splotched, leaving Manny embarrassed for his pal. Maybe the spots could be blamed on the nearly empty bottle of Canadian Club in front of Fontane. Manny searched for the soda water that Harry always mixed with his whiskey. He didn't see any.

Manola did not beat around the bush. His confrere in the New Orleans underworld, which hired out hit men for jobs across the United States, professed to be knowledgeable about the killing of that newspaper fellow in southern Illinois. Manny never knew his friend to be wrong.

Fontane remained motionless, his expression impassive, while his visitor recounted what he had. The two embers glaring out of Fontane's face did not waver from Manola, not even as Harry slowly stubbed a burning Chesterfield in the ashtray on his desk, a slow movement that caught the eye of Manny because of the brilliant sparkle of the two-karat diamond on Fontane's pinkie.

Cecil Langston clung to his isolation after the funeral of Marvin. He wanted only to be left alone inside his cubby in the repair garage, where he persisted in sitting hour upon hour with his shotgun and bible. It was awfully close to self-imposed solitary confinement.

The day the letter arrived, though, Cecil had been out roaming the farm and then had come into the house for lunch. After eating more than usual of what Dorothy put on his plate, she handed him the letter.

"This came for you today," she said.

Cecil opened it lackadaisically. The envelope contained no return address. It was postmarked at Oil City, a town over near the Wabash, but that was pretty obscured. Leading off with the salutation, "Dear Mr. Cecil Langston," the mailing went on to read:

> You do not know me but I know who you are. I read about the death of your son and I am very sorry about it. I am sure I can't begin to feel how much you miss him because I have never lost any of my sons. I saw you bearing witness to the love of our Great Lord and Savior Jesus Christ a time back at a revival meeting but I did not say any thing to you. But I know you would not have been there if you were not a Christian man seeking the true path through the love of our God. This is the reason I feel it is so important to tell you of what I have been told.

The next part of the neatly printed letter mesmerized Cecil.

> This came to me by way of my dear cousin who is a very fine man in spite of the fact that he does like to drink now and then. He knows that I know he does this but I do not hold this against him. He was having a drink or two (and maybe more) when he was told what I am telling you. My cousin never lies to me because he is very dear to me as I said. He says he was told this on the night next after the finding of your dear son's body when he was inside the Lost Creek Pub close by Oil City altho some claim it is closer to Grayville. Anyways, this little feller who is slopping drunk with liquor forces my cousin to listen to him talk even though my cousin is sitting alone and does not want to be bothered by this feller. My cousin said he's seen this feller in the tavern before and he is a no count oil field drifter called George or Little George. My cousin does not know his last name. Anyways, this George feller goes on to tell my cousin the

most sickning stuff about how your son Marvin died. My cousin said that no man could know so much about what happened if he was not there. My cousin got scared because this feller who my cousin said is real mean was talking like he was happy your son died because he does not like you and says you got a lot more coming to you. My cousin does not want to see this Little George feller again and says he is not going to the Lost Creek Pub any more.

Cecil stopped reading. He was biting his lower lip.

Little George. Little George. The palpitations of Cecil's heart soared at the thought of his name. Dorothy was watching, and she saw her husband's face contort into an expression of painful recognition, the most radical departure she had seen in days from the sober countenance since the death of their son.

"What is it, Cecil? What is in the letter?" She was frowning, steeling herself for whatever in the letter had brought her husband out of his stupor.

Langston did not answer his wife. He was skipping over the last segment of the letter, which began with the wording, "I feel you just should know this." He did want to learn who wrote it, but saw that the author identified himself, or possibly herself, as only "a friend."

Rising from his chair, still saying nothing, Cecil walked from the kitchen with the letter to a side room Dorothy used for sewing. She heard a grating sound that meant he was pulling open a drawer in an old chest that was stuffed with pictures. She detected from shuffling noises that he was rooting around in the drawer.

Dorothy had not moved from her seat in the kitchen when

Cecil returned, sank again into his chair across the table from her and laid down the letter along with a fading brownish photo. From where she sat, the picture was upside down. It didn't matter. She recognized it easily enough. Taken back in the era when the Langston gang was riding high, it was a shot of Cecil with outfit member George Bankheart. Crazy, demonic Little George, as he was known.

After first covering her mouth with her hand, Dorothy dropped it away and questioned with a gasp, "Could it really be?" The look on Cecil's face was her answer. "Oh, my God. Oh, my God," she said, her voice falling to nearly a whisper. Her hand returned to her mouth.

Langston pushed the letter and photo across the table to his wife. His eyes were plaintive and, at the same time, pleading. Dorothy had seen those eyes rarely in their many years together. They were beseeching her to forgive him for something he should have known or done but did not. She reached across the table with her hand. She forced a smile, a wan smile but a sign that she understood. Her facial language said that there was nothing to forgive. Although he averted his eyes, he stretched a hand over the table to hers. Their fingers intertwined.

Dorothy shifted her eyes down to the letter, still unaware of what it said but no longer gripped by morbid fear of what she might read. Her husband was showing emotion, and that counted more than anything else at the moment. Now she might entertain hope that the worst for them was over.

As Dorothy silently read the letter, Langston turned back the clock in his mind to reconstruct his history with Little George.

The two young men in the sepia picture were smiling. But, they were not grinning when they parted under most disagreeable circumstances. The Langston gang hardly was unfamiliar with roughhouse tactics, but Little George went out of his way to hurt people when it was not necessary, for no reason. Headstrong, he chafed under the leadership of Cecil. The last straw in Cecil's book was the bank job up in Danville pulled off by Little George and an impressionable lad who desperately wished to be accepted by the gang. Robberies were not part of the gang's business. When Cecil got wind of the bank heist, he lost his temper and pistol-whipped Little George in front of the rest of the crowd. Humiliated, Bankheart slunk off—but not before swearing there'd be another day for he and Langston. Cecil knew he'd made an enemy more vicious than most, but he had put Little George out of his head with the passage of time. The last Cecil had heard, a goodly number of years back, was that Bankheart got into trouble down in Texas and maybe had landed in prison. Langston had no idea the ornery cuss was alive, let alone back in Illinois.

Nevertheless, he could not shake a specter in his head that somehow he should have put two and two together and figured Little George might be out there.

After Dorothy finished the letter, her grief was suddenly outweighed by a rage for retribution. Cecil saw it in her face. He had gone from being melancholy just as quickly. His eyes, too, were brimming with fire.

"What are we going to do?" she asked in a voice much more demanding.

"I will do it, Dorothy."

"No, Cecil, I want—

"No, Dorothy," Langston interjected solemnly, "it is something I must do. You see God has answered my prayer. He has shown me the way." Motioning at the letter, Cecil affirmed what he was saying with a twitch of his thick eyebrows. "This is what I was waiting for, Dorothy, a message from the Lord."

Cecil was mustering his old gumption. If he didn't, there would be nothing left.

Chapter Twenty-one

The city room at the *World* was in a tizzy. A six-story furniture emporium in downtown St. Louis, just a few blocks away from the newspaper, was ablaze, a five-alarmer. Brosky's desk was one of only several by a window. He had a clear view of the ominous black smoke billowing into the cloudless sky, which he observed calmly, darn near oblivious to the scurrying of younger reporters and editors responding to the biggest breaking story of the day. Reporters not assigned elsewhere were being hustled into action on the fire. But not Brosky. Jake didn't cover fires. A gangster murder, yes, but not fires, floods or tornadoes. Rank had its privileges.

Yet, amid the excitement, he did hear his name called. Not by an editor but by the high-pitched voice of the copyboy manning the phones behind the city desk.

"Mr. Brosky, will you take a call from a Mr. Hawthorn or Hathern?"

Jake had to think for a moment. Hawthorn. Hathern. He didn't know anybody by...unless, wait a second, it was Lyle Hathorn.

Looking over at the pimply faced young man, Brosky nodded, the signal to put the caller through. Before putting on his spindly headphone, Jake carried out a time-honored ritual by dropping a deposit into the rusty spittoon by his chair. The veteran reporters were the only ones still parking spittoons by their desks. The newer guys, a number from Ivy League schools, found them disgusting.

Assuming it had to be Hathorn on the phone, Jake began simply. "Hello, Lyle."

"Hello, Mr. Brosky." It was Hathorn alright.

"I'm sorry I missed your call, Lyle, some time ago. I did try to get back to you."

"I have been gone from Grandville, Mr. Brosky, but I'm sure you know that." Hathorn sounded, Jake thought, slightly timorous.

"Am I to take it," Brosky asked, "that you're not sure you're going back to your newspaper?"

"Well, I haven't. I've been down here in Tennessee, where I'm from, sort of thinking about a lot of things, trying to figure out what I want to do."

Hathorn surely was not calling Brosky, either this time or before, for counseling, Jake surmised. Nevertheless, he'd best play Hathorn along until he brought up what really prompted the calls. So, Brosky opined that the *Banner* probably had to be having a difficult go of it without the services of Hathorn.

"That's a situation I just can't help. I don't know if I'm going back or not." A pause followed. Jake did not reply, not wanting to willingly extend the conversation beyond the subject that he had to believe Hathorn really wanted to bring up. Brosky didn't want the preliminaries prolonged. He got his wish.

"Actually, Mr. Brosky," Hathorn finally resumed, "I did not call to talk about the *Banner*." In a tone more halting, he went on. "It is really about Peter and, uh, what you said about calling you if I thought of anything that maybe you, uh, should know. Remember?"

"Yes, Lyle, of course I do."

"Well," said Hathorn, "after I missed you the first time I called, I didn't think I'd try again. Still, here I am sitting down here, thinking that I owe this to Peter since, as you know, he did a lot for me."

"Certainly, I know that."

"Telling you this, Mr. Brosky, still doesn't mean there's anything to it."

"I understand, Lyle."

"And another thing, please."

"What's that?"

"What you think or do about this is, uh, up to you, but I want you to, uh, keep my name out of it." Letting several seconds pass, Hathorn added, "Will you agree?"

"Yes, Lyle, that's absolutely no problem. None at all. If I say so, believe me." Having granted that assurance, Brosky, although trying not to sound impatient, felt compelled to ask, "Can you tell me now, Lyle, what it is?"

"Well, it's a telephone call that I got, or rather I should say I took, right after you left the *Banner* that day." Jake listened in silence as Hathorn related that the caller, an apparently old woman identifying herself as Miss Sadie, wanted to know when Peter Stine was coming to see her again to finish interviewing her for a story that she said Peter was going to write about her. This was news to him, Hathorn told Brosky, in that Peter had not mentioned a word to him about any story on a Miss Sadie. When Hathorn said he informed Miss Sadie of such, he quoted her as saying she did not understand because Peter had been to see her at her "retirement home" in Perkins and that he told her he was writing the story in appreciation of all she had done for him in the orphanage.

And that was about it, Hathorn said. When he informed Miss Sadie that Peter would not be returning to interview her because he had died, he said she became distraught and hung up.

Jake was not sure at first what to make of it. As Hathorn laid it out, though, the intuitive instinct that served Brosky well through the years, a kind of internal Geiger counter, perked up. Something was registering, just maybe. His nose for these matters had put ample bread on his table. But, he'd better proceed slowly with Hathorn. Must not go overboard showing

interest, Jake cautioned himself. Hathorn was, after all, sup-
posedly a reporter by trade—albeit one commanding little
respect from the hard-boiled Brosky.

One question begged to be asked by Jake. Pondering a
moment before posing it, he glanced out the window and
couldn't help but notice that the tips of the flames from the furniture store conflagration were shooting above downtown
rooflines, bringing to mind the fury of a volcanic eruption on
an exotic island.

"Tell me, Lyle, have you informed Sheriff Parkins, or anybody else in authority, like over in Indiana, about any of this?"

"Nope. No, I have not."

"Why not?"

"Well, I guess I admit I thought about it. But, you know, I
have decided I don't trust any of them anymore. Not at all.
Especially not Parkins. I am definitely going to avoid any contact with him."

Lowering his voice, Brosky sought to impart a vein of
comradeliness in replying, "Yes, I guess I can certainly see
that, Lyle."

"I am not mentioning this to anyone outside of you, Mr.
Brosky, because, like I said, I know I can trust you to, uh, just
keep my name out of it."

"I think you're playing it smart, and, yes, you know you
can count on me to keep you out of anything, if there is something, that comes out of this. I'm sure you know that I play this
game very well, Lyle. So, I'm telling you again, and for the last
time, quit worrying about it."

Brosky sensed that Hathorn would be uncomfortable talking much longer. However, holes had to be filled in the dwindling moments Jake felt he had left. "Lyle, did Miss Sadie give you her last name?"

"No, she didn't, Mr. Brosky."

"The Perkins you said she mentioned. I guess that would probably be the town down in Missouri. Don't you think?"

"Yes, I'm sure it is," Hathorn agreed. "Apparently Peter saw this woman on that drive he took over to Missouri, the one I told you about when you stopped by to talk to me at the *Banner*. Remember, I told you about that."

"Yeah, that's right, Lyle, you did."

"Another thing, too, the way she talked there must have been some connection between her and the orphanage where Peter went as a kid. The orphanage may well have been in Missouri, maybe around Perkins, although I just can't remember Peter ever telling me the location of the place. If he did, I don't remember. No, I'm sure he didn't tell me the place."

"Or the name, I guess."

"No, he never mentioned the name either. Don't forget. Peter always was real mum about his past."

"Is there anything else you can remember from her call?"

Saying no and adding that he had to run, Hathorn admonished Brosky once again to prevent his name from surfacing in any subsequent inquiry. Irritated at his caller's refusal to drop this worry, Brosky fought to hold his tongue, to avoid a snappish retort.

He settled for saying, "Come on, Lyle, there's nothing more to jaw over about that. Just remember who you are talking to. Remember, buddy." Then, quickly, Jake queried Hathorn about a phone number at which he could be reached in Tennessee. Hathorn hurled back that he was "moving around so much down here that there's really no number for me." But, he tacked on softly, "If I think of anything more, Jake, I'll call you." It was the first time during the conversation he addressed Brosky by his first name. Jake heard a click at Hathorn's end. The call was over.

Brosky, his headphone still on, turned again toward the window. The smoke pouring out of the furniture store had cast a sooty curtain across the sky, blotting out the sun.

Jake lost no time convincing himself that the Miss Sadie angle should be pursued. Hathorn smelled something there, or he would not have persisted in calling Brosky. Hathorn was just too spooked by the whole Peter Stine affair to do anything. No problem for Jake, though. In any case, he did not have much else going at the moment.

Perkins slumbered in the poverty-stricken Missouri boot heel, the only town of any size in a sparsely populated county where Sheriff Cotton Sesserman and Brosky were well acquainted. Jake caught Sesserman sitting in his office on the first call. Brosky needed a little information on the sly. Sesserman said it ought to be a piece of cake.

No more than two hours later Jake slid his headphone on again, to take the return call from the sheriff.

"Jake," Sesserman rumbled sonorously, "there is a woman by the name of Sadie Patrick, well up in years, living in Dixie Manor, an old boardinghouse in Perkins. I can't find any other gal named Sadie in the county."

"That's what I wanted to find out, Cotton," said Jake. Then he added, "Anything you know about her?"

"Only that my people tell me," came the reply, "that she ran an orphanage not far from here years ago." After asking whether he could assist further, the sheriff had a question of his own. "Is there something here that I should be let in on?"

"No, no, no," Jake responded without hesitation. "My interest in her has absolutely nothing to do with you or anything else in the county. Nothing in any way. Nothing at all. If it did, you'd be the first to know, Cotton."

"If you say so, old pardner. I'll take your word on that."

So far so good. Recognizing his next move was not difficult. Jake only had to hatch a scheme to pull it off.

Dinnertime was near. Brosky took off down the boulevard in front of the *World* for a nearby delicatessen on Jefferson that he preferred to the cafeteria run by the Greeks a few steps away from the newspaper's side entrance. Admit it or not, and Jake did, the place on Jefferson struck a responsive chord in him because it could have been a bigger version of the smaller but similar deli that his late Russian immigrant father ended up running out west on Delmar. The Reubens piled high and the long pickles stuffed into man-sized jars on the tables. Even the friendly guy operating the Jefferson deli resembled pop. The gray hair trying to escape from a paper fry-cook's hat. The same broken English. The camaraderie with regular customers. There was a kid too, sometimes helping out when not sitting down at one of the tables to bury his face in a book. That'd be the young Jacob Samuel of long ago.

For the father of Jacob Samuel, his tiny part of the world on Delmar was his share of the American dream. Jake's dad eventually had admirers, people who saw him as a person overcoming great odds to earn a sort of dignity. However, it was ironic, as Jake gradually came to realize, that pop never thought of himself as a loser at any stage of his life, but rather as fortunate to be his own person in a land of opportunity.

Brosky could relax in the deli on Jefferson. He could think there. The time he spent in the place amounted to a time-out.

As he walked along the boulevard to and from the eatery, the acrid odor from the day's fire still hung heavy in the air. Jake even sniffed it in his clothes. The fire was not on his mind, though. He'd decided during the interlude at the deli how to play it.

When he returned to the *World*, the hubbub of the day was over; only a cleaning crew and the night reporter remained in the city room. Good. The less background noise the better for Jake's next step. He asked Franny, the paper's night telephone operator, to put through a call to the Dixie Manor in Perkins, Missouri. Several minutes later, the woman who answered the phone at Dixie had Miss Sadie Patrick on the line.

Jake opened forthrightly, telling her who he was. After that, he began the lie, the approach he had plotted back at the deli.

"In recent years, Miss Sadie, Peter and I became close friends in the newspaper business," Brosky fabricated. "He talked of you often, and of how fondly he remembered his days with you. I know he was going to do a story on you. He told me that the last time I talked to him. His unfortunate death has hit me pretty hard. It's only in the last few days, while thinking of something I could do in recognition of our friendship, that I thought of the story he wanted to do on you."

Brosky expected to be interrupted, but she did not. Lowering his eyes to his desk, where he was fingering his pack of Luckies, Jake advanced to the punch line. "What I would like to do, Miss Sadie, is try to write that story myself, to not let Peter's effort go unfinished."

"Why, Mr. Jake," he heard her reply, "I would think that's a fine idea. Yes I would." He wished she didn't talk so courtly.

She could not have swallowed the bait more completely. Her ready compliance gave Brosky a twinge of guilt. Hoodwinking devious punks was one matter. Duping an old woman was not exactly honorable—even though some persons might look the other way if the trickery helped lead to the solution of a brutal crime. Judging by her voice, Miss Sadie was certainly up in years, although her speech was firm and polite at the same time. He was gambling that she was not too omniscient, but also saw little recourse for her if she detected his ruse.

Seeing no reason for foot-dragging, Brosky asked if he could journey to Perkins to interview her the next day. As he put it, "I don't have any excuse for not trying to follow up on what Peter started as soon as possible."

She agreed to talk to him the following afternoon.

Chapter Twenty-two

Was Brosky on a wild-goose chase? If so, it was a long and dusty one. Making it down to the boot heel without suffering a bad case of tedium was asking a lot.

His mind roamed aimlessly on the drive. Flashbacks of stories past floated in his head one minute, followed by unusually close attention to road signs. The Burma-Shave folks had been busy on this route. He seldom read the jingles for the shaving cream because, in order to digest a full verse, a traveler needed to read each one in a lineup of small signs. This day was an exception. Like skinning a cat, there were many ways to get across the message that a path to a gal's heart was through a smooth and cool face, not scratchy whiskers. And, a shaving brush wasn't the answer. No sir. "Shaving brush/all wet/and hairy," chanted one string of signs, "I've passed you up/for sanitary/ Burma-Shave."

The route also was littered with billboards. When he was forced to stop so several men could push a stalled car off the road, he was confronted by a flashy color-splashed panel featuring a handsome, brown-coated young actor, Ronald Reagan, plugging Chesterfield cigarettes. It was the first Brosky had heard of the Reagan fellow and the latest technicolor movie in which the signboard said he was starring, *Hong Kong*.

During a particularly desolate stretch of the drive, the 88's radio picked up a broadcast, or probably a rebroadcast, of one of the programs in the Fat Man mystery series. Whatever, this was a new one for Jake. He once had met the voice of the Fat Man, an actor named J. Scott Smart with links to Springfield, Illinois. Funny thing, Smart was in truth every bit as heavy in real life as the cynical, rotund private eye created by crime writer Dashiell Hammett. Brosky loved the tough-talking, witty, sarcastic characters fathered by Hammett, like Sam Spade. It distressed him that it was seemingly no falsehood that Hammett had been involved with leftist organizations, maybe had even been a Communist. That was difficult for Jake to stomach.

Brosky felt spent as the Oldsmobile 88 finally coasted out of a fertile floodplain and into Perkins. The sun was already past its highest point in the sky.

Southern agrarian towns were all the same. Perkins, smack-dab in the middle of cotton country, would have fit easily into Mississippi or Louisiana. A few blocks of fine old city homes of landowners, a handful still stately, and after that, a worn-out commercial district followed by emaciated neighborhoods of poor whites and the section reserved for blacks and true Dickensian squalor.

Dixie Manor was one of the larger residences. Romance novelists probably would have characterized it as a mansion of fading grandeur. Brosky found it right away, but did not stop. Instead he drove around a little longer, buying time for one last cigarette because of a suspicion that smoking might be taboo in Dixie.

Brosky's second-guessing of himself was now in full swing. He feared blind alleys, and he could not contain an increasingly gnawing feeling that he was on a fruitless mission. No question he was playing a long shot, betting he could discover something untoward, maybe even sinister, arising out of Peter Stine's contact with an old lady from his past. The hunch that had surged through Jake the previous day was barely flickering. If he struck out, it would probably serve him right for pulling the wool over the eyes of an old lady.

When Brosky parked in front of Dixie, a couple of kids were playing stickball in the street. No sooner had he killed the motor than the youngster with the broomstick slammed a home run. The ball, lightweight thank God, bounced off the hood of the Olds. "Hey boys!" Jake yelled. "No more of that!" After hurriedly inspecting to make sure the hood was not dented, Brosky walked up the sidewalk to the massive front door of the boardinghouse, cursing to himself that this just was not going to be his day.

He was greeted by the woman who had answered the phone at Dixie the day before. Ushering him into a heavily draped, musty sitting room, she motioned for him to have a seat on an uncomfortable loveseat with tasseled cushions, hardly a standard prop for a Jacob Brosky interview. One thing after another caught his eye. He assumed the decor of the room was vintage turn of the century. He gave a double take to a framed photo by the settee that coupled a solemn young army officer, somebody's son, with a smiling Clark Gable, resplendent in a creaseless tan uniform. Then his mind wandered to Gloria DeForest. He regretted cutting it short with her the previous night. Thinking of her had helped fight the boredom on the ride down, right along with the roadside advertising and the Fat Man. Suddenly, because the windows in the room were open, the noises on the street reminded him that the stickballers still were at it. He damned well better not hear another thud against the Olds.

Sadie Patrick entered the room. Tall and erect, with snow-white hair and thin lips, she greeted Brosky as "Mr. Jake." He was most struck by her eyes, bright and incredibly lucid. Although Brosky figured her to be an octogenarian, she wore no glasses.

Sitting stiffly in a tufted Victorian chair facing the loveseat, she folded her hands around a lace kerchief on her lap. How nice of Brosky, she began, to come "all the long way" from St. Louis to see her.

"Well," Jake replied, "as I told you on the phone...." Cutting the sentence short, he asked if she wanted to be addressed as Miss Sadie.

"Yes, please."

"Well, Miss Sadie, when I called you, I told you that this is something I knew Peter would want." As he spoke, Jake detected not one hint of doubt in her expression. "However," he continued, "I have no choice but to ask you to go over the ground you and Peter covered on his visit, since Peter did not share any of the information from the interview."

"That is perfectly in order, Mr. Jake," she said, "because I'm sure this was a story that Peter wanted to do alone." He couldn't recall anybody ever calling him Mr. Jake except for the bootblack up on Franklin Avenue.

As gently as possible, Brosky questioned her about the orphanage, her role there and Peter's tie to the place. From her answers, though disjointed, he gleaned certain basics.

Spinster Sadie Patrick, a schoolmarm from Arkansas, became the administrator during World War I of Thornhill Home, an institution for homeless children at a crossroad between Perkins and New Madrid. She retired from Thornhill about the time the United States jumped into World War II. Peter Stine was one of Miss Sadie's most precocious charges during her early years at the orphanage. She remembered that he was moved to Thornhill from the care of a foster mother who no longer could afford to feed and clothe him. Peter had been, based on Miss Sadie's best recollection, an abandoned baby. At Thornhill, in her words, "Peter was never a problem whatsoever. He was so well behaved. He learned to read very early, not like many of the other youngsters, and there were times I had to force him to put a book down. I'm confident he read every book in our small library." Brosky was sure he noticed a slight flush in her face when she allowed that "everybody came to think of Peter as the teacher's pet." To which she added, "And I suppose I could not deny it."

Nothing thus far had struck a particular chord in Brosky. He feigned interest as Miss Sadie reminisced about Peter, the model child at the orphanage who made his own bed, did not spill his milk, never strayed from the grounds. He sensed she was really talking to herself. Her clear eyes were staring aimlessly over his head.

Then, just like that, she fell silent. She dropped her face down toward her lap and put the kerchief to her forehead, as if she was feeling faint. He thought he heard her murmur about the heat smothering the room in spite of several electric fans struggling to circulate air. He didn't want to lose her, to even let her get out of his sight. Instinct told him not to let that happen. When she offered to bring him a fresh lemonade, which might have soothed his parched mouth and hoarse throat, he politely passed. Instead, he asked her permission to remove his seersucker suit coat. "Of course you may do so," she responded in a manner implying he need not have asked.

Unsure about the amount of time he had left with Miss Sadie, Brosky guided the interview, as delicately as he could, to an area he hoped might be more productive. "If you feel you can, Miss Sadie," he said gingerly, "I'd like to ask you to go over subjects that Peter talked to you about for his story." Anticipating that this might be his best and perhaps final approach, he explained that "only by knowing what Peter wanted to concentrate on will I be able to write the kind of piece that he would have done."

The tact showed promise of working. Picking up a cardboard fan by her chair, Miss Sadie flapped it back and forth, rapidly at first and then more slowly. She appeared to have collected herself, and when she complied with Brosky's request, she did so with renewed energy.

Stine had retraced with Miss Sadie, she related, his positive memories of Thornhill, especially his admiration for her strong influence. He said he wanted to particularly convey in his story that children who ended up in facilities like Thornhill were not doomed to failure. Far from it. Peter felt he was on the list of Thornhill kids doing well in the world, and he was sure there had to be others. She and Peter discussed several that he wanted to include in his article. One tyke whose parents drowned after his birth went on to become a doctor. Another was elected mayor of a town over near Kansas City.

And there was the little girl, that pretty little girl.

Brosky's unpromising day took on a radically different light with Miss Sadie's introduction of the little girl. Bringing her to the attention of Peter Stine had to have been even more riveting for Peter, Brosky could see. Miss Sadie said she had pointed out to Peter that the little gal's stay in the orphanage had overlapped his.

"Peter could not exactly remember the little girl when I told him about her," Miss Sadie ruminated. "But, I must say he showed great interest in her after I told him who she was. He certainly agreed that her life turned out wonderfully, and that, without question, she should be included in the story he was going to write."

When Miss Sadie first informed Brosky of the girl's identity in later life, it took all of a second for him to make the connection. The needle on the Geiger counter inside Jake immediately jerked into motion. What a small world, indeed.

There would be more. It had to do with the tragic circumstances that brought the girl to the orphanage. Miss Sadie was not as talkative about this segment of the girl's tale. After hinting around coyly, she divulged just enough in a whispery tone to propel Brosky's Geiger needle to wild fluctuations. But she warned Jake that this part of the little girl's past—the chapter about her "terrible mother"—must not get into the story. It was all "hush-hush" because efforts were made at the time to prevent people from tracing the little girl to "the awful woman" who was her mom.

"I told Peter he must not bring up any of that unfortunate situation," Miss Sadie said sternly. And, she admonished Brosky, "I trust, Mr. Jake, that you will also honor my request."

"You can believe me, Miss Sadie, when I tell you I will not write a word that you do not want."

Chapter Twenty-three

Never mind that he hadn't eaten or had a drop to drink since way back in the morning. The Brosky exiting Dixie Manor had a second wind.

His meeting with Sadie Patrick may have begun lackadaisically, but he was revved up when he left her. He'd gotten a lollapalooser from her, and he'd bet Peter Stine thought so too when Miss Sadie had leaked him the same information. Jake assumed Stine intended a follow-up, or was already trying to do so, before he was murdered. Whether Stine's reaction to Miss Sadie's bombshell had anything to do with his death was hard to say. Brosky certainly did not know enough about what he'd just learned to tie the two together. But Stine or no Stine, Brosky knew Miss Sadie had handed him the rudiments of a hell of a story. Key elements had to be nailed down, of course, before he could even consider going to his editors with what he had. Even then, he'd anticipate a great debate to ensue over whether or not to print the story. The editors would make that call. Brosky was a reporter, the bulldog kind. When he stumbled on a humdinger, or as in this case was handed one, he gave chase. And, the sooner the better.

Checking his watch as he sped out of sticky Perkins, Jake realized he still had a chance to reach the "morgue" at the *World* before everybody went home. Coming to a gas station and cafe a short distance from town, he abruptly turned in, parked and hustled to find a pay phone. Locating one momentarily, he hastily engaged an operator in the verbal jousting necessary for a connection from the remote boot heel to his newspaper. In spite of his great thirst, he was hit by a desperate urge to find an urinal. He was about to think he could not wait any longer when the welcome voice of an old hand at the morgue came on the line.

The morgue was not what it sounded like. It was the paper's reference library, a godsend for reporters with its huge collection of clips and pictures and cross referrals on everything appearing in the pages of the *World* through the years. Requests for assistance from star reporters like Brosky received priority.

Jake wanted clips or any other background on a public execution in Kentucky, roughly thirty years ago, of a woman convicted of murder. He ventured his best guess on the name of the woman. The morgue veteran vaguely remembered something about the subject, and he had to believe the files contained info on it.

"Good," remarked Brosky, "but handle the search on the qt because I don't know enough about what I am tracking to talk to anybody yet." Translation. It was premature for the editors to be alerted to what Jake was up to.

"Gotcha, Jake," the voice in the morgue replied.

Getting off the phone, Brosky headed for the john like a fellow possessed. Afterward, he succumbed to the aroma of fried chicken at the diner. A seat at the counter was open. He claimed it, and asked for cold water and coffee before placing his order. He was downing his third glass of water when the waitress plunked down before him a platter full of steaming chicken, and side dishes of all the stuff that went with it, including a favorite of the black cook, soft biscuits soaked in thick, brownish syrup. The fryer had been smothered in flour and allowed to simmer in a covered skillet overflowing with oil. Jake devoured it.

For Nat and Sloan, people who could afford a room at the Ritz, this was a most improbable spot for a rendezvous. Yet, here they were, snuggled together in the front seat of an inauspicious Crosley station wagon that Coyne had commandeered to avoid attracting attention, just two among the numerous lovers huddled in cars on the parking lot well after the setting of the late summer sun. Most of the others were kids who guzzled beer in between bouts of clumsy petting, suds obtained with no questions asked at the venerable veterans' hall that was the reason for the parking lot in the first place.

The setting was legendary. The old hall with the "members only" placard over the door, the big band dances attracting many besides veterans and the parking area that had spiced up life for neckers from one generation to another. Knowing winks always accompanied reminders of the time when so-and-so made out with so-and-so behind the hall on the edge of the quaint German farm village characterized by a sublime Catholic church with a sky-piercing steeple far out of proportion to everything around it. Once before, Coyne and Sloan had hooked up here, and unsophisticated as it was, they felt surprisingly safe for two individuals—well at least one for sure—with much to lose. Cops and watchmen and prying eyes, as far as Sloan and her paramour could tell, were not around.

His world had not been standing still. Sloan detected that something was wrong when Nat got through to her on the safe phone, insisting he had to see her that evening. Not in a luxurious St. Louis hotel room or one of their other sensuous retreats, but in this hamlet in the Illinois countryside. Nat sounded on edge. She couldn't suppress anxiety from gnawing at her as she gunned her white Ford convertible northward out of Grandville.

She refused to consider that her assignations with the mobster could ever end. She was schoolgirl starry-eyed over the trysts, and he had proven himself to her. The transitory hours with him, though painfully abbreviated, made her role as Mrs. Arkell Dillard endurable.

The affair between Sloan and Coyne had proceeded

without a hitch. And, at every stage, without remorse on her part. In her mind, it was a visceral progression destined from the moment they discovered each other.

The day that happened was one of those spectacularly golden ones of the previous autumn. A day that unfolded in a routine fashion for Mrs. Dillard—the footing of the bill for a fund-raising tea for the Rural Relief Society in the Foresters' Lodge in Grandville. Just standard fare for Mrs. Dillard, established procedure. Her life was full of it. When the tea party was over, one attendee, an out of towner, asked her friend Sloan to accompany her on a first-time visit, a quickie, to the famous Autumn Moon. Sloan, although not a frequenter of gambling clubs, saw no reason not to go along. After all, many women found nothing untoward, for instance, about the upscale restaurant at the club. Still, decorum being what it was, Sloan had nothing more in mind than a light drink, a weak gin and tonic most likely, as her friend satisfied her curiosity about the Moon.

When the two women were seated in the restaurant, which was nearly empty since it was the middle of the afternoon, nobody was within earshot. But oh how quickly, in a flash, a stranger surfaced at the next table. A man who looked fit to kill. A man who did not remain a stranger very long. Casual banter soon flowed between the two tables, stimulated by the gentleman's call for a round of whiskey sours, and another, and then another. Sloan had no inkling that initial afternoon that Nat Coyne was a gangster. What she did have was a desire that the interlude at the Moon not end. About the time the bartender was shaking bourbon, sugar and lemon juice into ice for a third round, Sloan and Coyne were oblivious to the presence of Sloan's companion. When the friend excused herself to sashay to the powder room, Coyne made a move that no chap in Sloan's backyard would have had the nerve to pull. He wrote something inside a matchbook, and slid it onto her table. As she picked up the small folder, he said, "You'll find a number in there that I can be reached through anytime." While their eyes locked, he went on, "I'd like it if you'd call me when you're going to St. Louis. I'd like to see you again, maybe show you some sights."

Mrs. Arkell Dillard, so aloof, so unapproachable to many in her part of the world, knew she'd take him up on it. Funny, but she never doubted this day would arrive. She had feared she might feel cheap when it happened. She didn't. For her, this juncture was overdue. And pangs of guilt? None. It was awareness, invitation and inevitable acceptance, all in a few moments.

Now, many months and clandestine get-togethers later, she still harbored no shame as she had sped toward her lover.

She'd drawn on a flimsier than usual excuse to get away from her husband for part of the night. The possibility of anything cropping up to threaten her relationship with Coyne pushed caution to the wind. No wonder she failed to notice her car being tailed by a pickup truck as she had scooted downwind.

She had reached her lover at the darker part of twilight. Her auto had turned heads in the parking lot, even though the top was up. Sliding out of the car, she had ignored wolf whistles from the area where a group of young guys were mingling outside their vehicles. Anyway, she could not have been certain she was the target since she was pretty far away for them to see her clearly in the semidarkness.

Nat heard the whistles too. When she jumped into the station wagon like a love struck sixteen-year-old, he swore in an exaggerated growl to "kill any of those young punks giving you the eye."

"Oh, baby, baby," was all she mouthed, shushing him with a finger to his lips to be quiet. Extending her hands around his face, she drew him against her as the woman inside started to stir.

"Nah, just kidding," Coyne whispered. "Nobody's getting killed tonight." Their lips meshed hard, and then their tongues entwined. He forced his hand between their compressed bodies and began to fumble with the buttons on the front of her thin cotton dress.

The door of the car closest to theirs, a jalopy, suddenly swung out, causing Sloan to stiffen and open her eyes. She watched a girl in short shorts, who was a real teenager, hop out, slam the door shut and stomp off. Through the open window of the junker, Sloan heard a whiny voice beg, "Ah come on, Lucy, don't be like that."

Relieved, Sloan shut her eyes again. Crushing her mouth against Coyne's even harder, she inserted her hand between them, pushed his down and expertly unfastened the middle buttons of her dress. He brought his hand back up and shoved it inside her bodice. He was rough, which was unusual, but she chalked it up to untethered desire. He wanted her and that, to her, was all that mattered. Whatever was bothering him, she silently reproved herself for even thinking that she might lose him. She just regretted they weren't in a hotel room.

Coyne explained the reason they were not. He had to surface at Fontane's headquarters for a late night conference decreed by the gang leader. Not showing up would be a mistake, Nat lamented to Sloan, because Fontane had become an impossible to please SOB since the state closed his Club Destiny.

Sloan hadn't perceived such reticence in Coyne before, not even where his boss was concerned. She never imagined Nat getting ruffled. Never. Not Nat. She also was not prepared for his zinger, the real motive for him having to see her that night, if only for several hours.

"I'm getting away, sugar," he blurted out into her surprised face. "It's drying up here. There's not enough left for everybody." Sloan was stunned. Straightening up, leaning back from Coyne, the spell from his hand under her dress abruptly broken, she asked, "What about us?"

"What about us? Us? I'll tell you what about us. You go with me, that's what about us." Alarmed at the tears welling in her eyes, he tried to inject the self-assuredness into his voice that she was used to. "I'll get it set up, don't you worry, and then you'll join me."

She turned her face away from him.

"You want me to join you," she cried. "Join you where?"

"Vegas. Las Vegas, sugar."

Las Vegas. Sloan Dillard in Las Vegas? She could not look at him. He talked about going legit, breaking into casino management, taking advantage of the growing opportunities in the desert boomtown. Still staring into the night, she could only think to respond, "Nat, I don't know anything about that place."

He moved to try to turn her face back toward him. Resisting, she uttered, "God! This is so sudden. I don't want to be without you. I can't...I can't even think about it." Her lips were twisting as she finally turned back to face him, trying to arrest a sob. "I thought," she said pleadingly, "you could not live without me."

"I can't, sugar, and that's why you're going to be with me." After a pause for emphasis, he added slowly, "You know if I say it, I mean it. You know that by now. Right, Sloan?"

"Yes, right. Of course. I know."

They talked on, their words drifting into the languid air of the humid night while his hand resumed its feverish movement beneath her open dress. Too soon for her, though, he forced an end to their time together. After sending her on a walk alone back to her convertible, and after hearing her car's motor start, Coyne hotfooted it out of the lot, hitting the road for East St. Louis and the meeting with a crime boss who had become insufferable.

As Sloan observed the Crosley's hasty exit, she overheard several fellows clutching bottles of Falstaff wisecracking about the guy trying to make a hot rod out of a station wagon. She had to clear her mind. She wanted to keep everything in place.

If she could, the world of abundance provided by Arkell Dillard. But also her secret lover, the dark, handsome and dangerous Irishman who gave her what her husband did not, could not. Retain both, that's what she had to do. She'd find a way. Just work it out, that was all.

First, she had to calm down on the return drive to Grandville. She wanted to have a plan by the time she got home.

While she steered out of the lot, Sloan paid no heed to anything else, including the pickup that had followed her from Grandville. Its lights flashed on after her Ford passed. Right after she turned onto the highway, the truck resumed the shadowing. The person in the cab, Johnny Bob Slocum, had plenty to report to Mr. Dillard. Slocum didn't know who Miss Sloan was making out with in the cozy quarters of the Crosley, but he caught enough to inform Mr. Dillard that Miss Sloan was a naughty woman.

More than a little digging was required, but Fritz Grimsley, the experienced hand in the *World's* morgue who took Brosky's call from the boot heel, came up with what he was sure Jake was looking for. The effort kept Grimsley at the newspaper well beyond his usual quitting time, but helping Brosky often meant that, later on, someone like Grimsley could feel he had contributed, if only in small measure, to one of the big stories that Jake regularly broke. Besides, Jake was always courteous to the morgue staffers, not treating them like inferior clerks the way some of the younger reporters did.

As Grimsley hustled to get out of the building in time to catch the next clanging streetcar heading to the west end, he dropped his find on Jake's desk so that it would be waiting for him first thing in the morning. The pay dirt was a blue envelope, like all the others in the morgue, containing articles about a woman named Marie Smith and the events that made her a public figure back in 1919 and 1920.

Chapter Twenty-four

When he wasn't in a rush, Brosky preferred to walk up to the news-editorial floor by the back stairs. Going that way, he could catch a glimpse of the cavernous room with the earsplitting roar where miles of newsprint in huge roles were fed into giant presses for the *World's* daily run of a half-million copies. Jake appreciated the touch of grandeur that the pressroom brought to the building.

But this morning, the elevator had to do because Brosky was anxious to reach his desk, to discover if one of the familiar blue envelopes was waiting for him. He was too tired anyway from the previous day's arduous drive to handle the stairs.

Riding up with him were two of the newsroom copyboys. "Good morning, Mr. Brosky," the older one said respectfully. He was the young guy who'd soon be passing out football parlay cards to the reporters and collecting their bets, but the only thing in his hand on the lift at the moment was the comics page from yesterday's *World*. When he caught Brosky skeptically eyeing the funnies, the copyboy blushed. "It's that Brenda Starr, Mr. Brosky. I keep up with her each day. I'm really hungry to find out if she sees the mystery man again." Brenda Starr, the voluptuous redheaded reporter adored every day in the strips by *World* copyboys and countless others. Too bad for all of us, Jake was tempted to tell these chaps, that the *World* did not have any Brenda Starrs on staff. But he didn't. That would be crossing the line.

Entering the city room, Brosky skirted without a side glance the horseshoe desk of the copy editors, the territory of stone-faced men, their shirt sleeves rolled up, fiercely attacking with black-leaden pencils the typed pages of reporters' stories. He did give a cursory nod to the editors at the city desk as he proceeded on to his desk by the window. Before reaching it, he spied the blue envelope. His spirit zoomed, but he was careful not to show it. Hanging up his suit coat, loosening his tie and putting a match to a Lucky, his fatigue from the day before was suppressed by his eagerness to explore the contents of the envelope. He even skipped the start of the day ritual with his cuspidor to get to the envelope.

Dumping out the contents, he sorted through a small mound of clips to ferret out several that he assumed would cover everything in the others, plus more

One article was headlined "Murderess Goes to Gallows in

Kentucky." The other, "Woman Pays Price for Brutal Slaying." Jake selected the first of the two to read. He had in his hand a page one story by the *International News Service* dated August 23, 1920, out of Lexington, Kentucky. The murderess was named Marie Smith, and she was hanged that day at a state prison for the murder of a payroll office clerk.

After providing a written picture of the hanging as witnessed by reporters, the yellowish clip delved into details of the crime that made an infamous woman out of Marie Smith. The following was read by Brosky.

On October 23, 1919, Smith and a male accomplice, Arthur Slater, held up the payroll office of Spencer Gun Works in Louisville. While the stickup was unfolding, armed guards from the nearby weapons manufacturing plant, alerted to what was going on, took up positions behind cars parked on the street outside the payroll office. One of the cars was a stolen auto the robbers intended to use for their escape.

Grabbing a sack stuffed with currency, Slater dashed first out of the office. The guards waiting outside yelled to him to surrender. Slater answered with bullets. The guards shot back. Slater was struck and fell to the sidewalk, mortally wounded.

When Smith, still in the payroll office, heard the exchange of gunfire, she loudly berated Joseph Abramson, a clerk with his arms raised behind a counter, for somehow tipping off the security personnel. Screaming obscenities, she fired point-blank at Abramson, a father of six children, killing him instantly. Running outside, she emptied her gun wildly at the guards before they subdued her.

The story went on to say that Marie Smith's notoriety in the wake of the crime ballooned because not many women cast as cold-blooded killers were as attractive as her. Crime magazines took it upon themselves to proclaim Marie the 25-year-old pinup queen of murderers, splashing her face on numerous covers. The article held by Brosky was accompanied by a picture of Marie Smith, a posed photo, the kind done in a studio. Jake readily understood how pulp magazines and the sensational press had a veritable field day with her.

Further down in the story, Brosky came to a paragraph that jumped up and bit him. Marie was from Madison, Indiana, described in the account as a picturesque town on the Ohio River not far up from Louisville. In fact, according to the INS piece, she was still living in Madison, working as a waitress, at the time of the robbery.

Madison, Indiana. Jake's mind was racing in numerous directions at once. Madison, Indiana. Peter Stine was shot to death on the outskirts of Madison. He had gone to Madison searching for records or background of some sort that took him into the courthouse and the local newspaper. Brosky's pulse was throbbing harder. Tracking situations like this, beginning to sense that something might be adding up, made his job great, reminded him why he'd stuck with reporting when so many of his early contemporaries drifted into public relations or other fields.

Jake did not believe in coincidences. Stine drove to Madison after Miss Sadie had told him the astonishing information she later slipped to Jake. Marie Smith was a central character in Miss Sadie's revelation, and Marie was from Madison. Stine was murdered when visiting Madison—Brosky did not doubt—to hunt for confirmation of at least part of what Miss Sadie had confided. Jake saw nothing accidental about any of it. Marie Smith, Madison, the killing of Stine. All tied together. No, Brosky did not subscribe to coincidences.

A key element still was missing in the story Brosky was reading. A scan of its concluding graphs made no mention of it. Jake thumbed through other clips from the envelope and picked out one, a feature, written when Marie was sentenced to die. Perusing it, he hit the jackpot. It was there. Marie was not married, but she had a five-year-old daughter. Predictably, nothing was said about the child's whereabouts.

Pieces of puzzles taken on by Brosky seldom came together as rapidly. What next? Roused by the way the chase was going, Jake knew from experience he had to keep his excitement within bounds, sit back and coolly plot his next move. Several steps obviously were in order. Brosky was on the verge of deciding on the first one when he became aware that the city editor had silently approached and was standing by his desk.

"Jake, this is yours," the editor said, gazing down at Brosky through horn-rims.

"Galligan just called from the East Side. They found that Fontane guy, Nat Coyne, in a ditch this morning with a bullet in the back of his head."

Chapter Twenty-five

In his obituary and the stories prompted by his violent death, Nat Coyne was cast as the Dapper Dan of the underworld. One of the wire services started it and newspapers dutifully followed, embellishing his reputation as a gangster who portrayed style and dash. Brosky was not keen on romanticizing hoodlums. He'd known too many, observed their vicious handiwork too often and, worse yet, too close up.

Nonetheless, the first edition of the *World* to carry the story of Coyne's killing, scanty coverage though it was, picked up on the Dapper Dan theme. Brosky's byline was on the article even though he had little to do with it. Most of it came from information the East St. Louis police supplied to old Daniel (Double Scotch) Galligan of the *World's* East Side bureau.

Coyne appeared to be the victim of a traditional mob-style

hit. His body was found after daybreak, lying in a roadside ditch near a vacant warehouse by the packinghouse strip in the north end of East St. Louis. Shot from behind. Cleanly, proficiently. Galligan, tipped by the cops, reached the site where the body was discovered before it was removed. The corpse was being photographed. Uniform officers in beat cars were the first to respond to the call on the body. Detectives dispatched to the scene arrived shortly afterward, followed by identification technicians, who were responsible for pictures, fingerprinting and evidence collection. The St. Clair County coroner showed up to declare the victim dead at the scene and conduct an initial medical exam, which indicated the fellow had been dead only five to seven hours because rigor mortis was still in an early stage. The ident of the victim was absolutely no mystery. Few cops around St. Louis would not recognize the face of Coyne. Besides, his wallet was still in the pocket of his trousers.

Searching for evidence where the body was dumped was fruitless because there would be none. Rubouts of gangsters were hardly ever solved. Even in the establishment of motives, the police seldom were more successful than the press. Nevertheless, in the case of Coyne, speculation about the who and why would be copious.

For the final edition of the *World* that day, the editors wanted Brosky to go as far as he could in both reporting on and theorizing about the killing. Nobody had to say that the *World* was expected to be ahead of the competition. Copy clacking out of the wire teletypewriters at the paper was spouting notions that Brosky found ridiculous. Coyne was killed, it was suggested, as revenge for the murder of Cecil Langston's son. Brosky did not believe that. Or, Coyne lost out in jockeying for greater clout in the underworld. Well, that was more believable, although Coyne had already been widely viewed as being groomed by Harry Fontane to be his heir. Might it be that Coyne had launched a move to prematurely replace his general? Jake couldn't swallow that either.

The *United Press* had an updated lead coming out of Springfield. Lawrence Dantello was ordering the Illinois State Police to assist local authorities in the investigation of the murder. Moreover, Dantello announced he had been directed by Governor Sanderson to pull out all stops in trying to stem further underworld violence in downstate Illinois. The deaths of Marvin Langston and Nat Coyne, contended Dantello, "are quite likely tied to old gang enmities inflamed in recent times by the lucrative flourishing of illegal gambling." Just as the state "stepped in to protect honest citizens against the gambling interests," crowed the state police superintendent, "we will not tolerate continued gang hostilities, whether deep-seated or not."

Poppycock, Brosky told the editor, who felt the Dantello angle ought to run near the top of Jake's final edition story. If Dantello was insinuating that Cecil Langston had something to do with the shooting of Coyne, which Dantello certainly looked to be doing, Brosky had only one word for it. Nonsense.

Getting Cecil to deny it on the record, though, was desirable. For several reasons. Langston had to defend himself and, secondly, Jake needed a last edition lead that nobody else would have. So Brosky had to get through to Cecil in the time remaining before the day's final deadline. Jake also knew he should get in touch with Mr. Brown, Norton Raven, to pick up the Fontane mob's inside line on the Coyne bump off.

No answer. Not at the phone at which Raven usually could be contacted. The Langston call was different. Dorothy was aghast at hearing Jake tell her that Nat Coyne was murdered and, furthermore, that some were depicting her husband as a suspect.

"Good lord, Jake," she protested, "they'd blame Cecil for starting World War II if they could!"

"Dorothy, you've got to understand that the past will always rear up at things like this. I wish that wasn't so, but it's nothing I can control, or keep out of people's minds. I wish I could."

"Jake, the Langston gang is long gone and buried. We've suffered enough for what happened years ago. Why can't people just let us alone? When is it ever going to end for us? Tell me, Jake. You know about these things. Tell me."

Brosky had no reply to ease her mind. But he still had to carry through on his call, and do it with Dorothy since she said that Cecil was not around.

"They are saying, Dorothy, that the killing of Coyne may have been revenge for the death of Marvin. State police detectives may be coming around to question Cecil and probably you too about it. At least, that's what they are saying."

"Jake," Dorothy said, her voice more firm, "you can write it up in the way you do to say that the Langston family is sick and tired of being accused of every bad thing that happens, and that we don't know one thing about the killing of that Coyne fellow."

Since he personally had no doubt of that, Brosky assured Dorothy that she could count on his story stressing a strong disavowal by the Langstons. He had gotten what he called for and was preparing to hang up when Dorothy abruptly uttered an addendum.

"The truth of it," she said, "is that we are pretty sure that this Coyne and that Fontane crowd didn't have a thing to do with what happened to our Marvin."

"How do you know that, Dorothy?" Jake asked, immediately interested in the new turn the conversation had taken.

"Well, Jake, we think we know who did this to Marvin, and—

"Dorothy, what are you talking about?"

"What I was saying, Jake, is we think we know who killed our son. And when Cecil feels like telling you about it, I'm sure he'll do it. It's not going to be something that you probably can ever put in your newspaper."

"Well, Dorothy, if there's something you know that can lead to the solving of Marvin's murder, then—

Dorothy was the one interrupting this time, saying resolutely, "Now listen, Jake Brosky, not one word goes any farther about what you've just heard. You are the only newspaper fellow I ever trusted. You know that."

"I understand, Dorothy," Jake rejoined, "but if there is something here I ought to know...." He let his voice trail off, hoping she still might elaborate on perhaps the latest significant development in the seemingly perpetual Langston saga.

However, she would add nothing more than that her husband "will confide in you when he thinks it's time, Jake. Until then, it's family business and nobody else's."

She left Jake suspended in midair. No question, though, that his call to Smithburg had raised the likelihood of another good story down the pike, an answer, maybe, to the mystery surrounding the murder of Marvin Langston. Virtually overnight, Jake had gone from a relatively empty plate to a feast of good stories. For sure, more than he could handle at one time. At the moment, the one staring him in the face was the killing of "Dapper Dan" Coyne.

The final edition of the *World* featured Brosky's story leading off with the Langston family denial of any connection to Coyne's murder. Jake took the liberty of dressing up Dorothy's quotes and of even manufacturing a couple more for added flavor. His rewrite man did not know anything differently, and he wouldn't have questioned Brosky if he did. Such was the case when a reporter like Brosky had exclusive command of his territory. Readers of the *World's* main competitor in the afternoon newspaper field learned only that authorities were considering an interview with Cecil Langston about Coyne's death.

Brosky's gut feeling was that the demise of Coyne was linked completely to the current state of affairs in gangland. The answer had to revolve around Fontane himself, but that would be a tough nut to crack. Brosky needed help, or at least someone who could feed him clews. Jake noticed, as the day wound down, that Raven had not called him, which was a bad sign if Jake expected the mob itself to proffer anything. He tried the phone for Raven again, but it still rang unanswered. Brosky did persuade a St. Louis homicide dick, friendly to him and familiar with the underworld, to agree to see him in an hour or so, but Jake's chance of providing much additional insight into the next day's follow-up piece on Coyne's death did not appear promising. The editors could pressure him all they wanted, but Brosky was going to need some time, a few days at least, to come up with something. In the meantime, the paper would just have to tread water with stories on Dapper Dan's rise from Kerry Patch to mob big shot, which was okay because *World* readers never seemed to tire of reading the life stories about the homegrown bad guys.

Homicide detective Asa Cundiff was one of the few St. Louis cops who did not hesitate to talk to Brosky in his office in the city's police headquarters at Twelfth and Clark. Most preferred back rooms of taverns or park benches. But Cundiff, who never was quoted by name, showed not the slightest trepidation at Brosky strolling into his office in plain view of his superiors and everyone else. Cundiff also was the only copper around with the audacity to wear flamingly red suspenders throughout the year.

The Coyne hit, Cundiff readily conceded to Brosky, "has us all baffled at the moment." Nobody, said Cundiff, "knows what it's over. There's no gang turf war around here, and even with

Fontane taking it up the ass on the Illinois gambling raids, there's still nobody with the muscle to get away with taking out Harry's top guy."

So, Brosky found himself asking the detective what he'd already begun thinking before he left the newspaper. "So you think, Asa, that the only guy could get away with a hit on Coyne would be Fontane himself?"

"Who else?"

Gloria DeForest was waiting for him in the dimly lit, cozy Sazerac lounge off the arabesque lobby of the President Hotel. Brosky was delighted she'd insisted on seeing him. Even better, she had volunteered to meet him in the little bar, only a short hike from his apartment on Lindell. He was dead tired when he left Cundiff's office, but perked up while walking to the hotel on an absolutely splendid evening. The graceful voice of bandleader Billy Eckstine was floating through the Sazerac as Jake joined her at a corner table. Gloria wore a pink chemise accentuated by sheer nylons, and an Ipana smile. As Brosky sat down, she thrust forward the day's final edition of the *World*.

"My, my, my. Another Jacob Brosky story all over the front page. Why I feel so honored to personally know you, Mr. Brosky." She laughed, and so did Jake. A waiter moved promptly to the table and set down before Brosky a tall glass of ice and a bottle of White Rock ginger ale. "I went ahead and ordered for you," she said. "I accept the sad fact you don't drink anymore, Mr. party pooper, but one of us still has to have fun." She was nursing a red vermouth even though no food was in the offing.

As she cooed over Brosky's article, she exclaimed without looking up, "You have such an exciting life, Jake! Dealing with gangsters, rubbing your shoulder against danger. Do you really know these Langston people in southern Illinois that I'm reading about here?"

"Yes, I do, Gloria. I sure do. And they are not bad at all. You might even like Dorothy Langston." But maybe not, he thought. No two women could be more dissimilar. One so unvarnished, the other a showcase for Dior and Schiaparelli. Yes, Gloria was right. Jake did lead an absorbing life, one that encompassed Dorothy Langston and Gloria DeForest in the same day.

"Since I am so lucky to have you all to myself, Jake," Gloria said after a slow sip of her drink, "what can you tell me about the murder of this man Coyne? It says here that he had a reputation for being a ladies' man. Do you think that his relationship with one of his women had something to do with his death?"

Jake replied that he had no reason to believe so, but that he might know more after a phone call that he needed to make. "How fascinating," she remarked softly, "getting to see you in action." Excusing himself, he found a pay phone in the lobby, took out his little black book and asked the operator to ring Raven's number. This time Raven answered.

"I want to talk to you, Mr. Brown," Brosky said gruffly.

"I can't talk to you now, Jake." Raven sounded very skittish. "I don't know nothin' at all about it. Nothin'."

Chapter Twenty-five

"That's not what I want to hear."

"Please, Mr. Brosky, I don't know what to say right now. I'll call you when I can." Raven sounded cold, and Jake noticed that he had switched from Jake to Mr. Brosky, a sign that he was trying to put distance between himself and Brosky.

"That won't do." But the stoolie did not hear the last comment because he had hung up.

Returning to the Sazerac, Jake was asked by Gloria if the call paid off. "No, it was a dead end," he said, adding, "For a guy who leads such an exciting life I run into a lot of dead ends."

"Oh, I wouldn't have thought that. I guess I should say I am sorry." As she talked, she put both of her hands around one of his.

Sorry. Gloria was sorry. Well, not as sorry as someone else is going to be, a simmering Brosky was thinking to himself. He had an idea, a plan of action that just might convince Mr. Fontane to shell out more than a little inside dope.

Chapter Twenty-six

Jake hatched his scheme the next day. He'd play it out in a story, to run twenty-four hours later, that would feed the voracious appetite of the reading public for further insight of any kind into the inner world of organized crime. The story's other purpose, the main one, was to tweak Fontane, to goad him into spilling the beans on what was behind the execution of Coyne. For Jake's ploy to succeed, the story had to zing Fontane's ego, his most vulnerable spot.

The article would be based on anonymous sources, which crime and political reporters got away with using in abundance. Especially Brosky and his peers covering the underworld, where the few individuals willing to talk to the press were scared shitless of being quoted by name. Editors seldom had any more idea than readers about gangland sources. Furthermore, hardly any newspapers, the *World* included, employed more than one really true crime specialist. As a result, a reporter like Brosky had all the leeway in the world to write whatever he wanted because nobody was qualified to second-guess him.

Of course, journalistic principles being what they were, no reporter—crime scribes included—was supposed to write anything he, or she, did not know to be true. To be fair, Brosky, in comparison to many, was pretty good about keeping the faith. But, he'd fudged his rectitude here and there through the years when he felt the situation demanded it. This Fontane story would be one in which there would be a lot of fudging. Much of what he dished up to his rewrite man was pure bunkum.

Later in the day, after Brosky had dictated the gist of the Fontane piece, Jake asked the paper's operator to place a call to a certain state official in Jefferson City. Sam Rabbit, deputy director of the Missouri Department of Social Welfare. A man with a noticeable name and a chap who owed Jake a big one and another big one and another big one. Brosky, and Brosky alone, had prevented Rabbit from being the fall guy in a nursing home inspection screwup by the department that the *World* disclosed a few years back. Still, he was as jittery as any bureaucrat would be when Brosky told him what he wanted.

"Jake," Rabbit reminded his caller imploringly, "those records are confidential by law. If certain people found out I let you see them, they'd hang me for sure."

"Sam," Brosky retorted, "don't give me this crap. Nobody would ever know it was you, and you know it. I want to get into that file, and I need you to handle it, and I don't think it's asking a hell of a lot."

Rabbit coughed nervously. "No, Jake, I guess maybe not. It's just that—

"Sam, we'll meet someplace away from Jefferson City so no one will even see us talking. I'd like to get together tomorrow evening if that's possible. And I'm sure, Sam, it will be."

Commercial production of petroleum in Illinois went back to 1885, but hardly anybody north of Springfield was aware of it. For a while in the early part of the twentieth century, when counties like Lawrence and Crawford were first heavily drilled, Illinois was third among the oil-producing states. A second oil boom in the lower part of the state erupted in the late 1930s and early 1940s, thanks to the discovery of the Clay City and Salem fields. Big production years resulted, but they would end with the absence of new major oil discoveries and the depletion of the known reserves.

If one place bucked the slump, it was Oil City. The flow of the liquid black gold hadn't ebbed since a hard drinking wildcatter, back from World War II and down to his last dollars, had pitched an empty Jim Beam bottle as far as he could out into a field of crusty southern Illinois clay near Oil City to show him where he should drill one final time. He hit a gusher so ferocious it couldn't be capped. Oil City still was bustling in 1950 with a steadily incoming stream of fortune seekers, showy sorts who flashed diamond stickpins in their loud ties and snakeskin boots on their feet. Theirs could not help but be a fly-by-night world, characterized by transitory roughnecks brought in by the catters to drill the test wells that either would hit oil or become dry holes. The dog-eat-dog environment was a natural for a lowlifer like Little George Bankheart to wander into.

Cecil Langston did not know how long Little George had been back in Illinois over in the oil fields, but he was around all right. When Langston got that confirmed, he had to quell an internal fit of violent wrath that easily could have driven him to run to the drilling sites near Oil City and shoot the bastard on the spot. Bankheart didn't deserve to get off that easy, though. He had to suffer, experience the terror that Little George had inflicted, Cecil did not doubt, on Marvin.

Working out in his mind the misery to inflict on Bankheart was therapy for Cecil. His spirit was finally uplifted. He never once thought that God would quarrel in any way with the steps he'd decided to take to protect what remained of his family and, while so doing, rid the world of a despicable evil. He honestly believed after all that it was God who alerted him to the presence of Bankheart. Cecil only had to call upon his old wile, clear away the cobwebs upstairs that he had let accumulate through the years.

By design, the dispatching of Little George entailed, at the beginning, pretty much the same extreme tactic Bankheart had used against Marvin. Little George would be shanghaied. Contrary to what the surviving Langstons professed, remnants of the Langston gang still were to be found. The old loyalty ran deep. There was one, Miles W. Wilson, who hit the county fair wrestling circuit after the gang broke up and later married a wealthy widow down in Cairo, no longer doing much of anything. Wilson hankered for the excitement of the old days, but not with Little George, whom he had despised. When Cecil requested a little assistance from Wilson, for old time's sake, Wilson jumped to oblige.

Cecil had done his homework. Bankheart was actually making it fairly easy. He was living alone in a dog-eared trailer on a dead-end road outside of Oil City. Although the tops of derricks could be seen on the other side of a nearby woods, surveillance by Langston led him to believe that Bankheart's trailer was rusting in seclusion.

If it went the way Cecil wanted, tomorrow would be judgment time. Wilson would hook up with him during the day, and the two would be waiting at the trailer to greet Little George when he wandered home from the oil patch or, more likely, the Lost Creek Pub.

Chapter Twenty-seven

Harry Fontane had yet to surface at his headquarters when a runner timidly placed a copy of the *World* on the desk of Theresa Carmody at high noon. The gang leader's gal Friday realized after reading only the opening paragraph of a story beginning on the lower left side of page one that those hanging around were facing misery once Fontane got in and saw the *World*. Without going over the rest of the article, she got up and carried the paper into his office.

Fontane had this to look forward to.

"Great Loss of Respect for Crime Boss"

By Jacob S. Brosky

Of the *World*

The status of Harry Fontane, recognized for years as the most feared underworld lord in the St. Louis area, has greatly diminished

among other organized crime figures as a result of major developments in recent days.

Long reliable sources in St. Louis gangland say that the prestige of the East Side-based Fontane has slipped so badly that many in the mob are labeling him a has-been. As a result, questions have been raised about how long Fontane will remain the chief coordinator in the St. Louis region for illegal enterprises of the Chicago underworld, which runs organized crime in the Midwest.

The most recent damaging blow to Fontane's stature was the execution-style murder several days ago of Fontane's top lieutenant and eventual heir apparent, Nat Coyne. Although East St. Louis police are being aided in the investigation of Coyne's death by the Illinois State Police and special homicide officers from the St. Louis Police Department, the inquiry has turned up neither a motive nor any suspects in the slaying.

The killing of Coyne is only the latest in a series of setbacks for Fontane. It has come on the heels of the collapse of Fontane's attempt to establish a gambling empire in Illinois. Acting under direct orders from Governor Elijah Sanderson, State Police raiders recently forced most of the illegal gambling clubs flourishing in downstate Illinoise to shut their doors. One of the most lucrative to be put out of business by a raid was Fontane's own Club Destiny located between East St. Louis and Belleville. Some of the other southern Illinois clubs closed forcibly or voluntarily as a result of the state crackdown had been targeted for takeover by Fontane, the *World* was informed. Furthermore, at the direction of Fontane, Coyne was leading the effort to muscle in on these other clubs. The undertaking reportedly was on the verge of success.

Police and other veteran observers say that reverses of this magnitude for a major underworld boss in such a short period of time are extraordinary.

As one of these persons put it, "Fontane looks like a guy who is losing it. First, people familiar with these matters couldn't believe that he did not put out enough money and have the clout to keep the Illinois officials from locking the door on his own club. That disgraced him in the eyes of many. Then we have his own top guy, his own fair-haired boy, getting shot in the back of the head and dumped in a ditch, and nobody knows anything about it. Fontane used to be the guy who ordered things like that done. They were not done to him. You just cannot believe how much respect Fontane has lost in recent days."

The killing of Coyne in particular has mystified authorities. His death had the earmarks of an underworld hit. There was early speculation in some places that Coyne may have been murdered by old southern Illinois enemies of Fontane seeking revenge. But investigators are discounting this possibility, saying there appears to be nothing to substantiate any validity.

Instead, the investigation is said to be focusing on other factions in the St. Louis underworld with a possible eye on the unseating of Fontane as the mob kingpin. For one, the Dutchmen gang on the south side now headed by the notorious Pashen family has long considered it time for Fontane to move aside. However, individuals close to the gang, as well as sources tied to other strong factions, steadfastly deny any knowledge of the Coyne killing.

"Until somebody gives, or the cops come up with something," insisted one source, "Fontane is going to look like a guy certainly losing control. It has got to be very embarrassing for him, not even being able to protect his own second in command."

If the article did not provoke the reaction from Fontane that Brosky needed, Jake did not know what else he could do.

One of the calls Brosky was expecting came through right after he returned from lunch. The *World* operator said it was from a pay phone in Jefferson City. Sam Rabbit sounded the way he felt, like a person reluctantly resigned to do something that he knew he should not be doing. He'd have the file requested by Brosky hidden in his briefcase when he left his office at the department later in the day. "Where's the safe place you want to meet, Jake?" Rabbit asked. Brosky told him what he had in mind. Rabbit agreed to see him there six hours later.

Jake was back on the road, piling up more miles on the Olds, heading for the hush-hush get-together with Rabbit that Brosky was banking on to yield one more piece of the puzzle that had him far more excited than the Coyne case. Before he left the newspaper, Jake considered briefly trying to call Cecil Langston, to pump him about Dorothy's intriguing revelation that she and Cecil knew who killed their son. Brosky intended to play the string of that subject out to the end, even if it required unreasonable pushing of the Langstons. If they were on target, Jake was certain he'd find a way to squeeze out a story and protect them at the same time. However, Brosky did not find time for the Langston call before taking off for the

Rabbit rendezvous. If Jake had, he again would have failed to find Cecil at home.

For Cecil and Miles W. Wilson had made their way into the trailer of Little George by mid afternoon to await his arrival. They'd had no need to jimmy the door; its lock was broken and didn't catch. Once inside, they were taken aback by a palpable stench. Langston thought it had the smell of sour milk. Good housekeeping was not Bankheart's strong suit, as evidenced by piles of dirty dishes on a card table, soiled clothes strewn about and a mound of moldy garbage. The intruders also were greeted by roaches—two kinds, the fat ones scurrying across the split linoleum and the butts of marijuana cigarettes sharing the sink with empty liquor bottles. The meager furnishings testified to the peripatetic existence of its occupant. He slept on an over-the-hill army cot, which was the best the trailer offered for sitting. So, the two men pushed aside the twisted sheet and parked themselves on the bed, hoping Little George was not bent on a long tavern night. They lucked out because he wasn't, or else he'd decided to stop off at home before going out for the evening.

Hearing a car pull up outside the trailer, Langston and Wilson sprung off the cot and lined up beside the door, one on each side. Flinging open the door, Bankheart stepped in, glancing neither left nor right. They pounced on him like cougars, kicking his short legs from under him and crashing him facedown to the linoleum. They did not want him to see their faces.

"Wha the hell," he uttered feebly. "Wha the hell is this...wha the hell...."

The mumbling ended abruptly as Wilson jerked Little George's head from the floor by his hair and jammed an oily rag into his mouth. He was powerless to resist since his attackers already had cuffed his hands behind his back. Next, a potato sack was slipped over his head, hooding him until the precise moment Cecil planned to reveal himself. Later, Cecil would tell Dorothy he couldn't recollect anybody being so flabbergasted, too overwhelmed by shock to defend himself. Only after the bag went over his noggin did George begin to really squirm, but it was pointless. The binding of his legs ended even futile resistance.

Within a few minutes following his arrival at his trailer, Little George—trussed and gagged—was tossed into the trunk of a blue Pontiac Torpedo sport coupe Langston had borrowed for the occasion. Slamming down the trunk lid, Langston quietly exchanged words with Wilson, the first they had spoken since the arrival of Bankheart. Langston then grasped his friend's hand before departing in the Pontiac. Wilson proceeded to his own car, which had been hidden nearby with the Pontiac. Soon he was heading for Cairo. He and Langston would refrain from further contact with each other for a good spell.

As Brosky was cruising down a busy highway in Missouri for his date with Sam Rabbit, Langston was sticking to back roads as he steered the Pontiac toward the conclusion of the "family business" that Dorothy had mentioned to Brosky.

To avoid going through Eldorado and Harrisburg, Langston made his way over gravel tops that treated his passenger in the trunk to a bruising jostle. Langston began to worry that the dust and heat might suffocate Little George before the destination was reached. Finding a harder road down near Carrier Mills, a little before breaking into the Shawnee Hills, Cecil hit a stop sign not far from a country inn he'd supplied in his previous life. With no other traffic in sight at the spot, an elderly gentleman peddling watermelons out of the back of a truck by the edge of the road walked up to the coupe.

"Like one, mister? They're real hard and juicy."

"No. No thanks," answered Langston, "not today." As he declined, he noticed that the puckered face under the straw hat was vaguely familiar.

The man himself was sure he recognized Langston. "Say, you was down in these parts in years back," he told Cecil with eyes that said he knew exactly who Langston was.

A dull thump emanated from the trunk, followed by another. The melon man's eyes shifted to the rear end of the car, then returned to the deadpan face of Langston. Cecil saw the fellow's lips twitch.

"I'll not be holding you up no more mister, no sir," he drawled. Langston, still unblinking, said nothing in return. "No," the aged one added, "I don't believe it's true I've ever saw you around here. Must've been some other man I was thinking of." He turned and walked back to his truck. Langston drove on, slowly at first, trying in vain to place the fellow. Cecil was not worried about the encounter, though. No question the man was a good old sock.

Several hours later, Langston was where he wanted to end up.

The gloaming of the day was at hand when the coupe reached the edge of the hardwood swamp fed by the Cache River below Grandville. Cecil encountered no difficulty in the dusk finding and turning onto a rutted trail leading to a decaying jetty protruding into the primeval muck.

All around was a murky wetland, the "forbidden bayou" of Illinois, where eight hundred-year-old cypress trees had "knees," birds stood almost as tall as people, bobcats might be seen and venomous snakes definitely were. The domain was infested with cottonmouths.

The jetty served as a safe haven for the Langston gang in the old days. A place to temporarily leave crates of hooch. A spot where an uncooperative individual might be brought for a heart-to-heart talk. Most folks shied away from the swamp. Were scared to death of it. Cecil remembered well one gang member who refused to go near it because he was terrified of the snakes smoothly gliding through the thick water. The same fellow in the trunk being escorted by Langston to the rotting old landing wharf.

After inching up as close as he could to the jetty, Langston yanked his prisoner up out of the luggage compartment and tossed him to the ground. Little George remained securely bound and hooded. Step by step, Langston dragged the shorter man by the back of his shirt across the splintery jetty, right to its far edge a foot above green-coated water.

The dark hadn't descended enough for Little George not to know where he had been borne the second Langston ripped off the hood. Staring up at Langston in utter panic, his blackish eyes pleading for mercy, Little George struggled against the gag to no avail. The discordant sounds of the swamp—the croaking of bullfrogs, the shrill screeching of birds, the buzzing of the skeeters—were interrupted only by the voice of Cecil.

"You have come to your favorite place, Little George." Swiping a wave of skeeters away from his face, he spat on the figure writhing at his feet. "I'll be leaving you with the moccasins. And when they are done with you, what's left of you will be going to that place where it's all fire. Fires, George, everywhere you step."

Kneeling, Langston plunged Bankheart's face into the water. But, not wanting to end it quite yet, Cecil hauled the head back up from the stew in the nick of time. Bankheart was still breathing. Good.

Crouching close to his enemy's ear, Cecil hissed, "Marvin is looking down on this, is loving this. He's going to watch you go all the way to hell, you little bastard."

The strong hands of Langston again thrust Bankheart into the gunk. This time the head stayed under until Little George stopped quivering. Rising up, Cecil kicked the rest of the body off the jetty.

Chapter Twenty-eight

" **A** nd now," the familiar voice on the radio intoned, "the latest news—brought to you by Old Gold cigarettes. Remember, the Old Gold people are tobacco men, not medicine men. Old Golds cure just one thing, the world's best tobacco." Brosky had an added reason for wanting to hear the news before the station faded from his car radio. Since the local newscasters unabashedly lifted much of their stuff every day out of the *World* and other St. Louis papers, Jake was curious to see if his Fontane story made it to the airwaves. It did not. What he heard before turning the knob to find music was a hodgepodge, the usual jumble.

He learned that Virginia Hill, the girlfriend of the late Bugsy Siegel, disrespectfully told members of the special United States Senate committee investigating gambling where to stick it at one of the panel's first hearings. What she actually said, according to the radio, was that she fervently hoped an atom bomb fell on every senator on the committee. What else? The *Washington Post* was refusing to print President Truman's angry letter to the critic who penned a bad review of a concert given by Truman's daughter, Margaret. In the letter, the President warned the reviewer that, if they met, the guy would "need a new nose, a lot of beefsteak for black eyes, and perhaps a supporter below." Truman was Brosky's kind of fellow. The news broadcast also turned to the president of Boston University and his warning that the craze over television sweeping the land was "destined" to create "a nation of morons" because of the idiotic level of the programs. The radio people were probably jealous, Brosky figured, justifiably wary that TV was cutting into their game. Jake could not see, though, those fledgling news programs on TV ever threatening the role of newspapers.

The top was down on the 88 convertible as Jake chased a radiant, setting sun in the west on the two-laner undulating through wine country. The Missouri River flowed nearby. Brosky's destination, the German-fed village of New Bavaria, was on the river. Before getting hamstrung by Prohibition, New Bavaria was one big prosperous winery, a community where every hill was blanketed with grapes. For years afterward, the old, idle terraces were a reminder of what the town had been.

Jake had used New Bavaria before for clandestine meetings. A safe place was needed, and he had one in a private back room of an inn known for mounted deer and elk heads and row after row of shelves filled with salt-glazed, pewter-lidded steins, a mirror of a Munich beer hall. The innkeeper was one Herr Helbig. Brosky's friendship with Helbig was a long story, starting with Jake's invaluable assistance in rescuing Helbig's dearest cousin in south St. Louis from a most personal and troublesome entanglement with an unscrupulous mother and son grifter duo. While Jake took umbrage at politicians taking freebies, he himself had not hesitated to accept free plates of bratwurst or Wiener schnitzel placed before him by Helbig.

However, Brosky had no desire to eat anything heavy as he waited for Sam Rabbit. The man from Jefferson City was late, prompting Brosky to begin to think he might have gotten cold feet. Jake was crushing out his third cigarette when Helbig ushered an apologetic Rabbit to the rear room. Extra time and a bit of legerdemain had been required to smuggle out the file, Rabbit explained. He could not overly stress, Rabbit rereminded Brosky, the sensitivity of state records on adoptions and orphanages, documents not authorized for public disclosure. Brosky himself was quite cognizant of the cold shoulder repeatedly given by lawmakers to proposals for easier access to files on adoptions and the identities of the biological parents of adoptees.

As Rabbit pulled a couple of large manila paper envelopes from a brown briefcase, he said to Brosky, "I hope this doesn't take real long."

"I still want to get them back in their cabinet at the department before the night is over," he added, handing the envelopes to Jake.

"These are all the records I could find, Jake, on the orphanage you wanted, Thornhill Home. I hope you see what you're looking for. If you don't, I'm not sure what else I can do."

Not replying, just nodding, Brosky went to work, employing his long-practiced eye in looking at official documents. The records seemed to be arranged chronologically, which was a break, as was the absence of the opaque language often used by bureaucrats to exclude or confuse outsiders. The print on the records also was clear, not in faded or smudged ink like on so many from the past. Some of the documents either were signed by or mentioned Sadie Patrick, who was listed, like she told Jake, as the administrator of Thornhill.

Glancing at his notes from the morgue clips at the *World*, Brosky was pretty sure that what he wanted to pin down had to have taken place very late in 1919 or, more likely, in 1920. He was on target.

There it was. In 1920.

In the fall of that year, Sadie Patrick certified that one Susan Smith, a five-year-old girl, was placed in Thornhill under a financial arrangement with a family apparently connected in some way with the girl's mother. She, the mother, was identified as "Miss Marie Smith, Madison, Ind., deceased." A subsequent reference in the records to Susan Smith gave her a middle name, which hit home with Brosky.

Further on in the documents, Brosky spied an insertion

noting that Susan was adopted in 1924 by a couple with "excellent character." The man's first name was misspelled, but there was no mistaking him for anyone else. Brosky had what he came for. The confirmation in the records of the information he'd gleaned from Miss Sadie allowed more pieces of the puzzle to be fit firmly into place.

Oh yes, Brosky also wanted to run back through the records to substantiate that Peter Stine was a young resident of Thornhill when Susan Smith was there. He was.

To where was it all leading? Every successful step in tracking a good story gave a reporter cause for gratification, maybe even euphoria. Nevertheless, the surge of elation that Brosky felt in New Bavaria, the sudden feeling that he was plugged into a high-voltage generator, surrendered during the return drive to St. Louis to a sober realization that he still was far from having command of this particular subject matter. He recognized without question that he was gaining ground on an elusive quarry, a revelation with the makings of a blockbuster. He was getting closer to its nexus. He sensed it, smelled it, could even envision the heat that reaching the nub well might generate.

But, he didn't have the whole story. To others, Brosky could see, the stuff he was turning up or corroborating still might appear to be little more than circumstantial, filled with much more than hairline cracks. Jake had to find a stronger tie, or maybe a visible thread was more accurate to say, crystalizing what had happened. He needed mortar to cement in place the loose bricks with which he was toiling. Jake's supposition was still just that, unless he unearthed more than he had.

Once back from the Missouri countryside, Brosky discovered a note from the building's concierge affixed to his apartment door.

Its message was brief. "Mr. Brosky, please call Mr. Brown. He says you know his number."

Chapter Twenty-nine

Jake phoned right away. Norton Raven picked up on the first ring.

"Mr. Brown, I've got a message here that says you want a call."

"Yeah, Mr. Brosky, that's right. We gotta talk."

"I thought you told me that you can't talk to me right now."

"That's what I said, yes. But now I'm telling you we gotta talk. As soon as you can. I can still make it tonight. Anytime tonight"

"No, tomorrow morning will be better." Then Jake could not resist asking, "What happened to make you change your mind?"

"Things, Mr. Brosky. Like maybe your piece in the paper today."

"Oh yeah?"

"That wasn't good. Not good at all."

"Well, you tell me about it tomorrow morning. Ten o'clock. Usual place. If I'm a little late, just sit tight."

Brosky contacted the city desk in the morning to check for any important messages, which there weren't, and to inform the desk he'd be out during the morning chasing an angle on the Coyne killing. Jake normally didn't notify any editor of his coming or going. He didn't have to. He really only checked in to see if anybody important was trying to reach him.

Black smoke-spewing engines chugging along in slow motion through the switchyard made Brosky more than a little late arriving at the greasy spoon. Like the last time, Raven was parked at the table most removed from the counter. Two of the red-topped stools at the counter were occupied by fellows wearing coveralls and train engineer caps. Each was stirring coffee poured by the same stumpy gal in the discolored apron. Acknowledging her with a quick downward move of his head, Brosky signaled with his hand for her to bring him a cup of coffee.

Brosky fully expected a fruitful meeting. One way to help ensure it, he'd concluded on the spin over to the East Side, was to be rough. He'd even thought of calling Raven by the hated name of Norton instead of Sam, but decided against it. He would not hesitate, though, to bully Raven in attempting to suck more out of him than Raven was instructed to tell him. Jake assumed, of course, that Fontane had ordered Raven to convey something. The mob leader had swallowed the bait, Brosky's story on his demise.

"So, you did not like what you read in the paper yesterday. So that's right, huh, Sam?"

"No, Mr. Brosky, it's not what I didn't like. It's what Harry Fontane didn't like. That's what there is to worry about."

Fine, Jake wanted to say. We are off to a good start. Now Jake had to keep the upper hand.

"Well, first of all, Sam," Brosky said firmly, "I don't understand why you're calling me Mr. Brosky at this time and not Jake. That seems to tell me that you don't trust me anymore. That I've done something wrong. Since I don't have any idea what that would be, I would like you to call me Jake. Okay?

"And secondly," Brosky continued in a stern tone, "I don't want to hear you say I have to worry about what Harry Fontane thinks. Harry Fontane can go to hell. My job is to call things as I see them, and if Fontane decides not to help me do my job the best I can, then that's his goddamn problem."

Points for Brosky. After several hurried gulps of coffee, the stoolie took on a submissive look. Still, he had to press on. "What is his problem is your story, Jake. It just ain't right."

Brosky sneered. "It takes a shit load of nerve for you to tell me this after I called you for help and you stiffed me. Now I'm supposed to give a damn what you or your boss thinks."

Following a moment's hesitation, Brosky gambled the time was already ripe for him to lead with his right hand. "So tell me, what was wrong with the story? The ones who talked to me think Fontane's going downhill very, very fast, like a chunk of concrete in a lake. Not one told me any goddamned thing different."

Chapter Twenty-nine

"I'm telling you, Jake, the story was way off."

"Why? Where wasn't it right?"

"I'll tell you, Jake, and then you'll see. But, I want you should know that when you called me the other night, I really didn't know nothin', I swear to God. If I had, I wouldn't have held out on you. You gotta know that. I always talk to you cause you play it on the straight with us. Up and up."

"All right, Sam, go on and tell me what I'm supposed to know but don't," Brosky said in a calmer voice. Staring at the pack of Luckies he just pulled out of his shirt pocket, Brosky's expression turned deadpan. "Go ahead, Sam, I'm listening."

"Believe me, I didn't find this out until yesterday." As Raven was about to go on, the two railroaders at the counter rose and walked out, curiously eyeing Brosky and Raven on the way. Raven, fidgety enough as he was, got distracted. Brosky's impatience immediately took over.

"For Christ's sake," he almost yelled, "what are you going to tell me?"

Snapping his attention back to Brosky, Raven came out with it. "Okay, okay, your story was wrong because it was Fontane who had Coyne killed. It was the boss hisself."

Raven went no further. He looked searchingly at Brosky's face, trying to gauge Jake's reaction. He saw Brosky raise his eyebrows in a look of amazement. Jake had figured as much, especially after the chat with his homicide detective friend in St. Louis. But he had to play the incredulity game, to string along his little canary as far as possible.

"Fontane had Coyne bumped off?" Feigning an expression

of disbelief, Brosky asked, "Why for God's sake?"

"He got out of line, Jake." Raven was talking more deliberately. Jake guessed he was determined not to go beyond what he'd been directed to divulge. "Coyne crossed Fontane. When somebody does that, then that's what happens to him. Even when it's Nat Coyne."

Good so far, Jake saw. There had to be a lot more to it, though. "What do you mean Coyne got out of line? What did he do, Sam, that would get him killed?"

"It's like I said, he crossed the boss. He just got out of line." Raven calculated the time had arrived for him to throw a right-hand punch. "That's what we want to see in the paper. That Fontane's still the boss, even though those birds you talk to say something else. They don't know what the hell they're talking about. If people screw Harry, it's going to be bad for them. That's what happened to Nat. Fontane is still number one, Jake. We want to see you write it that way. We want people to know the straight stuff...the true poop I guess you fellows call it."

"I've still got to hear more about it, Sam, before I can write anything," retorted Brosky, his voice rising with irritation. "I'd look pretty stupid if I didn't write any more than that."

Raven was turning panicky, evidently beginning to see that his mission with Brosky might collapse. "Harry says that's all he wants to see in the paper. What I told you." Please, he begged Brosky, his tone clearly plaintive, "put it in the paper the way I'm telling you."

Brosky took off the gloves. Browbeating time was at hand. Reaching across the table, he grabbed the lapel of Raven's coat and jerked him against the table hard enough to rattle the stoolie's coffee cup in its saucer. Brosky noticed his move got the rapt attention of the hardened woman behind the counter. He didn't care.

"Listen to me, you little shit," Brosky hissed, his face a foot away from Raven's, "I want to know what the hell's going on here. You tell me what Coyne has to do to end up in a ditch or I'll write a goddamn story that'll have Fontane putting you in the ditch."

Gaping, Raven's mouth was open so wide Jake caught the gold fillings in his cheek teeth.

"It's all over...a, a broad," Raven stammered.

"What broad?" Brosky barked. "Who is she? What's she got to do with Coyne's death?"

"I don't know her name. Honest to God, I don't. Nat went nuts over her. He screwed everything up on account of her."

A switch engine rolled by the diner. Usually, conversation would be suspended until it passed. Not today. Tightening his grip on Raven's lapel, Jake shouted, "How did he screw up so bad over this woman that he got himself killed?"

"I can't say. I don't...I don't know if I know."

"I'm asking you again. How did Coyne get himself killed over a woman?"

"You can't put it in the paper. It'd be real bad for me."

"I'm asking you one more time, Sam. Why did Fontane have Coyne killed over a woman?"

Brosky received an answer. Stuttering, his face marked by pallor, Raven sang. As he did so, Brosky gripped the stoolie's coat so tightly that his knuckles turned white. Jake, who thought he'd heard it all, was astonished at the lyrics of the canary's song.

Chapter Thirty

More than anyone else, Arkell Dillard was responsible for the rapid success in setting up a journalism education fund in the name of Peter Stine at the large university in the southern part of the state. Appropriately, Dillard joined the dean of the university's communications department on the lawn outside Old Main to announce the endowment.

As newsreel cameras whirred, Dillard readily replied to questions about leading contributors to the fund, pointing out with pride that he had solicited major donations or financial pledges from the *St. Louis World* and several other large newspapers. "It is gratifying to see," said Dillard, "that flagships in the newspaper field, like the *World*, are going to help perpetuate, through the Peter Stine scholarship program, the courageous kind of journalism that Mr. Stine exemplified."

Putting on his hat as the first president of the Progress League of Southern Illinois, the Duke of Windsor allowed as to how he did not foresee the reinvigoration of his region without a "healthy and unfettered press doing its job every step of the way. The press must be the bastion of truth—and for that to happen, the press cannot pull its punches irrespective of who or what may be involved." Dillard's words got wide play.

Governor Sanderson also got into the act by naming Stine the first recipient, posthumously, of the new Illinois Medallion of Honor. The governor cited the publisher for "great courage" in the *Cypress County Banner's* protrusive opposition to law-flouting gamblers. Sanderson came awfully close to blaming them for Stine's murder, leading to an assumption that he knew more about the Stine case than regular law enforcement officials, who had yet to find a culprit in the newspaperman's death.

One individual for sure who did not believe Stine was murdered because of his antigambling crusade was Brosky. His head was swimming with the incredible earful he ended up getting from Norton Raven. Jake needed a time-out for a day or so to absorb it all. He fully realized before he had even left the out-of-the-way cafe that he'd been handed dynamite. Assuming, of course, Raven was telling the truth. And Brosky's gut told him the stoolie had it right. To Jake, knowing what he already did even before sitting down with Raven, it was all very plausible.

But was it printable? Could Brosky get into the *World* more than a smattering of what he was playing with? Those were sixty-four-dollar questions.

As far as the editors were aware, Jake still was trying to track a possible breakthrough story on the Coyne killing. They'd understandably be asking him pretty soon for a progress report on his effort, meaning Brosky had to decide how much to pass on of what he had learned. Jake did not doubt he could get into print that Fontane now was said by gangland sources to have ordered the execution of his own top lieutenant. An article disclosing such, both readership appealing and wanted by Fontane, would be no threat to the mob boss since arrests hardly ever were made in killings of underworld figures. In the event Fontane was brought in for questioning, he'd simply ridicule the idea—and that would be that.

In addition, Brosky would have no trouble going a step further and saying that Coyne was murdered for getting out of line. Advancing beyond this point, though, required delving into the part about Coyne getting dealt out because of his involvement with a certain woman and all that came of it. This was where it became tricky.

If anybody at the *World* except Brosky had been working the story, the editors would have dismissed as too farfetched the allegedly catalytic role of the woman. However, Brosky was Brosky. He was paid way above the union scale for *World* reporters because he produced the kind of copy that readers remembered, that won prizes, that helped the *World* stay on top in the unending circulation wars.

Nevertheless, Brosky had to admit to himself that convinc-

ing the editors to go along with the whole story he was building might be an extraordinarily tall order. Ten to one, the publisher himself and the paper's ancient fuddy-duddy lawyer
would have to sign off before most of the story saw the light
of day. No question about it. The stuff from Raven especially
would be heavily second-guessed because it was based on the
words of an intimidated mob canary. Much of the rest was
attributable to the deductive reasoning of Brosky, which this
time around involved an unusually large amount of conjecture.

Magnifying the challenge for Jake in putting together his
story in its entirety was that it ran so counter to what everybody else believed. True, situations often did not turn out the
way they appeared, but Jake seldom, if ever, had found one to
go so far in that direction.

Because of what he was sitting on, Brosky was amused, and
also a tad annoyed, at a lengthy piece in the *World's* feature section. Sometimes Jake didn't even page through that part of the
paper, but he had pulled out the sports section to read about
the Phillies winning the National League pennant and Stan the
Man wrapping up the senior circuit batting crown. While doing
so, the feature section fell out and landed on his lap. Its lead
article, staring up at him, grabbed his attention.

The piece, covering considerable ground, resulted from
another visit to Grandville by the queen of the feature writers,
Martha Tanner. Her story emphasized that the forced cessation
of gambling at the Autumn Moon had left the community
divided. One of the most outspoken of the unhappy folks
remained Yvonne Fitzgerald, who had volunteered to lead the

southern Illinois end of a drive to get state voters to approve in a referendum the legalization of all kinds of gambling. An angry looking Yvonne, her hair still like Rita Hayworth's, glared out of a Max Slattery photo running with Tanner's article. Behind her loomed the shuttered Autumn Moon. Dayton Mansfield's attempt after the state raid to keep open the restaurant part of the club lasted only a short time.

On the other hand, the story was spiced by plenty of quotes from those overjoyed at the demise of illegal gaming in Grandville and the rest of southern Illinois—at least the wagering carried out in the open where everybody could watch it. Peter Stine was prominent in the article. Tanner had gotten ahold of Reverend Kincaid, who predictably blamed the gambling industry for the killing of Stine just as he did back at Stine's funeral. The minister was hardly alone. Tanner mentioned others in the story who assumed the same. Really, the piece left little reason for thinking that Stine was bumped off for any reason other than his crusade in his newspaper against gambling. Brosky barely suppressed a snicker over the extent to which one hand at the *World* often did not know what the other was up to.

In the end, though, Tanner's feature ignited in Jake a sense of urgency. Not much more time ought to be lost, he suspected, in trying to bring to public light a quite different version of the circumstances behind Stine's death. Brosky was close to putting it together, but that still did not mean he'd get the job done.

Crunch time was at Jake's doorstep. Wrapping up his hot pota-

to boiled down—anyway it was sliced—to one crucial interview. Or, unless he missed his guess, confrontation would be
a better word. In any case, once it occurred, Brosky would
have no more time to spare before getting into print with
whatever he'd manage to fight through the *World* hierarchy.
So, anything else entailed in the story had to be handled or dis-
posed of before Jake forced the final act.

Every story had loose ends. It was always best to tie up as
many as possible; there was no alternative on some stories.
However, this one was different. Much of the unfinished business about it would remain unfinished. Had to be. Parts of the
story could not be more than hypothetical. All the probing in
the world by Brosky could not obviate that.

Be that as it may, the inner voice in Brosky, the sixth sense
in any reporter worth his salt, urged him to make another stab
or two at shoring up loose fragments while plotting his big
windup. After considering the wisdom of doing it or not, Jake
opted to ask the *World's* crackerjack operator to place a call to
the office of *The Pilot* in Madison, Indiana.

"Who do you wish to talk to, Mr. Brosky?" the operator
questioned.

"The editor if possible, Glenda." Even as he said it, Brosky
still was not convinced this was a prudent move. Just when
he'd about decided it was not, he got the ring from the switch-
board. It was Glenda, informing him that "Mr. Pottman, the
editor in Madison, is on the telephone."

Sid Pottman's voice may have been youngish, but it
evinced no awe at the contact by a reporter, and a well-

known one at that, from the much larger *World*. Pottman noted right off the bat that he'd never seen the *World,* let alone heard of Brosky.

So what, he inquired, was of interest in slow-moving Madison to the *St. Louis World?*

"Oh yes, of course," Pottman said, as if he should have known the answer when Brosky mentioned Peter Stine.

"There's a lot of interest in his death over here in our area," Brosky observed almost matter-of-factly, yet taking care to measure his words. In attempting to put Pottman at ease and maybe lead him into revealing something Brosky did not know, Jake continued: "My editors feel it's time for another follow-up story. And the editors get what they want. You know that, right?"

"Well, we've got a couple of older reporters on the staff here who act like they don't know that," Pottman replied, cocksurely it seemed to Jake. He'd have bet Pottman was a whippersnapper out of one of those expanding journalism schools, or the publisher's nephew. Brosky felt sorry for the older reporters.

Jake cut to the chase. "Coming up with something new to write about the Stine murder is tough. But then I remembered that the law enforcement people told me he'd been to your newspaper office the day he was killed, and that he was looking at old editions of the paper. So, I thought that...well, since I don't have any new angle for this story the editors want, that maybe I could find out what years, or maybe the time period, were covered by the papers he was looking at." Brosky trusted his pitch was in a fashion insipid enough to not arouse any extra curiosity in Pottman.

"As you can see," said Jake, attempting to sound almost disinterested, "I'm really hard pressed to find anything new to write about on this case."

Brosky was prepared for the kid editor to give him the bum's rush, but he didn't. Jake calculated that the answer to his question may already have appeared in *The Pilot* at any rate.

"I was not here when Mr. Stine visited our office that day. But, I can tell you what we told the sheriff's people because they wanted to know the same thing."

"Sure. That's what I'm looking for."

"He wanted to look at the volumes of the editions from the World War I years up into the early 1920s. I guess you'd say it was about a ten-year period he was interested in." Pottman added that this was accurate because the cumbersome, black-covered books requested by Stine still were laying out the day after his visit.

"Janie O'Riley, our advertising saleswoman, was the one who talked to him and then went back to get the old editions. We store them in a big old bin behind the antique linotype machine in the composing room. There was so much dust on those old editions—which shows you how much we look at them—that she got, she had a white dress on that day, that she got it filthy getting them out."

Clearing his throat, Pottman went on. "It seemed like he only got a start that day on going through the volumes."

"How'd you know that?"

"He asked Janie if it was okay for the books to stay out so he could look again the following day. That's why the books were laying out. They were waiting for him. But, of course, as you and everybody else knows, he didn't come back."

Brosky suspected that pushing his luck with this fellow might invite trouble, but he decided to inquire a bit further anyway. "You don't have any idea, do you, what Stine was searching for?"

A moment expired as Pottman expelled his breath noisily. "None at all. He didn't say what he wanted to find. Nobody here has any idea. If we did, I can definitely tell you that you would have read about it in *The Pilot*." It was the answer Jake deserved.

"Yes, I'm sure of it. That was a pretty dumb question." Jake sensed the conversation had lasted long enough, but Pottman apparently felt differently.

"With all the attention this killing has garnered," Pottman said, "it would be pretty embarrassing if we were scooped over here when they arrest someone for the killing or figure out what's behind it."

"Yeah, sure, I can understand that," Brosky felt he had no choice but to answer.

"Does anybody over your way think Mr. Stine was killed by some person other than those Illinois gamblers he was taking on?" Pottman asked.

Oh boy. The sooner Brosky got off the phone line the better. But he had to reply to the question.

"People around here think the gamblers killed Stine, or had

it done. That's what they think as far as I know." Pottman's next query put Jake in a real bind.

"You don't think, do you, that this fellow was killed for some reason that had nothing to do with gambling?"

Responding that he did not know, Brosky was about to say he had another call when Pottman plowed on. "We can't come up with anything in those old editions Mr. Stine wanted to see that would have any connection to gamblers in Illinois. I haven't been around here that long, but those who have can't figure it out.

"Hey," a suddenly coy Pottman suggested, "maybe you know a little more about this than you're letting on. For all I know, you may know a lot more about this."

Brosky had to end it, but amiably if possible. Forcing a laugh so guttural it may have sounded strange, Jake managed to kiss off Pottman with the parting words, "I'd like to know more about this case, you can bet. I'll certainly admit that much."

Jake's premonition was right. Calling *The Pilot* turned out to be dangerous. Still, Brosky was left feeling even more certain, based on Pottman's information, that Stine went to Madison seeking background from the years during which Marie Smith gained notoriety while living in the Indiana town. Therefore, the call was helpful.

Mulling over loose ends, Jake weighed whether a call also was in order to the sheriff's office in Jefferson County. There was always a chance new stuff was available on the Stine murder, and a deputy named Hoskins had been of assistance where possible—a far cry from the hostility toward Brosky by

Sheriff Parkins in Cypress County. However, Jake decided against the call, concluding that it might lead to the same awkwardness as in the Pottman exchange. Hoskins came on as a straight shooter. If Brosky phoned him, he'd want to know if Jake had stumbled on anything the Jefferson County sheriff should know. Hesitant to lie to Hoskins, Brosky put the call on the back burner.

Jake also considered, before dropping the thought, a call to the clerk in the Jefferson County Courthouse who had been approached for help by Stine. The clerk had been quoted as recalling that Stine inquired about the county's birth records and that he, the clerk, had directed Stine to a small room housing copies of birth certificates of individuals who entered the world in Jefferson County. The clerk then left Stine alone and, consequently, did not know what Stine may have discovered or even how long he stayed in the building.

Had he so desired, Brosky could have explored other passageways that might have led to even firmer footing for his story. He concluded, though, that none would add much to or subtract from the picture in his head of what had transpired. No more preliminaries. Concentrate on the main event. Get to it. Get it over with.

Chapter Thirty-one

Once he figured out exactly what he intended to do, the countdown began. Brosky would be on a beeline the next three days, or as long as necessary, a falcon with his prey in range, streaking down—if all went well—for the kill.

The first day he'd put together a story going with some of what he had. It would run the second day while he prepped for the do-or-die hour.

The editors were antsy. *The Bugle*, the *World's* afternoon rival, had hit the streets with a piece saying the Coyne killing, based on all the usual parameters, just did not add up. The competitor had to be only a step or two away from raising the specter that maybe Fontane himself was not clean in the execution of his top guy. Nobody was aware, for one thing, of any revenge killings of rival gang members, which you certainly would have expected Fontane to order if another gang had done in Coyne.

Too, Mr. Brown had placed a call to Brosky at the newspaper. Jake missed it, and he couldn't catch Raven when he tried to get back to him. That worried Jake since he could picture Fontane hammering on Raven until the *World* ran the piece that the stoolie fed Jake. Brosky could not rest easy knowing that Raven might succumb to temptation to leak his info elsewhere.

His biggest dilemma, hands down, was the woman. To what extent should he bring her into the story? Maybe he should only allude to her, or not mention her at all. Identifying her in any case was certainly out of the question. Not yet. No, he was ill equipped to go to the mat with the editors on this one—at least not until he worked through the final stage of his game plan.

The editors could be a big stumbling block. All of them would have a say in the final disposition of Jake's effort, not to mention the tip-top of the *World* organization. A crew of editors, headed by the managing editor, rode herd over the news department. The city editor, who never lost frontline responsibility for dealing with the local reporters, was the one closest to Brosky, which was good since that was the way it was supposed to work. Jake's rapport with some past editors on the city desk had not always been as positive. Unlike some of them, the current city editor had been a solid reporter himself. True to form, the managing editor and his assistant, to whom the city editor answered, were typical higher-ups who'd never gotten their hands dirty working a real story, the slam-bang kind that registered with readers. Never having done so, they failed to appreciate or understand the delicate footwork, the emotional energy, the element of luck going into the tracking and landing of the big stories. Damn if they weren't sometimes even the bane of reporters, including the rare ones like Brosky who operated day to day with a relatively free hand from the editors. Jake couldn't remember where it came from, but he'd known editors who fit the saying that went something like: An editor was a person employed on a newspaper whose job was to separate the wheat from the chaff, and then to ensure that the chaff was printed.

So, among the editors, the city editor was closest to kinship for Brosky, and that was because he'd also put in his time in the reportorial trenches like Jake. The city editor always was being pulled in a hundred directions at once, but he made time when Brosky signaled him that the moment had arrived to talk turkey on Jake's endeavor. After the final edition of the day was put to bed, the city editor turned his seat over to an assistant and went over and pulled up a chair by Brosky's desk. Since the city editor rarely joined a reporter at his desk, everybody in the news room had to assume an important conversation was going on. If the city editor had made a contribution to Jake's spittoon, it would have been a show of ultimate camaraderie. But he didn't.

Brosky laid out what he knew for sure, as well as what he strongly suspected—the juiciest stuff, the sensational part. The time it took him was enough to drag through two Luckies and survive a coughing spell. Jake could not remember the city editor ever smoking, the only worthwhile reporter Jake could think of who didn't.

The city editor listened intently. White-headed, with eyes never seeming to flinch behind the horn-rims, his expression seldom changed as he sat hours on end absorbing a flood of calls and subsequent copy chronicling triumphs, heartaches and, God knows, everything else. Attached to the man was a stoical quality, a lack of demonstrable passion that excitable young reporters easily mistook for indifference. The veterans saw it as remarkable composure.

Even when Jake got to the heaviest, most ticklish part of his story, his listener showed little reaction beyond a slight puckering of his lips. He hinted at a smile, though, when he opined to Jake that maybe the tattletale rag, *American Informer,* might be a more appropriate harbor for Jake's story in its entirety.

"But seriously, Jake," the city editor continued, "going the distance with your story is likely to involve a hard sell. I'm sure you know that.

"However," he added, "I'll support you in pushing ahead with the interview needed to bring this to a finish, one way or the other. I'll handle the managing editor. We are far from reaching the point on this paper that a reporter can't pursue an interview because it steps on big toes. After you have the interview, if you can get it, then we'll just have to see where we go." Of course, he concluded, "the more you make of it, the better."

Back to the first story, the one Brosky would dictate to his rewrite guy the next day, the city editor and Jake doped out how much territory to cover. The piece would contain enough new twists to be titillating. The city editor was confident it would get a green light from the managing editor. It did. Brosky spent the following day constructing it with his wordsmith. Later, that night, he went to a movie, not any flick but one he'd seen before. *Body and Soul.*

The Vienna Theatre down on South Grand featured art films and second runs. After grabbing a pastrami on rye at a market up from the Vienna, Brosky ducked into the darkness of the small, cool cinema in time to catch the credits on a movie he hadn't gotten out of his mind since its first showing in the city a few years before. Brosky was quite caught up with John Garfield, hadn't missed any of the actor's string of films after World War II. *Body and Soul* was Jake's favorite, the one in which Garfield was Brosky's supreme alter ego. Seeing again the fight film, raw and powerful, would be an emotional workout for Brosky on the eve of his own championship fight. Perfect timing.

Body and Soul lingered in Brosky's imagination as an allegory of himself, of the visceral Brosky, the deep-seated Brosky. Most tellingly at the movie's end. The boxer played by Garfield had agreed to throw a fight, but he rebels in the final frames, changes his mind and wins, costing the underworld a lot of dough. As the battered but triumphant Garfield is escorted away from the ring, he catches the deathly stare of the criminals he has double-crossed. "What can you do, kill me?" Garfield snaps. "Everybody dies." Brosky loved those lines, couldn't wait to hear them come off the screen again. And, for icing on the cake, Garfield's girl was played by none other than Lilli Palmer.

It was written that Garfield was a tough, vigorous young man from the streets of New York, a Jewish boy from Brooklyn with a sort of square face who had learned early on that you sometimes had to sustain a couple of punches to land one. Brosky knew he, too, had a gut strength, natural instincts that never had been tamed. Yet, it went further than that, the brotherhood that Brosky felt with Garfield. Jake had known his own mean streets, his own rejection early on of certain things the way they were. He still had not quite figured just where he fit, his niche in the life game beyond the job into which he poured his energy and was given license to satisfy his bent for questioning the traditional structure of things. A penchant for the underdog always lurked right under his skin, gave him an appetite for confronting the rich and powerful.

Brosky never shed the hard-shell coating that defined him, and fearfully so, to others. It served to camouflage an empathy in the man that burned on with a fire that his professional success never extinguished. He would not have wanted anyone to know it, but remorse gnawed at Brosky when he learned of the death of Miss Foster, the kindly English teacher back in public school who suspicioned there might be hope for the rather coarse youngster too often a battler in scraps on the playground. She encouraged him to read Horatio Alger books and gently guided him to James Fenimore Cooper's *Leatherstocking Tales*, which turned Brosky on to an early hero, Natty Bumppo, the courageous and resilient settler who was taught by the American Indians and adopted so many of their ways of life.

Three years before, in 1947, Brosky did not let on to anybody why he had to be in the stands in the ballpark the initial time that Jackie Robinson accompanied the Brooklyn Dodgers to St. Louis. Jake even entertained the idea of sitting that day out in the "pavilion," the name for the right field bleachers behind the big screen at Sportsman's where black fans roosted apart from everybody else in the park. But he chickened out. Nevertheless, Brosky couldn't stay away from the park because he discerned in the arrival of Robinson, the first black player in major league baseball in the century, a salve for his, Jake's, own inner discontent with the established order. Brosky wouldn't reveal to anyone either—there really was nobody in his life who'd understand anyway—his eager anticipation of the coming of each Garfield movie.

There he was, right up there on the screen, Brosky himself. Garfield, the rebellious hero, not always pretty but restlessly second-guessing the old values so protective of some and unfair to others. Brosky recognized himself more in the celluloid persona of John Garfield than he ever did looking in a mirror. He fed off Garfield, was nourished by him. *Body and Soul*, with that terrific ending, was a spark plug for Brosky.

Chapter Thirty-two

The story hit like a thunderbolt.

Minutes after the *World's* first edition rolled off the presses, it was snatched up by the wire services for transmittal far and wide. Within a few hours, afternoon papers in Chicago and other parts of the region were giving it a good ride.

The contention in the flashily displayed article in the *World* that St. Louis area mob honcho Harry Fontane was behind the execution-style slaying of his own gangland heir apparent was big enough news in itself. However, a greater stir was caused by the allegation, also based on an unidentified but "reliable" source, that Nat Coyne well may have had a major hand in the killing, back in the summer, of southern Illinois newspaperman Peter Stine. Speculation all along held, of course, that Stine was rubbed out by gambling interests. But the piece by

Jacob Brosky in the *World* bolstered the widespread belief with a new degree of credibility. Going far beyond innuendo, the *World* pretty much flatly laid the death of Stine at the feet of Coyne. Who could take issue with it? The *World* was the most respected and widely read paper in the Midwest south of Chicago. In addition, the Brosky byline made the story even more plausible. One couldn't forget that gangsters and cops alike talked out of school to Brosky. Everyone knew that.

According to the Brosky article, Coyne's link to Stine's murder—which Fontane became aware of after the killing—amounted to a death warrant for Dapper Dan. One thing Fontane or anybody else running an Illinois gaming club never wanted was the brutal slaying of a small-time newspaper fellow crusading in his columns against gambling, Brosky wrote. That was tantamount to waving a red flag in the face of Illinois officials, leaving them no choice but to take action against the up to then largely undisturbed gambling places. Thus, Coyne's involvement in Stine's killing, Brosky reasoned, "had to be starkly counter to the interests of his boss."

The article stated that Coyne, although known to have used his own hands in past murders, did not actually shoot Stine. The triggerman was believed to be a professional killer brought in by Coyne from another part of the country, the *World* related, most likely New Orleans. Nevertheless, whether Coyne pulled the trigger or not, his alleged transgression in the killing of Stine could not be tolerated by Fontane, especially after the state's forcible shutdown of Fontane's Club Destiny, his cash cow gambling establishment near Belleville.

"As if the loss of his lucrative club did not sufficiently enrage him," Brosky's story explained, "the discovery that his own top lieutenant was said to have greatly precipitated his adversity pushed Fontane over the edge. A mob boss like Fontane does not retain power by tolerating a loose cannon right under him in the organization. Coyne's fate was sealed."

Brosky omitted any reference to the involvement of a woman in the downfall of Coyne. A follow-up story in a couple of days would deal with that, if Brosky could pull it off. Meanwhile, it did not take long for the story already in the paper to trigger a merry-go-round.

In East St. Louis, Theresa Carmody was sure she heard Fontane chortle for the first time in days as he read the story. He mumbled that bigger things might be in store for the little weasel Norton Raven now that the whole damn world knew that Harry Fontane was still the king of the turf. Fontane had a mixed reaction to bringing in the stuff about Coyne and the murdered newspaper guy. But what the hell. The story said clearly in black and white that Coyne was behind the killing and not Fontane. So really, what the hell. Nobody nowhere could prove one thing about anybody anywhere in the Stine case. Or in the Coyne one either. There was just nothing to worry about. Hell, for all Fontane knew, or cared, Nat maybe even did do in Cecil Langston's son. That murder could not have been more poorly timed. Fontane was truly surprised he had yet to pick up one bit of scuttlebutt about that one. It was strange that he hadn't, quite out of the ordinary. If the

Langston kid was anything like his old man, he'd gotten his just dessert. But what god-awful timing.

In the final analysis, they could not hang Harry Fontane for any of it. Just in case, though, he ordered Theresa to have his legal beagle, Saul Slisher, get his fanny over pronto. Just in case. Fontane might need him.

Harry smelled it right. He'd need the services of Slisher. A young hotshot had recently arrived in the office of state's attorney of St. Clair County, a conveyor of fresh blood to the top prosecuting post in the county, of which East St. Louis was the largest city. He displayed his get up and go within hours after spying the *World's* story. Standing on the front steps of the old brick and stone county courthouse on the public square in Belleville, famous for its circular fountain, he revealed that a special grand jury would be impaneled within a few days to investigate and bring to justice "the person or persons" responsible for the slaying of gangster Nat Coyne.

The first individual to be subpoenaed to appear before the jury, the state's attorney disclosed, would be none other than Harry Fontane. Then, waving a copy of the *World* before him, the prosecutor added that Jacob Brosky would be invited to share with the panel "the inside information from secret sources that Mr. Brosky obviously must have to write a story professing to answer the questions we all have about the murder of Mr. Coyne and certain related matters.

"I certainly hope," the prosecutor declared, "that Mr. Brosky will voluntarily consent to assist us in this proceeding since he surely is desirous, like any good citizen, of helping proper authorities do their job." Should Brosky not agree to questioning before the jury, the state's attorney pointedly added, "we will seriously consider issuing a subpoena to him, too."

There was more. Over in Jefferson County in Indiana, law enforcement officers who had come up empty handed in the investigation of Peter Stine's murder said they could not ignore the contention about the crime in the *St. Louis World*. They were likely, they said, to request assistance from the FBI, if necessary, to get Harry Fontane into a hot seat for interrogation. They also expected cooperation, they were quoted as saying, from the *World* reporter who possibly seemed to know too much about the Stine killing for maybe the reporter's own good.

What about Brosky on the day his story was kicking up so much dust? He was ensconced at his desk by the window, putting together a memo. Even though it was intended only for the city editor and anyone else he'd choose to share it with, the memo still would be reviewed by Jake's rewrite man before anybody saw it. Brosky was not even a good typist let alone a writer.

While the newsroom was abuzz with talk over his story, Brosky remained undisturbed at his desk. The younger reporters always gave him a wide berth anyway, and the old hands knew better than to approach him when he obviously was working a big one. The only interruption came early in the afternoon when the city editor waltzed over to Jake's desk with a story that he suggested, with a wry smile, that Brosky read.

From the *World* bureau in the Illinois Statehouse, the piece centered on a claim by the state attorney general that "recent unsavory events" in the southern part of Illinois clearly demonstrated a need for greater investigative power at the state level. A politically ambitious fellow, the general—as those in the know called Illinois' top elected legal official—revealed a plan to ask the General Assembly to authorize for the first time the use of statewide grand juries at the behest of his office. Without them, he argued, all the ruckus downstate over the illicit gaming, gangsters and murders would lead only to continued mayhem. To back up his demand for new prosecutorial authority for the state, the general revealed a scathing, previously undisclosed report by Lawrence Dantello. In it, the state police head concluded that events in past weeks in southern Illinois confirmed that local authorities, cops and prosecutors alike, just did not have the resources, or often the gumption, to confront big-time criminal activity with tentacles reaching far beyond local jurisdictions.

What it all boiled down to was easy to see. The murder of Peter Stine had unleashed a chain of events, still perhaps far from over, affecting life and limb, livelihoods and now, it seemed, the makeup of the criminal justice system. It had all happened like wildfire.

Brosky knew what was next. He needed to connect on a phone call if he was to carry out the game plan that, so far, was working to a tee. He invited Glenda to get a certain person on the line, and crossed his fingers that the *World* operator could come through one more time.

There it was, the jangle of his phone. Putting on his headset and flipping the switch, he heard Glenda say those magic words. "Mr. Brosky, your party is on the line. Go ahead, please."

Brosky had heard the woman's voice once before, and he remembered it being composed and aloof. That hadn't changed. Yet she conveyed a tinge of surprise at his request to see her, to talk to her.

"If I may ask," she questioned, "why do you want to see me?"

"It concerns a story I am working on," Brosky replied, attempting to sound matter-of-factly, "and I think you can be of assistance."

"Can you tell me what the story is about?"

"No, not on the phone. It's a matter that needs discussing, but not on the phone." To pull it off, Jake knew he had to see her face-to-face, preferably alone. It would be too easy for her to just hang up if he tried to proceed on the phone.

She asked to be excused for a moment. Brosky waited nervously, but his persistence paid off.

Returning to the line, she said that she would see him, but only on the condition that he come to her home at ten o'clock the next morning. He agreed.

"Do you need directions?"

"No, I do not," he replied. "Thank you. Good-bye."

It was going too smoothly.

There was no time to lose now. He'd have to wrap up the memo and get out. He'd meet Gloria for dinner, but he'd call it an evening early. Tomorrow was a big day. He had to be ready.

The memo had to be complete, though. The city editor wanted it, in the event questions came up when Jake was not around. Too, it made sense for Jake to put it all down, to think it all through in a kind of rehearsal for his encounter the next day. He tried to include everything, starting with his astonishing discovery during his visit with Miss Sadie at Dixie Manor and up through his last grilling of Mr. Brown at the greasy spoon on the East Side. It was hard to believe, this real story behind all the other stories breaking in Illinois since the middle of the summer. As discomforting as the real story might be when it got out, and Brosky believed it would, the fact remained that it was the truth. And, pretty or not, the truth was the currency of Jake's profession. He'd heard somebody say that, and he'd never forgotten it.

With the memo tucked away in a drawer of the city editor's desk, Brosky exited the building by the back stairs, his mind firmly fixed on what lay in store the following day. As he traipsed downward, he heard the footsteps of a person coming up the stairs. Only a few individuals at the *World* besides Brosky ever used the stairs. Brosky had a feeling he knew which one of them he'd be passing in a moment. He was right. The publisher. A long legged man, full of energy, he often went up the stairs two at a time on the way to his top floor office. When he came upon Brosky, the publisher stopped.

The potentate of the *World* never appeared in the newsroom and could match the faces of few reporters with their names. But he knew Brosky.

"That's quite a story today, Jake," the publisher offered. "Finding a connection between that dead hoodlum and the murdered Illinois editor is a big surprise to all of us, I must say. You've uncovered a terribly dreadful situation."

"Thank you, sir." The publisher was the only person at the paper Jake addressed in such a respectful manner.

"You deserve a bonus, Jake, for your hard drive in getting to the bottom of this matter, and I intend to see to it."

The publisher grinned and held it, Cheshire cat style. Jake forced a smile in return, his preface to a simple reply, "I appreciate that."

As the publisher resumed his climb, Jake began to wonder if the exalted one still would feel as positive about Jake's effort after his foray tomorrow, an expedition designed to deal with the situation's real bottom line.

Chapter Thirty-three

Jake's day began early, shortly after the sun should have been coming up. Instead, it was raining and gloomy. He hoped it wasn't an omen of what lay ahead.

When he crossed over to Illinois, though, the shower ended. The sun broke through, and the land and its bounty glistened from the rays. For a brief spell, an exquisite rainbow arched across the sky, its dazzling hues in stark contrast to the sombrous clouds still off to the east.

He drove the way so familiar to him, the shortest path he knew, the route he'd taken going down to Peter Stine's funeral service and the raid on the Autumn Moon. The morning traffic was light and uninterrupted, meaning no farm tractors or lumbering hay wagons clogging the roads. He had time to stop at the cafe on the square at Pinckneyville, to grab two eggs sunny-side up, toast limp with melted butter and bacon the way he liked it, which was not well done. He even hung around for a second cup of coffee and a smoke. The baldish fellow behind the counter caught him glancing up at the black glass panther on a shelf above the coffee urn and the blown-up pictures on the wall of jubilant high school basketball players clutching a fancy trophy. "Them's our Panthers, mister," the counterman said. "You must have heard of 'em. They won state two years ago." Jake nodded absently. He may have been staring up at the wall, but his thoughts were miles away.

Back outside, Jake found several locals admiring his car. "I'll betcha," one remarked, "you'll have the top down before this day's over."

"Yeah, probably," Jake answered. But he wouldn't. The day was business, all business.

He went over it again in his mind. He had not fully realized how well everything had fallen into place until he'd done the memo yesterday. Nonetheless, he held no illusion that his quarry was about to roll over and play dead.

How much more convenient it would have been if he really knew what lay in store for him. He couldn't foresee any ready capitulation, followed by begging for mercy, a plea for him to go as easy as he could in the story that he planned. A nice thought, but not likely. No, Jake would be toyed with. Or, maybe just stonewalled. Hell, he might not even get his foot in the door. He might have to resort to machismo, a turn he pulled routinely with the creeps. But how would that go over? Jake definitely was not venturing into one of his run-of-the-mill settings.

Brosky remained in solid shape time-wise when he arrived in Grandville.

He'd not argue that the city didn't have a good face. Passing by blocks of trim homes before going through downtown, Brosky observed a gentle pace of life humming along with a pleasantness far removed from the rude cacophony of St. Louis. Not a care in the world was evident on the surface. Not about the Korean War. Not about the murder of the town's newspaper publisher. Not about anything.

Jake actually did need to ask for direction to reach his destination. Two places at which he would not stop for help were the county courthouse, the abode of Sheriff Parkins, or the office of the *Cypress County Banner*, which Jake spied out of the corner of his eye as he cruised along. He got the guidance he needed at a five-and-dime on the south side of the city. Really, just about anyone could have told him where to go.

In the few miles he still had to cover, Brosky noticed how the land rose sharply, an immediate introduction to the Shawnee Hills, the terrain many labeled the Illinois Ozarks. Had he stayed on the highway running down from Grandville, he'd have gone through a break in the hills and on toward that torpid little river crawling into the scary swamp that everyone in Brosky's memory but Cecil Langston avoided. Jake wasn't going that far, though. Soon enough he came to the final leg of his drive, the narrow road from the highway up to his journey's end.

Climbing, the roadway afforded him a much closer view of the thickly wooded bluffs and knobs leading in short measure to steep, rocky cliffs. He was watching for a particular ridge, which he was assured he could not miss because of the house. Advice proven true.

There it was, the stately white mansion, up through the trees. He could see the shafts and cornices of the columns and what appeared to be a captain's walk atop the structure. Looking out from it had to be breathtaking. To reach the house, Brosky eased the Olds up a driveway bounded by Douglas firs. He half expected to encounter fancy iron gates across the drive at its start, an obstruction maybe even accompanied by a guard. But there was no such hindrance. The drive only widened and turned to brick as it leveled off in front of the house. All around were plants, gobs of them. If Brosky had any inkling of such things, he'd have spotted silver bells, gauzy ferns, coneflowers and buttercups, enough to stock an arboretum. But Jake couldn't tell one from another.

He did know one thing. He suddenly felt uneasy up here all alone by this elegant aerie, where nothing was rustling except for a morning breeze through the pines. Suppressing a yearning for a last Lucky, he was tempted to open the glove department, slip out the Smith and Wesson snubby and slide it under his belt at his backside. He took nothing for granted. However, he decided against the gun.

A glance at his watch revealed he'd arrived a few minutes before the appointed hour. Snatching a notepad from the front passenger seat, he slid out of the Olds, advanced up several steps to the columned porch and marched to the front door. He still did not detect anything stirring. A big brass ring was hinged to the door for knocking. Before he could grasp it, the door opened.

He stood face-to-face with Arkell Dillard.

"Good morning, Mr. Brosky."

The Duke of Windsor bore a tenuous smile on his lips and a wariness in his eyes. As Brosky returned the salutation, Dillard motioned to him to cross the threshold of the door and enter the foyer of the home. Wanting without delay to get a feel for the game to be played, Brosky dispensed with any beating around the bush.

"I called Mrs. Dillard yesterday and arranged to see her—

"Yes," Dillard broke in, "I know you did."

"I want to talk to her about—

"Please, Mr. Brosky, join me over here." Dillard gestured with his hand palm up for Jake to proceed from the vestibule into an expansive living room. As Jake passed a set of French doors, he caught a brief glimpse of her. She was seated in a white wicker chair in a glass-enclosed veranda off the southern side of the parlor. Her back was to him, and she made no effort to turn around. Her hair—more flaxen than he remembered from the one time he'd seen her—was swept up and secured by a black bow, revealing a tan on the nape of her neck. Smoke from a cigarette in her uplifted hand curled lazily skyward. Everything else about her was motionless.

The room into which Dillard motioned Brosky made him uncomfortable. Inlays on the mosaic floor created a dazzling pattern. The white marble mantel above the fireplace ran under a massive gold leaf mirror that visitors, on other occasions, were told came from France. The reflection of a crystal chandelier in the mirror made the parlor seem endless. Brosky guessed he was looking at the price of his Olds in the furnishings alone.

Jake had already observed enough to know the Dillard residence had vestiges of the grandiose interiors of palatial mansions on private streets in the west end of St. Louis, domains of exclusivity not frequently penetrated by reporters. Any other time, Dillard might have explained to a guest displaying appropriate admiration for his home that the style and layout were fashioned after a well-to-do planter's house down in Natchez that Dillard visited as a young man. To be sure, though, Jacob Brosky of the *St. Louis World* was not an invited guest in the home of Arkell Dillard. He was an interloper, and an unrefined one at that judging by his rumply suit and face, a face whose chin and nose and cheeks seemed to Dillard to be chiseled out of cold granite. There were women, Dillard hardly doubted, who'd find Brosky ruggedly handsome. His face had just enough of a granulated surface, accentuated by a scar or two or three among the furrows of a man well into mid-life. Dillard could have easily believed that Brosky had boxed some in his salad days, although his nose didn't show signs of being flattened.

Dillard detected a deadness in Brosky's eyes, like the hunters who sat unmoved on cold mornings in southern Illinois waiting for geese. Of course, Brosky was a hunter too, just as deadly. He preyed on people. No, this crude man Brosky was not a welcome visitor. Dillard would skip small talk because he held no illusion that this intruder had any taste at all for idle chitchat.

The Duke of Windsor wanted to get one thing straight right away.

"My wife is not feeling well, Mr. Brosky. It is her wish that I discuss with you whatever is on your mind. I trust that this will not present any problem."

Brosky did not want to get off on this foot. Not at all. He'd come down here to talk to Sloan Dillard and had no choice but to try to do exactly that. He had to play one certain card even though he realized he might be whistling in the wind.

"Mr. Dillard, the reason I want to talk to your wife is because the story I am putting together at this time concerns her. I do not see what role you might have had in what I am writing about." Jake always told outsiders he could write. "Naturally, I am certainly agreeable to you sitting in on any conversation between Mrs. Dillard and myself."

"No, I just told you, my wife does not feel up to talking to you. Whatever it is that has brought you here, you will have to discuss with me."

Dillard paused, waiting for Jake to reply. When he did not, Dillard continued. "I will tell you that we are leaving tomorrow for a cruise through the Greek Islands, something we have put off until the Communist threat over there was repulsed." So, he concluded, "if you want to talk about the subject on your mind, or I should say perhaps this story you are writing, you will have to settle for talking to me. And, it will have to be today because, frankly, I cannot say when it might be possible for us to get together again."

Brosky fixed him with a drop-dead stare. He wanted a few moments to think. But about what? This rich bastard, who had to be really out of place down here, had Jake in a corner. They both knew it. Thinking he could get Sloan alone on her home turf was probably expecting too much in the first place. Hell, if he was in St. Louis trying to pull off something like this with one of the powerful families, he would surely have to submit questions through a phalanx of lawyers or, not much worse, encounter plain old stonewalling. Here at least he had gained entry to the hunting ground. However, a formidable obstacle stood between Sloan and Brosky.

Jake remembered meeting Arkell Dillard, if only briefly, after Peter Stine's funeral service. His initial impression was that everything about the fellow carried a big price tag. His suit. His wife. Oh yes, Dillard had moved back then without hesitation to secure an upper hand on Brosky by bringing up the publisher of the *World*, intending to get across to Brosky that Dillard had access to an individual who could pull Jake's chain. An ill-disguised ploy at intimidation, but often effective. Except on Brosky, Jake liked to think. Truthfully, persons who had invoked the name of the publisher in dealing with Brosky through the years seldom ended up winning. Brosky always assumed the device would not work. You could never know for certain, though. The man he was confronting, Brosky suspected, might stop at nothing to protect his world. Nothing.

From somewhere in the place, Jake could not tell if from a

phonograph record or a radio, came the distinguishable sound of a classical piano piece. He was not into highbrow music, was not aware that he was hearing a composition of Frederic Chopin. When Gloria DeForest proposed that Jake escort her to the symphony, he told her that he was not a dilettante, his word for anybody heavy in the arts. He recalled his first impression of Dillard was that of a dilettante, a weak sister. The image did not last. Dillard, Brosky later sensed, was not to be taken lightly.

Now, facing Dillard in his imposing home, Brosky assumed, did not doubt one bit, that this fellow, although far more cultured than Brosky, could be a most earthy adversary. Jake just might discover that a joust with this high-hatter could get lower down than having an alley cat by the tail.

"So, Mr. Brosky," Jake heard Dillard repeating, "what is it that you want to discuss today? As I said, my wife and I have a hundred details to attend to before we depart for the islands. I'm sure you can understand that our time is getting limited."

"Yes, sure, I understand."

"Oh, by the way, you are certainly free to smoke in here if it pleases you."

Brosky did crave a cigarette. There were not many times when he didn't. He refrained, though, having decided beforehand against reaching for the pack while he was in the house. Anyhow, the way Dillard made the offer smacked of a put-down.

Comprehending that any further delay in addressing the subject of his visit would work against him, Brosky got to it. What was that tingle? Was it from a knot in his stomach? If so,

Jake was embarrassed. Anybody who refused to back down from the Harry Fontanes of the world shouldn't sweat this fellow. Jake knew for sure his voice must not hint at any trepidation, any hesitancy in spelling out what he knew and what he intended to do with it.

"As I know you are aware, sir, there have been some pretty far-reaching events in this part of Illinois in recent weeks," Brosky began in a firm tone.

"Being the *World* man who for many years has handled big stories in Illinois, especially down here, I've been assigned to cover what's been going on."

"Yes, of course," Dillard interjected, "I do recall meeting you outside the funeral home after the service for Mr. Stine."

Good. Dillard's mention of Stine supported the tack Brosky was taking. Jake jumped on it immediately. It was the murder of Stine, noted Brosky, that in the opinion of most persons had set off the chain of developments bringing unwanted attention to southern Illinois. Nevertheless, the reason for Stine's murder continued to elude authorities—in spite of the pressure exerted on numerous individuals, including reporters like Brosky, to pin down the cause.

Wait just a minute, Dillard interrupted. Was it not taken for granted by everybody that Stine was killed because of his crusade in his newspaper against the wide-open gambling?

"True, that is assumed by many people, Mr. Dillard."

"Well, I've heard no talk from anyone who thinks otherwise, Mr. Brosky. Even the governor. You may or may not be aware that I am heading up a big campaign to try to boost the economy in my part of the state. This has put me in contact with Governor Sanderson, and I can assure you he sent in his state police to shut down the gambling around here because he has no doubt the gambling people, or someone hired by those people, killed Mr. Stine. Really now, do you know anyone who does not believe that?"

Only moments into the conversation, noticed Brosky, and Dillard was already informing him he talks to the governor of Illinois. Predictable. Let it ride.

"The governor, and anybody else for that matter, is certainly entitled to believe whatever he wants about the Stine case," Brosky resumed. "But nobody has been arrested and charged with the crime." The preliminaries were out of the way. Jake proceeded into the main event.

"Taking it a step further, Mr. Dillard, I don't think anybody will be arrested for the murder of Stine because I believe he was murdered by a professional killer. In fact, I am positive he was killed by a hit man out of the organized crime mob down in New Orleans. I said so in a story in yesterday's *World*." Added Jake, "I guess you didn't see the piece."

"No, I did not," Dillard replied. Brosky could not tell if Dillard was being truthful. But he kind of doubted it when Dillard asked, "Did your story mention who got this professional killer to murder Mr. Stine?"

"Yes, I did say." Studying Dillard's eyes closely for a reaction, Brosky stated that "the person was Nat Coyne, the top lieutenant to Harry Fontane in the East St. Louis underworld." Dillard did not blink; his eyes remained impassive. The Duke of Windsor was a good actor, Jake thought, or else he really did not know what was coming.

"This man Coyne you mention," Dillard said, "was with this Fontane up in East St. Louis...who I understand is tied to gambling. So, if this Coyne was responsible for the murder of Mr. Stine, how can anyone say that the gamblers were not behind his death?"

"Thank you for asking, Mr. Dillard. That happens to be the reason for my coming here today."

Dillard's facial composure gave way to a look of incredulity. Asking Brosky what in the world he was talking about, Dillard added that he could not "see how any of this unfortunate business could have any relevancy to me—or to my wife."

"Let me explain."

First off, Brosky related, neither Fontane nor any other underworld figure in his right mind bumped off newspaper people. Those killings were no-no's because they spurred public clamor for action against the real or imagined perpetrators, such as in the Stine case when the state cracked down on illegal wagering clubs. Since Coyne arranged for the killing of Stine without the approval of Fontane, Jake went on, the gangland boss ordered the execution of Coyne. "All of this," Jake pointed out, "you would have known if you'd seen my story in yesterday's *World*."

"Mr. Brosky, I am sorry but I do not see your paper every day. When I do, I must say that stories about gangster shootings usually escape me." Dillard gave his wristwatch a conspicuous glance. "I still fail to see just what about any of this caused you to come down here," Dillard went on, his voice hinting at growing testiness. "Like I told you, I do have to watch the time since I have a lot to do for the trip."

"Fine," Brosky said, "let me get to the point."

"Peter Stine was not murdered because of his articles against gambling. It was because of something he was planning to write about your wife."

"About my wife? You cannot be serious!"

Dillard could not have appeared more dumbfounded, but Brosky was not buying. He charged on.

"Stine had uncovered, or you might say discovered, information about your wife that I am certain he planned to write about. He informed your wife of this, and she in turn told Coyne, with whom she was acquainted. Coyne then directed or hired the killing of Stine to protect your wife and her reputation."

Dillard's countenance twisted into an angry contortion. He wasn't faking it.

"What are you talking about? You actually believe this, Mr. Brosky? Or expect anyone else to believe it? I am sorry, but this is ridiculous! No, it's more than that. It's rubbish! This is far below you, Mr. Brosky, or your newspaper."

"It is the truth, and I intend to have a story in the paper laying out the real reason for the death of Stine and certain other things that have happened as a result."

Dillard, his face flushed, opened his mouth, but no words escaped. Instead, Jake blurted out, "Now don't get me wrong. I am not saying or writing that Mrs. Dillard is guilty of anything. However, she is part of some pretty strong stuff that has happened in downstate Illinois in the recent past, and I have a duty to inform the readers of my paper of the whole story. I don't have a job that always makes everybody happy, but it's a job that I try to do well...and that job is to tell the truth as I know it."

"The truth as you know it? I am going to read in your newspaper the truth as *you* know it?"

"Yes, you are," Brosky uttered, as if there was no doubt whatsoever that the story that had brought him to this encounter would run in the *World*.

"What really happened, Mr. Dillard, was that Peter Stine was, as they say in my business, working the story on your wife when he was killed. He had gone to Madison, Indiana, where he died, to dig up background for the story. The hit man was obviously tracking him, and he decided Madison was the right place to do him in. Stine drove onto the grounds of a college by the town that was closed for the summer, like schools are. The hit man figured that was a safe place to pick him off, which it was."

Dillard raised a hand like a traffic cop for Brosky to hold on. "I don't think," he barked indignantly, "I have to stand in my home and listen to any more of this."

Jake was snappish himself in retorting, "You certainly don't."

When Dillard did not counter, Brosky said in a more temperate voice, "I will leave if that is your choice. I'm here because I have a responsibility as part of my job to inform your wife, or you, if that's your desire, of what I am writing and to give you or your wife a chance to comment, to react." And, Jake thought to himself, he was there to try during a confrontation like this to learn or pry loose additional information that could make the story more solid or revealing.

"I've found," Jake said, "that most people like to know what is going to be written about them." He refrained from adding that the thing most persons did not want was to get hit cold with a story about themselves in the *World* that they had no idea was coming. Jake calculated he would probably get the boot from Dillard, but not before Dillard got a better grasp of what Brosky had. Human nature was human nature. The Duke of Windsor was not an exception to the rule.

"Very well, Mr. Brosky," Dillard questioned in a tone somewhat subdued, "just what is it about my wife that is, or was, of such great interest to Mr. Stine and, I presume, to you too?"

"It's this. Stine found out, whether he intended to or not, that Mrs. Dillard is the daughter of a woman very much in the public eye in America thirty years ago. Her name was Marie Smith."

With that, Brosky hesitated before going on because it occurred to him that Sloan Dillard likely was still out on the veranda. At least Jake had not heard any sound of movement from that room. He wondered how much she knew about her mother, whether Sloan was even aware of as many details about her as he was. She surely knew enough, after Stine approached her, to realize that the need to suppress public airing about her momma was sufficient to justify murder. So, what Brosky was relating to Sloan's husband probably was not news to her. Anyway, the sounds of Chopin easily may have been reverberating loud enough to prevent her from hearing the exchange in the parlor.

Jake continued.

"Marie Smith was hanged in Kentucky in 1920 for the murder of a man at a factory payroll office in Louisville. The crime got sensational headlines for a lot of reasons. It was cold-blooded, and Smith was a good-looking woman. Everybody knew who she was."

Dillard's body noticeably stiffened. Jake was prepared for him to break in, but Dillard remained silent.

"Madison was the hometown of Marie Smith. She was living there at the time she committed the crime. Marie was not married, but she had a daughter, four or five years old—your wife.

"After Marie Smith was executed, her daughter was placed in an orphanage in Missouri called Thornhill Home. The girl's name was Susan Sloan Smith. She lived in the orphanage for about four years before being adopted by a minister, Sterling Kincaid, and his wife. Kincaid, your father-in-law, has gone on to make quite a name for himself over here in Illinois as a big opponent of gambling. I saw him preach at Stine's funeral. He has a lot of followers."

Brosky stopped to give Dillard a chance to say something. But he didn't, so Jake went on.

"Stine knew about everything I'm telling you. By coincidence, a hell of one, Stine himself was in that orphanage when your wife was there. He discovered that when he was doing research for a story on the orphanage. There's no question he was chasing the angle about your wife and her mother. If he wasn't, why did he go over to Madison, her hometown?"

Jake was not quite certain where to venture next. Surely, the man standing so rigidly before him would weigh in. The reporter foresaw Dillard asking how Brosky or Stine, for that matter, could be so positive of all this since orphanage and adoption records were not supposed to be open to the public. In replying, Jake would make damn sure he protected the proud old woman sitting in the boardinghouse in Perkins, Missouri. And Sam Rabbit, who let Brosky look at nonpublic state records in Missouri that erased any doubt that Sloan Dillard was the daughter of Marie Smith and the adopted child of the Kincaids. Yes, Jake would say or do whatever was necessary to not betray Sadie Patrick or Sam Rabbit.

"I have a question," Dillard said. Okay, thought Brosky, here it comes. Sadie and Rabbit had to be kept out of it. But, Dillard brought up another matter. And a good question it was.

"How could you possibly know that Mr. Stine made contact with my wife about this subject that you've raised? I mean the gentleman is dead; this man Coyne is dead, and I cannot believe my wife would have singled you out to inform you of this stuff. So tell me, if you will, how you could possibly be aware of these contacts you say happened between my wife and Mr. Stine and this gangster? I really would like to know."

Smart. Dillard was speeding to the weakest segment of Brosky's story. Its part closest to an Achilles' heel. If the game between the two were football, Dillard would be running his best back at the weakest guy on Brosky's line. This was the toughest link for Jake to maintain in the chain of developments in his story. If he couldn't say that Coyne got rid of Stine after learning from Sloan Dillard of Stine's pursuit of her background, Jake well could be flirting with a nonstory—or at least a flimsy foundation for introducing the mystery woman drama. There'd be little or nothing really new beyond the story under his name in yesterday's paper.

Of course Jake had anticipated Dillard's question, if not from Dillard then from those above Brosky at the *World*. He'd give Dillard the same explanation spelled out in his memo laying in the city editor's desk. Underworld sources.

Underworld sources. The fuel of Jake's success. The fountainhead of information milked and jealously guarded by Jake, not that very many other reporters had tried to grab a piece of that particular action. Since second-guessing Brosky on material he attributed to mobsters seldom occurred, he had gotten virtually unlimited mileage out of his contacts in the netherworld.

However, the present situation was different. Underworld sources were not being used to bring down other nefarious types. The target was an alluring woman, raised by a widely known clergyman and married to one of the most powerful men in southern Illinois. In her case, the underworld sources amounted to one individual, Brosky's Mr. Brown, the little informer Norton Raven who insisted on being called Sam Raven. Brosky had squeezed out of Sam the inside dope on the Coyne execution, had bled the canary into roping Coyne to Sloan. Before he let Sam off the hook that last time at the greasy spoon, Jake had more than enough to believe he was on sound footing with a whale of a story.

Coyne carrying on with this rich society babe in Illinois. Coyne livid about this local newspaper guy threatening to do her great harm. Coyne so head over heels about her that he arranged for the demise of the newspaperman without the knowledge of Fontane and without recognizing that the news-paperman would have been the last person on earth the gam-bling proprietors wanted murdered. In light of what he'd turned up before pinning down Sam Raven, Brosky knew the stool pigeon was reluctantly dishing out the straight goods. Had he not felt secure about it, Jake would not have pushed for this climactic story, the last word on the death of Peter Stine.

In the memo back at the *World*, Brosky took care to not mention Raven by name. Jake never identified his underworld sources. This time would be no different—although the high-er-ups at the *World*, Jake assumed, for once would be press-ing him very hard about the "reliability" of his informant or informants. The odds were good that the bosses at the *World* would be contacted on this specific matter by Dillard or his lawyer before Jake even made it back to St. Louis. Brosky had to be ready to encounter in his own shop some of the same skepticism he was facing on the spot from Dillard.

When Brosky replied to Dillard that rock-solid underworld sources revealed the interaction between Stine, Dillard's wife and Coyne that led to Stine's killing and then Coyne's, Dillard scoffed.

"Really unbelievable," sneered Dillard, his bearing full of insolence, "that you would smear my wife and me on the word of gangsters. I cannot conceive of anything more despicable than your kind of journalism."

Brosky let the polemic pass because it suddenly hit him that another maneuver was in order.

"My underworld sources are reliable, but I'm willing to see if your wife has a different version of what I've been told. Why don't you ask her—

"No! I keep telling you she is not feeling up to this."

"Well, it seems to me that it would make sense, if you are so sure I'm wrong, for your wife to deny to me that Stine approached her on the information he uncovered and left her very upset over what he intended to do with it."

"I would not let her lower—

Brosky did the interrupting this time. "Also, I would think she'd be willing to tell me to my face that she did not tell Nat Coyne that Stine was going to write a story about her that would be very damaging to her. I would think—

"I do not care what you think!"

Jake was no stranger to conversations going downhill. They were an occupational hazard. He had not taken one note on anything Dillard said, and it was not likely he would. Opening up his tablet at this stage might push Dillard over the edge. Convinced the visit was nearing a dead end, Jake reckoned the moment had arrived for his exit, civil or otherwise. Apparently, though, Dillard wasn't finished.

Publication of any story in the *World* "defaming my wife,"

Dillard warned, "will result in a libel suit by me or her father, or both. We will not sit peacefully by and permit you to darken our names. My family has commanded the utmost respect for a very long time. You are doing a shameless thing to all of us."

Brosky, always one who took pleasure in tweaking the high and mighty, relished the moment. If nothing else, he had this muckamuck squirming. Brosky anticipated the libel suit threat and wondered what was next.

Dillard did have one more thrust in mind. Jake kind of expected this one too, but was surprised at the abrupt return by Dillard to a quietly composed tone in his voice.

"I am asking you not to proceed with this story," he said slowly, almost solemnly. "I am asking you as a gentleman to consider the ramifications of what you are doing. You are committing a great disservice to my family, to your newspaper's fine reputation and even to Mr. Stine, whose memory is held in the highest regard because of the belief by so many people that he lost his life as a result of his writings against the gamblers.

"I am asking you to reconsider the matter that has brought you here today," entreated Dillard. "What I am requesting," he continued in a voice falling darn near to a hush, "is to please leave well enough alone."

Brosky was now confronted by the persuasive Dillard. Jake could easily see this version of the Duke of Windsor prevailing over persons in southern Illinois whom Dillard needed to control to keep his financial empire in place. Just like that he was off his high horse, abandoning the overbearing manner for silky smooth beseeching, imploring of Brosky. A man capable of such supplication would get his way a lot. But not today. Brosky wasn't biting.

"I'm sorry, Mr. Dillard, but nothing has been said that would make me rethink my story. I'd like for you to understand that the story is not intended to hurt your wife because of who her mother was. The basis for my story is that a man, a newspaper publisher, was killed because, rightly or wrongly, he was going after the story on your wife and her mother.

"That remains the truth of the matter, and it is more important than any other consideration."

Jake was not sure how else to end it. He had not sat down, had not even taken off his coat. He was poised, ready to get out of the house. Before turning to leave the room, he said rather matter-of-factly, as he did at the conclusion of most interviews, "I will be available in my office in St. Louis if you want to talk to me about anything." He hoped those would be the final words. They were not.

Brosky had taken only three or four steps toward the foyer when he heard Dillard call his name. Jake stopped and turned to face the man. The strain of Chopin seemed to have picked up. But Jake was pretty sure he heard Dillard's parting words.

"You are making a grave mistake, sir," Dillard said.

Outside, Brosky fished a Lucky from his pack as he walked to the Olds. He'd wait to light it until he was in the car because the wind through the pines had grown stronger. The sun, so bright on his drive earlier in the day, was obscured by clouds. Jake felt chilly for the first time in the changing of the season.

Once settled in the driver's seat, he fired the cigarette and pushed the key into the ignition. As he revved up the engine, he swiveled for another look at the mansion. He noticed Arkell Dillard staring at him through a window. Funny as it might seem, Brosky took more comfort than usual in knowing that his revolver was handy.

Chapter Thirty-four

Dillard stayed at the window as Brosky's car descended down the winding drive. When it disappeared behind the evergreens, he returned to the living room. Sloan was standing under the chandelier. He went right to her.

"You little bitch," he muttered.

He slapped her face, whacked it hard.

Wincing, suddenly flushed crimson, she recoiled, one hand raised shakily, precariously, as if she could not decide whether to strike a return blow. She didn't. But as the hand went down, and her composure sprung back, she leveled a smile of derision at her husband.

"You bastard. You insufferable bastard." She spoke the words slowly, softly, laden with contempt.

"You bought me. You've gotten your money's worth."

Then, as her smile faded into a grimace, she added, "But I've never gotten what I needed from you! Nat made me feel real. He—

"For God's sake!" Dillard yelled, interrupting her. "You're talking about a gangster, a low-life hoodlum! He was nothing but scum."

"Oh no, Arkell," she countered, her voice now infuriatingly calm, "being with him made it possible for me to keep tolerating you." Mocking her husband, watching the last bit of color drain from his face, she continued, "Nat died for what he did for me. But, he had more than you have, Arkell. He had me—really had me. And I loved him!"

"You ungrateful slut. You thankless little hussy."

He stormed toward her. She stepped back, abruptly raising her hand. "Don't. Don't you ever hit me again, or I'll call that obnoxious newspaper fellow and give him Mrs. Arkell Dillard's true confession right out of my own mouth."

He stopped cold, then turned and retreated to the kitchen. Snatching up the receiver of the telephone, he placed a call to his loyal servant, the chap who'd snared catfish out of backwaters with his bare hands. He was always out there, waiting to be summoned.

"Come on up," Dillard said matter-of-factly into the receiver. "There's more work to be done."

Then he hung up.

Taylor Pensoneau, a native of Belleville, Illinois, spent twelve years as the Illinois political correspondent of the *St. Louis Post-Dispatch*. He is the author of the widely acclaimed *Brothers Notorious: The Sheltons*. He is also the author of *Governor Richard Ogilvie: In the Interest of the State* and coauthor of *Dan Walker: The Glory and the Tragedy*. The *Chicago Sun-Times* called the Ogilvie book one of the ten most notable political books of 1997, and both the Ogilvie and Walker books were awarded the Illinois State Historical Society's Certificate of Excellence. *The Summer of '50* is Pensoneau's first work of fiction.